James A. Brakken

Alias Ray Olson

The complete story behind the 1939

Chequamegon Forest Manhunt

Alias Ray Olson

The complete story behind the 1939 Chequamegon Forest Manhunt

Copyright 2017 James A. Brakken

ISBN: 978-0-9976249-1-5

Badger Valley Publishing
45255 East Cable Lake Road
Cable, Wisconsin 54821
715-798-3163

BADGER VALLEY PUBLISHING

Cable, Wisconsin

An independent publisher for independent authors.

TreasureofNamakagon@gmail.com
BadgerValley.com
715-798-3163

— • —

For the legions of dedicated
historical society volunteers
who keep the past alive and
make books like this possible.

— • —

IN APPRECIATION

To President Jim Ferguson, past-president Barb Williamson, and all the Sawyer County Historical Society volunteers for your efforts to collect and share glimpses into the rich past of northwest Wisconsin. And to the Cable-Namakagon Historical Museum, the Historical Societies of the counties of Bayfield, Douglas, Ashland, and Waukesha in Wisconsin and the Tacoma, Seattle, and Spokane Historical Societies in Washington for help with research.

To the late Eldon Marple. His many articles about northwest Wisconsin's past enhance knowledge of our region's history and enrich our lives. Eldon's efforts remind us of the importance of writing down what you know while you can. Everyone should.

To the public officials in the counties of Sawyer and Bayfield who tolerated my scouring of county records in search of details I know my readers will appreciate.

To Susan and Mike Reynolds, whose dad, Sidney, was there, rifle loaded, ready for action. To Fred Meyer, perhaps the only surviving witness to the Olson affair. To Clancy, who knows old cars. Thanks for the lift! To Jim from Deerfoot Lodge and Bill from Musky Tale Resort, places quite familiar to Ray Olson. To Charlie and Julie from the old Moose Lake Store, now Charlie's Fine Foods. To Dell's son, Dave Anderson, and others I'm sure I've missed. Know that you all helped give life to this story.

For your on-the-mark reviews of the text, I thank Lorna Dreher, Howie Gold, Sybil Brakken, Susan Reynolds, Abett Icks, and my often brutal but always delightful Yarnspinners writing critique group. You all help me get to the station on time and keep the train on the right track.

Thanks, too, to all you readers who encourage independent authors by purchasing our books. It makes all the difference.

And above all, thank you Sybil, my love, my wife, my partner in life, for your around-the-clock confidence in my work, for your praiseworthy patience, and for contributing in so many ways.

A NOTE TO THE READER ...

This novel is not intended as history. Rather, it is historical fiction based closely on newspaper articles, court documents, interviews, and anecdotes regarding the life and death of August Buelo, *Alias Ray Olson*. It is the story of a man who many considered to be gravely misunderstood, maligned, and misrepresented.

Today, eight decades after Olson's arrival in northern Wisconsin, controversy remains regarding his case and the three resulting homicides.

Readers seeking more information on Ray Olson are encouraged to visit the Sawyer County Historical Society Museum in Hayward, Wisconsin, where visitors, new members, and contributions are always welcome. JB

Pronunciation of two Ojibwe
terms used within this book:

Chequamegon   she-WAM-ah-gun
Namakagon   nam-ah-KAH-gun

The spelling of the river is Namekagon.
The spelling of the lake is Namakagon.
Both are pronounced the same.

Sheriff George Seehuetter's name is pronounced SEE-hut-ter. August Buelo's last name sounds like BEW-low. Police Chief Fred Sieh pronounced his last name as SEE.

A section in the addendum offers many of the facts that inspired this novel. Readers are encouraged to *not* read the addendum before the novel, as some of the twists and surprises in the story will be spoiled.

Press photos that appeared in newspapers and magazines during and after the 1939 Chequamegon Forest manhunt are posted on James Brakken's website, BadgerValley.com where you will also find the author's other engaging books, ordering information, and special offers.

Captions for a few, selected images:

Alias Ray Olson

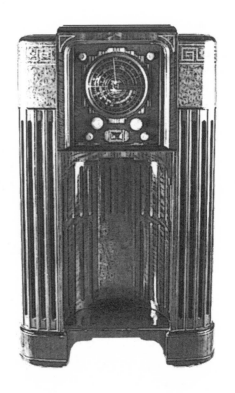

Prologue

As I trudged toward the final pages of my manuscript, a novel about the life and death of a man born August Frederick Buelo but who died as Ray Olson, I thought back.

I was a boy when my father told me the story of a small-time crook who changed life near our northern Wisconsin community during the summer of 1939. Dad said Olson, a man about his age, had eked out a living as a fishing guide and by doing odd jobs at some of the resorts near our home. But Olson, Dad said, fell in with the wrong crowd and had some sort of slot machine troubles. Before Ray knew it, he became the subject of Wisconsin's largest manhunt, hiding out in the Chequamegon National Forest from lawmen and armed volunteers for nearly two weeks.

It was a fascinating tale to hear, especially for a boy of twelve. The story stayed with me.

Years later, I mentioned the Ray Olson manhunt to my editor, wondering if this might be a captivating subject for a novel. Intrigued, he gave me the nod … and an advance. But before I left his office, he said something that struck me as odd. He asked if I could handle it.

"Handle it?" I replied, "of course I can handle it."

Now, with the manuscript nearly finished, I wonder.

Chapter 1
June 17, 1939

*T*wo Sawyer County patrol cars sped down Highway B toward northwest Wisconsin's Chippewa Flowage. Turning onto North River Road, Sheriff George Seehuetter signaled the car behind to stop.

"I want three men to drop back into the woods and circle the cabin from the right. Three more from the left. At exactly eight forty-five, Deputy Hamblin, Cullie, and I will move in. If he runs for it, don't let him get past you. But remember, Olson hasn't been convicted of anything yet. Nobody shoots unless I give the order."

The three teams of three men took up their positions and waited until time came for the circle to tighten. Then …

"Ray Olson, this is the Sawyer County Sheriff. Come out with your hands where I can see them."

No response.

"Give up, Olson. It's the only way out."

Again, nothing.

"We don't want any trouble. Come out with your hands up."

Still no reply.

Hamblin tried the door, finding it locked from the inside. Cullie Johnson grabbed a shovel leaning against the wall. He broke the latch on the second swing. Seehuetter pulled the door open. A hooked screen door came next.

"C'mon, Ray," said Hamblin. "This is your last chance. Either you come out or we're comin' in."

Still no response.

The sheriff nodded to Cullie who forced the shovel between the screen door and jamb. He gave a twist, then kicked open the door. The three lawmen peered into the dark room. There, with one foot on the bed, the other on a wooden crate, loomed the figure of Ray Olson aiming a shotgun at them.

Each man felt his blood run cold upon hearing the click of the hammer being cocked.

Chapter 2

Six years earlier.

Trouble followed him like Mondays follow Sundays. Had he taken any other road, this farmer's son from Waukesha County, August Frederick Buelo, may have turned out to be just another regular fella, some poor sap working his way through life, trying to make ends meet. But that wasn't Augie's style. To him, life was all or nothing—full throttle—winner take all.

The smoke from his cigarette gave him up twice. The second time it happened on a remote island on Lake Namakagon in northwest Wisconsin. The first, a cold October night in 1933, at a farm on the end of a long, narrow lane, not far from Milwaukee.

No lights on in the farmhouse, upstairs or down. No car in the driveway other than his rattletrap 1926 Model T Ford. Augie stepped to the porch, struck a match on the door jamb, and lit a Lucky Strike. He stood there, listening, looking, smoking his Lucky about half-way to the butt before he knocked. No one answered. Augie turned the knob. The door opened. He walked in like he owned the place.

"Anybody home?"

No answer.

"Ma? Pa? Anyone?" he said.

No answer.

He went to work.

The beam from his flashlight lit up the contents of the top left desk drawer. He hoped to find money. Instead, he found a revolver. Augie slipped it into the pocket of his coat, a long, blue-denim oilskin he swiped from God knows who down at the National Avenue truck stop. Probably some truck driver fortunate to have a job. In 1933, Augie didn't. Applying his twisted, junkyard logic, he figured he had the right. After all, the chump hung it on the coat rack, didn't he? Right there by the door. Easy pickin's. What a sucker. Besides, the Journal said it might rain that night. Augie thought a raincoat might come in handy.

He pulled the next drawer open, then the next, then turned his light toward the kitchen. He opened the first cabinet to find plates, cups, saucers, then closed it. The cookie jar! He lifted the lid. Stale oatmeal cookies. Stuffing two in his mouth, he shook one tin canister after another until a Chase & Sanborn coffee can sang out like a church bell. He dropped his cigarette butt on the floor, crushed it with his foot, and pulled the lid from the can, slicing his thumb on the sharp edge.

"Dang it!"

The twenty-two-year-old, six-foot-two, broad-shouldered, dark-eyed thief dumped the contents of the can on the counter. He scooped up the bills, stuffing them into the pocket with the pistol. Coins came next, same pocket.

Augie heard an upstairs door creak open and the snap of a light switch. He froze.

"Papa, that you?" The child's voice sounded weak. "Papa? Somebody with you? I smell a cigarette."

Augie crept toward the kitchen door.

"Papa, who you with? Why don't you turn on the lights?"

"Go back to bed."

"Where's my papa?"

"Go back to bed! Hear me?"

"You ain't my papa. You get outa here."

Augie dashed out the kitchen door. He tripped, fell, got up and stumbled to his car. Stepping to the front, he fumbled for the crank, smearing blood on it. One quick turn and the Model T shook to a start. He jumped in, jammed it in gear, released the brake, turned on the headlights, and sped out of the yard just as the porch light came on behind him.

Clattering down the narrow, dirt driveway between the farm and the highway, he seemed to hit every rut and rock. Far ahead he saw headlights coming. Closer now, he slowed, pulling as far to the right as he dared. The other vehicle, a Chevrolet truck, did the same. As the driver rolled down his window, Augie pulled the throttle lever down. Chevrolet and Ford fenders met, screeching like rusty hinges on a jail cell door.

Rocks and ruts didn't slow him now. And he didn't stop when he reached the highway. Cranking the wheel, he laid on the gas again, squeezing all the speed he could from the old engine.

Another car came toward him. A single, flashing red light. A howling siren. He slowed. It passed. He exhaled. Then, a flash of headlights in the rearview mirror said they made a U-turn. They'd be on him before he could make another mile. Augie opened the throttle again, searching for any way out. A curve ahead! The instant the red light disappeared from his mirror, he slammed his light switch in, then cranked the wheel hard right. Tires squealing, his car bounded and bounced down the shoulder into a cornfield. Lights still off, he floored it again, plowing down row after row of six-foot-high cornstalks. Behind, a flicker of light said the patrol car passed by, its siren fading into the cold night air.

Augie stopped. There'd soon be more cops. He couldn't risk the highway. He couldn't use his headlights. Even with them on, all he would see is corn falling before his car. He slammed his fist on the steering wheel. "Dang it! Dang it all!"

He crept forward in low gear, dry cornstalks polishing the car's undercarriage and wedging tight against the hot exhaust pipe. The car filled with smoke.

"Jesus! The corn's on fire!"

Augie pulled the throttle down again, picked up speed, shifted into high, and rattled through the corn, flames behind. With a thump-bump, his front wheels left the last cornrow and climbed onto the shoulder of a gravel road. He swerved away from the glow of the city and turned on his headlights. Speeding off, only a thin trail of smoke followed.

The neon sign in the front window blinked MAUDE'S COFFEE CUP. Augie's Model T rumbled to a stop near the garbage cans out back. Smoke gone now, he walked around his car, pulling cornstalks from the front axle and fenders. Next, he pulled a comb from his shirt pocket and stroked his black, wavy hair before entering the diner through the back door.

7

"Hey, stranger," said the young brunette behind the counter, "what brings you out at this hour?"

"Couldn't sleep, Delores. Thought I'd go for a drive."

"You been burning leaves?"

"Why?"

"You smell like smoke."

"Yeah? Well, maybe I burnt up a pile of leaves down at my Pa's house."

"What can I get for you?"

"Gimme a Coke. And cut me a piece of that raisin pie there. And put a scoop of ice cream on it, Baby."

"Raisin pie *à la mode,* comin' right up, Sweetie."

"Yeah. That's it, Doll. *À la mode.* A nice, big scoop."

"This isn't on the cuff, is it? Maude doesn't want me to serve you anything you can't pay for. Says your tab's too high and she's not running some Chicago soup kitchen."

"Maude said that? She's got a lotta nerve. Thinks I'm some kinda bum."

"Well, you know Maude."

"She got no right. I ain't no bum, Delores. Not by a mile. Here, take this." He pulled a twenty from his coat pocket. "That'll cover my tab, this here piece of pie, and the rest you can keep for a tip."

"Twenty bucks? Holy cow!"

"I got big plans for you and me, Baby."

"Where'd you get twenty bucks? You rob a bank or something?"

Augie stared at Delores, saying nothing.

"Oh, Jeez Augie. You stole this money?"

A police car pulled up to the diner.

"Naw, I earned it," he said, watching two officers exit their car. "But, if anyone asks, I been here over an hour. Maybe an hour and a-half, see?"

"Sure, Augie."

"Say it. Say it!"

"Hour and a-half, Augie."

"Thanks, Baby. I'll make it up to you."

"Aw, forget it. I'd do anything for you, you big Palooka. Anything. You know that."

The bell over the door rang as a patrolman entered.

"Evenin', Delores."

"Hi, Officer Benson."

Augie ignored the patrolman.

"Say, Delores, you didn't see a Model T Ford go zippin' by a few minutes ago, did you?"

"No, not that I noticed. Ever since the supper rush things have been pretty quiet."

The officer set his hat on the counter. "Not so quiet out on the highway."

"High schoolers racing again? Those crazy kids are sure to get themselves killed one of these nights."

Augie slipped off his stool and walked to the men's room.

"Racing? No. Somebody robbed Pete Robertson's place. Cut through McCarry's cornfield to make his getaway. Corn caught fire. Waukesha Fire Department is on the way now to put it out."

"Jeez! Maybe it was John Dillinger. You think?"

"No, Delores. Just some penny-ante thief too dumb to put out his smoke before robbing Pete and Martha of their milk money. Poor little Sarah was upstairs in bed with the chickenpox. Scared the bejesus out of her. Kid wasn't too scared or too sick to call us, though."

Delores poured coffee into a cup and placed it on the counter for the officer. Augie returned to his pie as the back door opened. The second officer came in through the kitchen, revolver drawn. He glanced at at his partner, then Augie. "There's a Model T out back. Motor's hot."

Officer Benson turned on his stool. "Your car, young fella?"

"Me? Uh, yeah. That's my Ford out back. So what?"

"Why not park in front like regular folks?"

"Oh, it's just a rusty old rattletrap. I never park it out front of a joint if I don't have to. Might give a place a bad name or somethin'.

9

Even this dump."

"Say, don't I know you from somewhere?"

"Me? Naw. Unless you saw me play football in high school."

"You played for Waukesha?"

"No. Mukwonago."

"How long you been here, son?"

"Twenty-five years and then some."

"I mean here, wise guy. In the diner."

"Oh, 'bout long enough to chow down, chew the fat with Delores, read yesterday's funny papers, and gobble up some of this raisin pie."

Delores poured another cup for the second patrolman. "Augie stopped in here about an hour and a-half ago, Officer Benson."

"Son, can you explain why your engine's still hot?"

"I left it running awhile. On chilly nights like this the motor's hard to turn over. Gotta keep her warm. She's just a rusty old rattletrap, y'know."

"Hard starter, huh?"

"Hard starter? Try no starter. It's busted. Gotta crank my dang arm off when it's cold."

"There's some corn hangin' underneath," said the other officer. "How come?"

"Say, what is this? Why you asking me all this stuff? How should I know? Maybe somebody's pullin' a fast one. Why, for all I know, *you* coulda put that corn there yourself, see?"

Officer Benson stood. "Son, I want you to empty your pockets out onto the counter. Nice and slow."

"Or what?"

Benson pulled out his handcuffs. "Or we take you down to the county jail and sort it out there, Augie. Now quit stalling. Empty your damn pockets and don't give me no lip."

"All right. All right." Augie pulled his Luckys from one coat pocket and matches from the other. He placed his wallet on the counter along with a jackknife and less than a dollar in change. "You cops got no right to pester honest people. You oughta be out lookin' for that crook," he said, placing a rabbit's foot on the counter. "There. That's it. Now what? Want me to take off my coat? My shirt? My pants? Right here in front of Delores?"

"Turn around, son." Benson patted Augie's pockets. "Okay, go ahead and put your things away. How come your coat smells like smoke?"

"As I was tellin' my girl before you butted in on us, I raked up some leaves at my pa's tonight and burnt 'em. No law against that, is there?"

Delores added, "That's right, officer. Augie said he was burning some leaves earlier."

"How long did you say he's been here?"

"Gosh, must be going on a couple of hours, I'd say."

"You sure about that, young lady?"

"Sure as shootin', Officer Benson."

Benson sat again. The other officer walked toward the men's room.

Augie finished his pie. "I still say the both of you should be scourin' the highway for that robber instead of here botherin' somebody who's just tryin' to mind his own business."

"Yeah, well, you can be sure we'll nab him. Small time crooks all slip up sooner or later."

The men's room door opened. Pistol drawn again and a waste basket in hand, the second officer approached. "Kid, I want you to put both hands on the counter."

"Why? What the heck for?"

"Hands on the counter. Right now!"

"All right! All right! For cripes sake, you don't have to get so riled up."

"Found this under the sink." He dumped the wastebasket on the counter. Paper towels, bills and coins scattered.

Augie grinned. "Well, look at that. You're one, lucky copper, that's what. Wish I woulda seen that stash. I s'pose it's 'cause I don't spend my time rummagin' through the trash like some garbage-grubbin' pole cat."

Officer Benson pulled out his handcuffs as the second officer said, "And I found this here revolver in the toilet tank."

Augie shook his head. "This ain't got nothin' to do with me. You coppers are barkin' up the wrong tree. I'm tellin' ya, you got the wrong guy."

"Wrong or right, we're takin' you in, son."

Augie jumped off his stool and charged straight into the chest of Officer Benson, knocking him across the diner. Both sprawled across the floor. Augie jumped up and over the counter, dashing out the back door, wedging it shut with a garbage can. He raced to his car and cranked and cranked and cranked until Officer Benson's nightstick ended his escape with a sharp *crack*. He dropped to the ground, then felt the handcuffs' cold steel biting into his wrists.

Delores watched as the officers stuffed her boyfriend into the back seat of the patrol car, blood trickling from his head.

"Bail me out, Baby. Bail me out soon as you can."

"Augie, I don't have the money."

"You'll find it, Baby. I know you will."

Chapter 3

"All rise."

Judge Henry Broadmore stepped up to the bench. He lowered his head to peer over his glasses at the defendant, then sat. "August Frederick Buelo, it says here that you broke into the home of Pete and Martha Robertson, robbed them of their milk money, and frightened the daylights out of their daughter. Is that so?"

"No, sir. Well, yes, but not ..."

"Well, what is it, son? Did you or did you not steal from these good folks?"

"I didn't break in, Judge. The door was open. I knocked first, then called out to see if anybody was home."

"Was there? Anybody home, I mean."

"Nobody called back so I figured the place was empty."

Judge Broadmore turned toward the Robertsons. "Gus Buelo isn't the only unemployed fellow willing to relieve you of your money if given the chance. You folks need to get into the habit of locking your door. You hear me?"

"Yes, your Honor."

Broadmore turned back to the defendant. "So, because the Robertson's door was unlocked, you thought you'd help yourself to anything you want. Right Gus?"

"Augie."

"What?"

"Folks call me Augie, Judge."

"You got a job, Augie?"

"Nope. Not right now. Used to work at Munson's doing masonry until they lost the business and the bank shut it down."

"What do you do for money these days? A young man like yourself needs some cash coming in. How do you pay your bills? What do you do?"

"Oh, I do this and that."

"This and that?"

"Yep."

"By this and that you mean robbing good folks of the money

they labored for?"

"Aw, I didn't do no harm. Just took a few bucks outa an old coffee can, that's all."

"Officer Williams, here, says he found twenty-one dollars in bills and another eight in silver. Is that about right, Augie? Is that what you stole?"

Pete Robertson stood. "'Bout twice that much, Judge."

"Augie, just how much did you steal?"

"I never really had the chance to count it up. Besides, for all I know, one of them officers might have pocketed a twenty."

"I will disregard that last statement, son."

"You're the judge."

"Yes. I am. And what I'm hearing you say, Augie, is that you entered the Robertson home in the dark of night and stole their money. Is that right?"

"I s'pose. But I woulda paid it back. When times are better."

"You stole their money, frightened the daylights out of their sickly daughter. Then you sped off down the road, right?"

"I s'pose."

"You s'pose?"

"Yes, Judge. I s'pose you're right."

"And when you saw the flashing red light of a county patrol car, instead of stopping, you tried to outrun them by cutting across a corn field? Is that right?"

"I s'pose."

"And later on, when Officer Williams and his partner found you in the diner—what's the name of that diner?"

"Maude's Coffee Cup."

"Yes. Maude's Coffee Cup. When they came in, you hid the stolen money in a wastebasket in the men's room. We know you did because they found a fresh cut on your hand, blood on the starting crank of your car and blood on some of the bills. Around here, we call that an open and shut case. Do you know what I mean by open and shut case, Augie?"

"Well, uh, yes, I guess so. But ..."

"No buts about it. You entered someone's house uninvited, stole money from good, hard-working, law-abiding, tax-paying citizens, avoided capture by driving through a cornfield, ruining acres of corn, causing a fire that brought two firetrucks and ten men out into the countryside in the middle of the night. Then you tried to slip out of the problem by hiding the stolen money in a wastebasket in the restroom of a diner. Is that not right, Augie?"

"I s'pose it is, Judge."

"And the only excuse you have for your behavior is that you're out of work? Is *that* not right?"

"Yes, sir, that's right."

"And it was you who robbed the Vernon Grocery Store. Is that not right?"

"What? No. I didn't rob no grocery store. Who told you that?"

"You have anything else to say for yourself?"

"No, well, only that I'm awful sorry for what I did that night and any grief I caused at the Robertson place and I'd like to pay back the money I stole and maybe I can do some farm work to make up for the corn and such."

"Hmm. Well. That's nice of you, son. But, like you said, I am the judge. And folks here in Waukesha County would put someone else on this bench if they learned you were not held responsible and taught a good lesson for your actions that night. The State of Wisconsin has a new work program that will allow you to learn a trade and keep you out of circulation for a while."

"A work program? What kind of a ..."

"It's for inmates of the penitentiary, Augie. I'm sending you to the Waupun State Prison."

"Jesus, Judge. You're sending me to prison for snitching a few dollars? How long?"

"Son, the theft charge would be one year if not for the fact that you also stole that pistol. Committing misdemeanor theft while in possession of a firearm makes it a felony punishable by a term not less than three years."

"Three years? But ..."

"Behave yourself and you might be out in two. August Frederick Buelo, I hereby find you guilty and sentence you to three years hard labor at the Wisconsin State Prison in Waupun. And, while you are there, I hope you learn your lesson and find the Lord and a worthwhile trade, son."

Judge Henry Broadmore smacked his gavel on the bench.

"Next case."

Chapter 4

The gray-green hallways and cells of Waupun State Prison served as August Buelo's home for the next two years. During that stay, he made a few friends—friends who taught him more about getting into rather than staying out of trouble. He didn't mind the training he'd been given in the prison kitchen, though peeling carrots, onions, and potatoes wasn't his idea of a future career. Still, it was better than that month when his on-the-job training had him scrubbing floors and toilets, again not his career choice. He found the six-week-long stint of interior painting far more to his liking. His steady hand proved to be useful when painting trim. His reputation as a skillful painter grew within the prison walls. Enough so, that his next assignment was in the outer office of Warden Oscar Lee.

A tall, thin prison guard watched him in silence as he mixed his paint, stuffed a clean rag in his back pocket, and climbed the ladder to paint the crown molding along the ceiling. When near the open transom over the door to the inner office, Augie overheard the warden speaking into the mouthpiece of his desktop telephone.

"Mornin' Governor La Follette. I trust you're doing well today?"

...

"Marvelous. And the missus? She's fine, too?"

...

"Wonderful. Say, you sure hit the jackpot when you hitched up with her, Governor."

...

"Yep, you, sir, are a lucky man, you are."

...

"What? What's that?"

Augie descended the ladder, then moved it closer to the door. He climbed, dipped his brush, and listened again while painting.

"Why, thank you Governor," said Warden Lee. "I truly appreciate that, sir. We Progressives have to stick together. I believe we are key to the future of both state and nation.

"Say, I have several proposals that will get you noticed in the newspapers, Phil … er … Governor. Some improvements in our penal system policies that will be good both for the inmates and for the citizens of Wisconsin. If you're willing to go along, I am certain the changes they bring about will make a real difference when the next election rolls around. Might just clinch it for you, in fact."

…

"Well, I don't know about that, sir. But I do know this—the press will eat this up, Governor. Eat it up like strawberry ice cream on Independence Day."

…

"What's that? Oh, no, Governor. This won't become something the Democrats can use against you. On the contrary, it's sure to be a feather in your cap. Look. Let me spell it out for you. Three major changes in how we rehabilitate our inmates."

…

"First off, I think we should dispense with the practice of handcuffing the men to their cell doors overnight."

…

"Hmm? Yes, I know this has been the practice followed over the past six or seven decades. But to me, the warden of this institution, that doesn't matter. These men aren't going anywhere. They know it's no use to try to escape. We've got things buttoned up tight here, Governor. Only a fool would try to break out."

…

"Escapees? Well, sure. There's a man now and then who lusts for freedom. But nobody's tried to escape for twenty years and the men all know it. Shackling them to their cell doors is no deterrent, Governor. It only serves to foster discontentment among our inmates. Besides, it's just plain wrong. Dehumanizing, in fact. No other state prisons shackle their inmates any more. Only Wisconsin. You give the word and I'll pass the order along today."

…

"What's that? Oh. Thank you. The men will appreciate it. And sleep better beginning tonight, I'm sure."

"Okay. Item two on my list. I say we get rid of the black and white prison stripes and give the men blue denim uniforms and, I might add, some dignity. These are modern times, Governor. The men deserve better outfits than prison stripes. I know you'll see it my way on this. It's a matter of humanitarianism. You'll get a pile of good press out of this. Coast to coast."

...

"No, sir. I can order bolts of blue fabric and have some of our inmates in the laundry room sew the uniforms. Good experience for them."

...

"Good. Good. Okay."

...

"Third item on my list is this. I say we expand our efforts to train some of our inmates—give them the skills they need to make a go of it on the outside. If we were to put the most trustworthy of our young men to work building homes, bridges, roads, and such, they'd have the knowledge and abilities to get a decent job after their term is up."

...

"Come again?"

...

"Joking? No, I'm serious, Governor! Most of our inmates are quite capable. My plan is to give them on-the-job training and experience that will help them contribute to society once they're released. Help keep them out of trouble, too. By offering our best men, the cream of the crop, jobs on my prison construction crews, we'll help them get a leg up. A chance to make something of themselves."

...

"Cost? Well, sure there's a cost, Governor. Name one thing in Government that doesn't come with a cost. But, other than a thousand dollars-or-so for tools, supplies, and such, this program won't cost taxpayers much. Might even make a profit for the state."

...

"No, sir. We'd run it like any other business. Our earnings from each project we finish would pay for the security guards' wages, transportation costs, and living expenses of each work detail."

...

"Runaways? With all due respect, Governor, I disagree. You see, we'd hand pick each team of workers to make sure we have only the most trustworthy of men. I'll select only those men who have demonstrated their intention to abide by the law. And my crews will consist mainly of short-timers. A man with one or two years left to serve out of a five or ten-year sentence isn't likely to abuse my program. Those who we feel are a flight risk or might jeopardize the welfare of the public will not participate."

...

"Oh, I'd say about two dozen men on each prison work crew. Depends on the size of the job, I suppose."

...

"Well now, I agree there will be some public concern, Governor. However, I feel the good newspaper coverage you will get from this will assure you of a win come November. We can work with the press prior to beginning—make sure folks understand this is a safe, worthy program that will reduce their tax burden in the long run."

...

"A test run? Why, yes, I can have a pilot project up and running in a couple of weeks. In fact, I have been anticipating this for a while and have the perfect job lined up. It's a cabin on a lake in the far northwestern corner of the state. Up near Lake Superior."

...

"Yes, sir. Bayfield County. A sleepy little town called Cable. Not far from Hayward."

...

"You've been there? Well good. Then you know it's quite remote. I don't suppose folks in the southern half of the state will mind us conducting this pilot project way up north."

...

"Yes, I'd like to ship the materials this week. I'll hand pick the first work crew myself and send the men up in one of our prison buses."

...

"Middle of June. We'll set up a camp on the property. If all goes well, we should be finished by the end of August at which time the men will return to the prison until the next project comes along."

...

"Governor La Follette, I thank you. Like I said, these three improvements are bound to muster up nationwide attention—attention for your progressive policies. You won't regret this decision, I assure you."

...

"I will, sir. You can always count on me."

...

"Yes. And tell your wife that Harriet and I really enjoyed that blackberry pie she served us last time we were in the capital. She's a keeper, Governor."

...

"Why, thank you. And good day to you, too, sir."

Oscar Lee set the phone on his desk and hung the receiver on the cradle.

In the next room, August finished painting the molding. He descended the ladder, then rinsed his brush in turpentine. His painting supplies in one hand and the ladder under one arm, Augie left the warden's outer office, escorted by the guard.

Chapter 5

The prison guard led August Buelo down the hall and up the steps, stopping before a large oak door. He read the name etched into the polished, brass nameplate, "Oscar Lee – Warden."

"Hey! What is this?" Augie grumbled to the guard. "I ain't done nothin'. Why you takin' me here?"

"Quiet, Buelo. You'll find out soon enough."

"You got no reason to pick on me. I been clean since my first day here. Clean as a whistle."

"Tell that to the warden. He'll be here any minute." He shoved Augie into the chair before the large mahogany desk.

"Hey, take it easy, will ya? You dang screws got no right to push a fella around like that."

"Shut your mouth or I'll shut it for you. And try to have the good sense to show some respect when the warden gets here."

A sandwich in hand, Warden Lee entered his office from a side door, stopping briefly to study the inmate. Then, with a scowl, plopped down in his chair and stuffed the remainder of the sandwich into his mouth, licking his fingers. He then pawed through a pile of folders, stopping at one. Opening it, he belched, then looked up as Augie spoke.

"What's this all about, Warden? I ain't done nothin' wrong. If somebody fingered me, they was lyin'. I'm clean. I tell ya, I'm clean."

"Take it easy, Augie. Nobody fingered you." He belched again. "I swear to God, as much as I love these limburger and onion sandwiches, they're gonna be the death of me."

"Then why am I here?"

"It says in your file that you're in for armed robbery."

"Yeah, well, I got a raw deal."

"You and every other inmate, Augie."

"Look. All I did was swipe some dough out of an old coffee can, see? And I found a gun in a drawer and took that too. Thought I could pawn it, that's all. Most time I shoulda done is ninety days in county. But, no. Judge Broadmore called it armed robbery even though he knew it weren't. Gave me a three year stretch. I got a raw deal, I tell ya. I shouldn't be here."

"Maybe I can help you."

"Sure ya can. Sure ya can."

"You underestimate my ability to improve your situation."

"You? Help me? Why would ya? I ain't nothin' to you and your kind but another poor slob behind bars. Sheesh. You help me. That's a knee-slapper."

"Says here in your file that you know something about masonry. Is that true?"

"Maybe. So what?"

"And you're quite good with a paintbrush. I've seen your work."

"What of it?"

"How'd you like some time on the outside?"

"Come again?

"I said, how would you like to spend some time working for me beyond the prison walls?"

"Sure, Warden. I'll tell you what. You hand me my walkin' papers and I'll skedaddle faster than you can say twenty-three skidoo. I'd give anything to see this joint in my rearview mirror."

"I can't do that, Augie. However, what if I told you that you could spend the summer beyond these walls, teaching your masonry and painting skills to other inmates?"

"You serious?"

"You bet your bottom dollar I'm serious. I can put you on a special work detail right away."

"S'pose it's better than rotting away in this God-forsaken hellhole."

"Watch your mouth, Buelo," snapped the guard.

"It's all right," said Lee. "Even I don't like being cooped up in this place during the heat of summer. Augie, if you play your cards right, you'll soon be building a cottage by a lake way up north."

"What's the catch?"

24

"No catch. No strings. What do you say? How about spending the summer up north camped out with my crew?"

"Some chain gang? No thanks."

"No, not a chain gang. Imagine a couple dozen inmates, mostly short-timers like you, all willing to gain skills and improve their chance of getting a job by learning how to build a house. It's a plan I developed to help men make it on the outside once they get paroled."

"Seems to me I got wind about this before."

"Augie, I plan to have ten crews workin' around the state, building houses, repairing bridges, logging off state woodlots."

"Ya don't say."

"That's only the tip of the iceberg. I want to give every man in here a chance at a new, productive life and no reason to end up in prison ever again."

"What's in it for you?"

"Me?"

"Ya, you, Warden. What's your angle?"

"Look, Augie, plenty of others will want in. I can find someone else."

"All right, all right. I'll do it. Anything to get out of here. Anything. You name it."

"All I ask is that you keep your nose clean and teach the others what you know about the building trade."

"I'm your man, Warden. Long as it gets me outa here."

Oscar Lee turned to the guard. "Officer, escort Mr. Buelo back to his cell. And on your way, tell the kitchen I'd like another limburger and onion sandwich with extra mayonnaise."

"Extra mayonnaise. Yes sir."

Shortly after dawn on a misty June morning, the doors to the prison bus closed with twenty-four inmates inside, each with one hand shackled to the seat. The driver, a prison guard named Bert Stinson, called out each man's name one last time, marking the roster as they shouted, "Here!" August Buelo sat in the third seat, behind Sam Campbell (seven years for extortion) and Clarence "Spike" Brown (two-to-three for check fraud). Behind Augie slept Harley Crandon (two years for assault). Wilbur Wilcox shouted the last "Here." Roll call finished, the driver turned the key. The engine revved and the bus rolled across the prison yard and out the gate.

A mile down the road, Augie leaned forward. "Spike, Whaddaya think got you onto the warden's work crew?"

"Is that what this is? A work detail?"

"You didn't know?"

"I thought we were being transferred to another joint. What's this all about, anyhow?"

"It's a special work detail. Something Warden Lee cooked up. He figures he's going to teach us how to build houses and such. We're headed someplace up north to build a cottage."

"Say, you on the level?"

"You bet I'm on the level. Got it straight from the horse's mouth, I did."

"You mean ...?"

"Yep. Warden Oscar Lee told me himself. Wants us to build a home on some lake up north. I'll tell ya, Spike, this is a dang site better than scrubbing toilets and peeling spuds."

"You said it, pal."

"So, why do you s'pose they picked you, Spike?"

"Me? Well, I worked for a plumber till I got sent up for cashing bad checks. Can't say I was much good at either one, though. How 'bout you?"

"I can lay brick and sling paint."

"What you in for, Augie?"

"My rap sheet says armed robbery but all I did was swipe a few bucks and a pistol from some farmhouse. Got me three years. Can you imagine that? Three years?"

"Aw, you'll be out in two. Who was your judge?"

"Broadmore."

"Sheesh! Lucky you ain't doin' a twenty-year stretch in Alcatraz. Ol' Henry Broadmore comes on like your long lost uncle then slaps you with the max. I oughta know. I was up for two counts and that jerk gave me eighteen months for each count. I think he's out to fill up every jail in the state."

Augie turned around. "Harley, what kind of work did you do before you got sent up?"

"Loan collection."

"Huh?"

"I used to break a few fingers here and there to help remind freeloaders they had to pay up."

"Must be something else you done before that."

"I did some carpentry in the army. Mostly building barracks. Why?"

"We're being sent to build a cottage someplace up north."

"You stringin' me along, Buelo?"

"Warden said so himself."

"Any change of scenery is better than bein' on the inside."

"I ditto that, Harley."

"Say, Augie, this place we're goin' to, you s'pose there will be any dames around?"

"Danged if I know."

"Maybe they'll let us have visitors."

"Yeah. I'd give my eye teeth to see my gal, Delores."

"And, oh, what I'd give for a chance to give my gal a good squeeze again."

"You said a mouthful, Harley. You said a mouthful."

Ten hours later, three trucks loaded with lumber, hardware, and tools rumbled down a crude logging road, stopping by a lake. Behind them came a white prison bus with twenty-four inmates handcuffed to their seats. The drivers set their brakes. A tall, uniformed man at the front of the bus stood.

"Fellas, my name is Stanley Van Camp. Mosta youse know me as Dutch. Warden Lee has put me in charge of keepin' you healthy, happy, and toes to the line. From here on out, you take your orders from me, see?

"Now, men, I want you to take a look out there at that lake. Ain't that something? Ain't that better than lookin' at the inside of a prison cell? Not only is it a sight for sore eyes, but it's clean and clear and full of big fish ready for the catchin'. The warden even got fishin' licenses for you mugs so you won't end up in front of another judge. For the next twelve weeks or so, we will be sleeping in tents right here by this lake. We are building us a cottage—a lodge such as most of you never seen before. After each day's work you'll be able to swim, fish, or, if you want, you can sit around playin' checkers, readin' magazines, and so forth and so on. Of course, if you'd rather, you're welcome to go back to the prison. Anyone want that?"

Nobody spoke.

"That's what I figured. Men, Officer Bert Stinson and me, we're gonna come 'round pretty soon and unlock your handcuffs. From then on, your only shackles will be knowin' that if you run off you will be hunted down, captured, and carted back to the prison—away from this little piece of God's paradise you see out there. Understand?"

"Don't you mean shot in the back and left in some swamp for the wolves?" came a question from the back.

"Nobody's gettin' shot, Harley. If you could see past the nose on your face, you woulda noticed me and Bert are not armed. And we'll be your only guards."

"What about them drivers in the other three trucks?"

"They're headin' back tomorrow as soon as you men unload the supplies. Anything else, Harley?"

"Sheesh! What kind of prison is it that don't even give a guard a shotgun to keep us mugs in line? Makes me feel like I'm gettin' gypped, Dutch."

"Harley, you are not getting gypped. The poor slobs back at Waupun—they're the ones gettin' gypped. Compared to them, you'll be livin' the life of Riley. Any more questions? No? All right. You'll find tents and bedrolls in the first truck. Make camp and get some rest, men. Tomorrow we start work."

28

The gang of inmates, a cook, three drivers, and two unarmed guards pitched tents, built a fire, and soon ate supper by the shore.

"Dutch," said Augie, "if you don't mind me askin', who's plannin' on takin' over this lodge after we get done with it?"

"Buelo, there's some questions better off not bein' asked."

"Aw, c'mon, Dutch. I won't spill the beans. Spit it out, wouldya?"

Dutch eyeballed Augie down and up. "You didn't hear it from me, but what we are buildin' here … this lodge on this lake?"

"Yeah?"

"It's for him."

"Him?"

"Three truckloads of supplies, two guards, and twenty-four convicts. All working for him."

"For Pete's sake, Dutch, quit beatin' around the bush! Who?"

Dutch glanced left, then right. "Lee."

"Oh, so that's his angle."

"Yep. We're buildin' Warden Oscar Lee of Waupun State Penitentiary his very own lakeside lodge. But keep it under your hat. If the newspapers ever found out, he'd be in the hot seat and we'd all be back in the pen. I don't want that any more than you."

"Mum's the word, Dutch. I bet there ain't a man in camp who'd let the cat out of the bag as long as the mosquito dope don't run out and Warden Lee don't make us eat limburger and onion sandwiches."

"With extra mayonnaise, Augie."

Chapter 6

A coffee and oatmeal breakfast was ready before dawn. Bert Stinson slapped the bottom of a copper pot with a wooden spoon and tent flaps soon flung wide. One by one, the bleary-eyed inmates held out their tin bowls as the cook, Marvin Waters (five to ten for stealing a Sheboygan delivery truck packed with bootleg Canadian whiskey) scooped oatmeal from a pot. The men ate, watching the rising sun peek through the trees across the lake.

It didn't take long for the gang to dig the trench and construct wooden forms for the outer wall and fireplace footings. Bags of cement were mixed with sand, rock, and water from the lake. One wheelbarrow at a time, they filled the forms with the concrete. Augie and Sam Campbell finished off the footings using trowels as others cleaned the cement troughs, shovels, and wheelbarrows.

Sam rested his trowel and walked over to the water bucket. He lifted the dipper and drank.

"So, Sam," said Augie, "Marvin tells me you'll be out by this time next year."

"Marv talks too much."

"What ya plannin' to do when you're out?"

"Me? I'm gettin' as far from this lousy part of the country as I can. I'll be on an express train headed for Tacoma before the door on my cell slams shut.

"Tacoma? What's out there?"

"I got friends out by Tacoma. Good friends."

"They can get you a job, then?"

"Me? A job? That's a good one, Augie."

"You got no work, then?"

"I'm allergic."

"To what?"

"Bosses. Never could get along with 'em."

"How you figurin' on gettin' by without a job?"

"Job? Don't need one. I got me other plans."

"Like what for instance?"

"With all the money there is changin' hands out there from the

31

timber mills to the shipping docks, I'll be in the money in the shake of a lamb's tail. How 'bout you? You got plans?"

"Me and my gal, Delores, are gonna settle down, raise us a batch of kids, enjoy the sunsets."

"Where?"

"Someplace quiet, that's all. Someplace we won't run into trouble with the law."

"Ain't no such place. I got news for you, pal, once they stamp ex-con on your record, there's no place in the Midwest where they won't be watchin' you like a hawk. You should think about comin' to Tacoma. Out there, you can get a fresh start."

"Naw. Me and Delores, we're gonna put down roots by Milwaukee someplace. I'm walkin' the straight and narrow, see? I've had enough of them prison bars to last me till I die."

"You? Goin' straight? That's a good one, kid. What kinda dope do you think's gonna hire an ex-con what's got a rap sheet showin' armed robbery? There's plenty of chumps outa work that they can pick from. You'll be just one more jailbird, some Joe standin' in the soup lines, buddy."

Augie picked up his trowel.

"I'll find work, I tell ya."

"Well, when you don't, you look me up out west. I'll fix you up."

"Think you could help me find a straight job out there?"

"Sure, sure, buddy. You just say the word."

"Well, maybe so. Maybe I'll get in touch if I can't find good work back home. Gotta be honest work, though. Delores won't go for anything that ain't legit."

"You gonna let some skirt run your life?"

"No, I ain't lettin' some skirt run my life. Besides, Delores ain't just some skirt.

"What is she? Some kind of a Harlow?

"More like Hedy Lamarr."

Augie put down his trowel. "Say, Sam, looks like we're 'bout done here. You go ahead and clean up your tools. I'll finish this off and we can join the others for chow."

After supper, Sam and Spike cast lures from shore, hoping for a largemouth bass or a northern pike. Other men fished from the boats provided by the warden or played cards by the fire. Stretched out in his tent, Augie read a letter from Delores. In it, she asked if she could visit him. He didn't read on. He jumped to his feet and ran to the mess tent.

"Say, Dutch! Dutch! My gal says she wants to come see me. Whaddaya think?"

"Jeez, Augie. I don't ..."

"Aw, c'mon, Dutch. See it my way, won'tcha? We have visiting time at the prison, don't we?"

"Yeah, Dutch," said Stubby Gilman (two years for bunko). "For cryin' out loud, Let the poor kid see his girl."

Dutch scratched his head. "Golly, fellas. Don't put me on the spot. I can't okay somethin' like this."

"Sure you can, Dutch," said Jimmy Johnson (former bookie), "I'd like to see my wife and kids one of these days, too. And Augie's got a point. We got visitin' rights in the joint. Why not here?"

"Have a heart, Dutch," pleaded Augie. "It's no big deal. Just say the word and I'll send Delores a letter tellin' her to come up on the train."

"All right! All right! I s'pose there's no harm in it long as it's not during work time. She can't stay here, though."

"There's a couple hotels in town," said Jimmy.

"Tell her to bring a tent and camp out," said Pete Walker (three years for grand theft auto). "Plenty of woods 'round here."

"Camp out?" said Augie. "Not my gal. No siree! No pup tent and bedroll for her. My Delores is a top-notch, first-class gal. A regular Hedy Lamarr."

"Well, let her know that she can come, but tell her she'll have to find a place to stay in town. She can visit you here in camp after work and on Sundays."

"Jeez thanks, Dutch. You're a pal—a *real* pal."

33

By the morning of the sixth day of work, the prison work crew had the first floor exterior walls up and were preparing for the second. Meanwhile, Dutch and Augie were out with the truck, scouring the area farms for fieldstone for the fireplace. Rumbling down woodland roads, they passed many pristine lakes and crossed bridges over picturesque rivers and creeks. In the hot, mid-afternoon sun, they tossed stone after stone onto the truck bed. On their way back to camp, they came to a resort.

"Say, Dutch, I sure could go for a cold root beer right now. I wonder if they don't have a pop machine in there. What say we pull in there and you loan me a nickel for a bottle of pop?"

"Naw, we better not, Augie. I don't want to risk getting called onto the carpet by the warden."

"Aw, Jeez, Dutch. Wouldn't a cold soda pop taste good right now? C'mon. Nobody's ever gonna know the difference."

"All right. All right, already! Quit yer yappin', will ya? I'll pull in and see if I can get us each a bottle of pop. But you have to stay in the truck. We got a deal, Augie?"

"You bet, buddy. I'll stay put."

Augie lit a cigarette as Dutch Kowalski entered the Westview Resort's main lodge. Beyond, a long row of small cabins lined the shore, each with a boat tied out front. Children played on a sandy beach. Adults relaxed nearby, some reading, some resting, others chatting.

"Howdy," came a voice from behind. "I'd like you to move your truck. This area's for guest parking only."

"Oh, my boss is comin' right out. Just went in for a bottle-a-pop."

"Well, just pull it up a few yards. Right under those trees, there. He'll find you."

"Sure, sure," said Augie, sliding behind the wheel. "You run this place?"

"Yep. Own it. Say, you fellas lookin' for work?" The tall, thin, mustached man jumped onto the running board as Augie turned the key. "I'm lookin' to hire a couple of fellas who aren't afraid of putting in an honest day's labor for good pay. Half-a-dollar an hour."

"Half-a-dollar? Jeez, thanks, but we've got work." Augie put the stick in first and let out the clutch. The truck slowly rolled forward. "We're building a lakeside home near here. I'm in charge of the masonry crew. Fieldstones in the back are for the fireplace."

"You don't say. You look like a hard-workin' honest fella. You ever need a summer job, you can get ahold of me here, son. Never a shortage of work, spring to fall."

The man stepped off the running board as his words registered with Augie. "An honest day's labor for good pay." Then, as he sat there behind the wheel, he realized his opportunity. Without further thought, he revved the engine, let out the clutch, turned the wheel, and headed for the town road. He was free. Free as a bird on the wing! Free to find Delores. He could be in Milwaukee by the next morning, Chicago by noon.

But, wait! His gal was on a train heading north. He was broke. He'd get caught. This was wrong—all wrong! She'd be sad, mad, maybe even hate him for it. They'd be on the lam for the rest of their lives. Augie slammed on the brakes, turned the truck around, and rumbled back up to the main lodge just as his boss came out of the front door.

Dutch stood near the driver's door, looking up. "What are you up to, Augie?"

"Me, Dutch? Nothin'. The owner of this place told me to move the truck, that's all."

"Don't play wise with me, kid."

"Honest, Dutch. Honest! Ask him yourself if you don't believe me. Go ahead! That's him right there." Augie waved at the tall, slim, mustached man who waved back. A pop bottle in each hand, Dutch approached the man, spoke, listened, and returned.

Augie slid over. Dutch handed him his root beer then climbed into the cab.

"See, Dutch? See? Didn't believe me, didja? Think I was gonna run off? Steal a state-owned truck and run off? You figure I wanna get sent back to the joint? Do more time? Whaddaya take me for? Stupid? That what ya think, Dutch? That I'm stupid?"

"Aw, I'm sorry, kid. I shoulda known better. I s'pose it's in my nature. Don't be sore."

"Sore? Naw, I'm not sore. Ol' Oscar Lee would be, though. But don't worry. You can trust me, Dutch. I won't rat on you for leavin' the keys in the truck. No, I'll keep it under my hat, pal."

"You do that. Now, drink your root beer. They want the bottles back."

Chapter 7

Wearing a blue dress and carrying a red and yellow plaid coat in one hand, a small valise in the other, Delores Olson boarded the Chicago Northwestern passenger car. She found a seat and raised the window to say goodbye to her grandmother standing on the platform.

"Delores, honey, you can still change your mind."

"For the last time, Grandma, I'm only going to visit Augie for a few days and nothing more. He's been locked up two years for a crime that amounted to little or nothing. He needs to know somebody back home still cares about him. I'll be back by Monday afternoon. You and Papa needn't worry."

"Oh, honey, don't go. You know that man is no good for you. Stay here. Spare yourself the heartache."

"I wish you didn't feel that way. Augie's treated me so well. Never even raised his voice to me. Can you say that about Papa? How often has Papa raised his voice to you? How many times has he slapped you? Or worse? Augie would never do that to me. He's a good man at heart. A good man who got a raw deal. A good man who needs me."

"He's a jailbird, Delores. Your mama would say the same if she was alive. Do it for her sake. Please?"

"Last call for Milwaukee, West Bend, Oshkosh, Ladysmith, and all points north," shouted the conductor. "All aboard." A burst of steam rushed from below the locomotive.

"You've got Augie all wrong. He's a good man. He needs my support, needs to know I care. I know Mama would approve. I'm going to go see him, Grandma, and I'll be back real soon."

"I love you, honey. So does your father. You be careful."

"I'll take care, Grandma. I love you, too. And, for Pete's sake, don't worry."

The train pulled out of the Waukesha depot, steam rushing and smoke billowing. Delores settled into her seat, pulled a copy of *Silver Screen* magazine from her valise and flipped through it. Outside, the city scenery dissolved into country landscapes.

Five stops and four hours later, the train pulled into Marshfield, Wisconsin. As it did, a young man carrying a briefcase took his seat across the aisle from Delores. The train left the station, rumbling north, the farms, fields, and woodlands gleaming in the summer sun.

The young man winked. "Where you headed, darlin'?"

Delores pretended not to hear.

"I said, where you bound to, miss?"

"Me? Oh, up north."

"How far up north?"

"Resort country."

"Really? That's funny, me, too," he replied.

"Looks like you're on business."

"Yep. Might say I'm in the real estate game on this trip."

"So, you buy and sell land?"

"Not exactly. My boss is sending me up to Hayward to look at some property and figure out what it's worth. He wants to build a house on one of the lakes up there. Told me to look it over to make sure he's not getting a bum deal."

"No kidding? He's building a house? My fella is helping to build a house on a lake up there right now. Maybe he could help your boss out."

"Maybe. This fella your husband?"

"Oh, my, no. He's my beau."

"What kind of work does this fella of yours do?"

"Masonry, mostly. But he's a darn good painter, too. And he can help out with plenty of other jobs. You should tell your boss about him."

"Sure I will. Say, you got a name?"

"Augie. Augie Buelo."

"No, no. I meant what's *your* name, darlin'?"

"Delores Olson. But Augie Buelo is the one your boss needs on his crew."

"So, Delores, this beau of yours ... is he on the train?"

"Augie? No he's working."

"Working where?"

Delores paused. "He's way out in the forest someplace. But you can always reach him through me. So, how do I get ahold of you? What's your name?"

"Johnny Moran. My uncle is Billy Moran. Ever heard of him?"

"Can't say as I have, Johnny."

"He's in the trucking business. Hauls liquid cheer from Canada to Chicago. Get my drift?"

"Hmm?"

"Joy juice, darlin'."

"I don't follow you."

"Uncle Billy's drivers bring booze across the border."

"Your uncle is a bootlegger?"

"He's in management, you might say. His drivers do the haulin'."

"Bootleggers."

"Sure, some call 'em that. Bootleggers, rum runners, other names, too. But to tell you the truth, they're just truck drivers tryin' to make a living. Not easy nowadays."

"Don't I know it!"

"So, what's your game, darlin'?"

"Me? Oh, I just work at a Woolworth's lunch counter back home in Mukwonago. It's down by Milwaukee."

"A waitress, huh?"

"That's me. Augie calls me his five and dime dame."

"Darlin', you can do better than that. Lots better," he said with a second wink.

"For instance?"

"Uncle Billy's got himself a string of nightclubs—nice joints—strictly upper class. Why, with your looks, you could be making tips that would put you on easy street in no time flat. You get my drift?"

"Yeah? Where are these upper class joints of your uncle's?"

"Mostly Chicago. One in Racine, one in Milwaukee, a couple in St. Paul. You interested?"

"Maybe. Can't say right now. Depends on how things go."

"With your fella, I suppose?"

"Augie has big plans for us. No telling what I'll be doing in the future."

"Any girl as good lookin' as you has the future in the palm of her hand, darlin'." Johnny pulled a flask from an inside coat pocket and slid off his seat, crossing the aisle to hers. "Say, let's have a little drink to your future." He unscrewed the cap. "Here's to a dame what's got it made, whether she takes me up on my offer or not, strikes it rich or not. Darlin', I wish you all the best." He handed the flask to Delores.

"No thanks," she said, pushing it back.

"Aw, come on. This is top shelf hooch!"

"I never touch your so-called *top shelf hooch*. I saw what it did to my father and too many others."

"Y'know, it's downright unlucky not to drink to a toast made in your honor. Here," he said pushing the flask her way again, "have a little snort."

"I said, no," she said louder, pushing it back.

He put his arm around her.

"Aw, c'mon."

She ducked out from under his arm and pushed him away. "Look! I've never in my life taken a drink with a stranger and I don't mean to start today. Now you get back to your own seat before I report you to the conductor."

"Now don't go gettin' your feathers in such a ruffle. I didn't mean nothin' by it. We got a long trip ahead of us. I just thought we could have some fun on the way," he said with a third wink. "You get my drift. Right, darlin'?"

"So all this talk about your uncle building a home and having restaurants, is all baloney, right? All part of your come-on line?"

"No, no. It's all true. True as true can be." He took a long pull from the flask. "Come here and sit next to me, darlin'. I don't bite, least not much. Let me fill you in, give you the full story."

"How do I know you're not just some masher stringing me along?"

"A masher? Me? Why, I'm nothin' but a passenger on a long train ride, just like you. C'mon, darlin'. Have a seat next to me, will ya? We can have some fun. Get my drift?"

Delores closed her magazine and moved into the aisle. Johnny grinned, slapping the seat. "Atta girl, darlin'."

Delores leaned in close. "Listen, Johnny *Moron*, and listen good. My fella, Augie, is an ex-football player. He's six-two and solid muscle and if he ever got wind that you were trying to get me to drink with you, get me to make nice with you, or do damn near anything else with you, why, he would rip your arm off at the shoulder and beat you to death with the bloody stump of it. Now, do you get *my* drift?"

"You ... you ain't gonna tell him, are you, darlin'?"

"So help me, Johnny, one more wink or *darlin'* from you and I swear to God I will!" Delores turned, walked down the aisle and exited to the next car.

At five-thirty that afternoon, a stationmaster directed Delores to a nearby farm on a quiet lake. She knocked on the farmhouse door.

41

"Yes?" said a short, stout woman.

"The stationmaster said you have rooms to rent, ma'am."

"Oh, he did, did he?"

"Yes, ma'am. Is it true you have rooms?"

"Well, of course it's true. Have you got any money? We don't cater to penniless tramps, y'know."

"Madam, I'm neither penniless nor a tramp and I resent your words." Delores turned. "Good evening."

"Oh, for heaven's sake, don't be in such a twitter, missy. Where's your sense of humor? I didn't say you were a tramp, I said we don't cater to 'em. What's the harm in that? C'mon in, for cryin' out loud."

Delores hesitated, then entered the woman's kitchen.

"Have you had your supper, yet? You look all skin and bones. Don't they feed you where you come from?"

"How much are your rooms, madam?"

"Dollar a night is fine and two bits for each meal you eat but only if you're at the table when we say grace. Six-thirty, noon, and six o'clock sharp. Now sit yourself down and I'll fix you a plate of something or other."

"You needn't do that."

"Well, I know I don't have to. I don't have to do anything that I don't want to. But that don't mean I can't get you a plate of food and a glass of beer to hold you over."

"Do you have milk?"

"Milk? You're askin' me if I have milk? Ha! Wait till I tell Pa that one. This is a dairy farm, for Pete's sake. Of course we have milk! I take it you're from a city. Chicago? Minneapolis? Milwaukee? St. Louis? Well, which is it, city gal? Spit it out, where the heck you from?"

"Waukesha, ma'am."

"Where in tarnation is that?"

"Near Milwaukee."

"See? Didn't I say so? City gal. Yep. I figured as much. So, what's your name, city gal?"

"Delores. Delores Olson."

"Well, Delores Olson, I'm Beatrice. Bertram's my hubby. Beatie and Bertie, they call us. He's tendin' to the barn chores right now. So are the boys. They'll be in soon as they finish up."

The door suddenly burst open. "Ma! Ma! Bossy's havin' trouble droppin' her calf. You gotta come right now. Pa says so!"

"All right, all right. I'll have to leave the dishes till later. Missy, your room's at the top of the stairs just to the left of the biffy. Go make yourself to home. I'll be back when the calf comes."

After breakfast, Delores laid an envelope on the table and placed a dime on top.

"Can one of you boys take this to the men who are building the cabin up the lake?"

"The prison gang?" asked their father.

"I'll go!" shouted Ozzie, the oldest.

"Me, too," said Ollie, the youngest.

"Wait one minute, Miss Olson," said their father. "What business do you have with them convicts?"

"I came to visit my beau, that's all. He's building a cabin up there. I need to get word to him that I'm here to see him."

"So, you are the gal of one of them bums?"

"He got a raw deal, that's all. He was sorry for what he did and shouldn't have been put in jail for more than a few weeks. Instead, they gave him three years. Put him on a work gang and now they have him building a house for the warden. It's not a fair thing to do to a fella who is good deep down in his heart."

"What did your fella do to get himself in such a jam?"

"Oh, I'm not saying what he did was right."

"What did he do?"

"Stole some money, that's all. Not much. Thirty, forty dollars. For that, they put him in Waupun State Penitentiary. It's not fair."

"Ozzie, you take the rowboat up to the camp where they're putting up that new cabin. Just leave this lady's note on the dock. Put a rock on it so it don't blow away."

"Sure, Pa."

"And don't you stop and talk to anyone there. You hear me?"

"Yes, Pa. I won't talk to a soul. I promise."

"And give this young woman back her dime."

"Oh, no, sir. I want Ozzie to keep the money. It's only fair."

Later that morning, Benny Dinkles (five years for swindling an old woman out of her life savings) ran up from the lake.

"Mister Dutch, Mister Dutch," he shouted, "I found this on the dock." He handed the envelope to the foreman.

Dutch tore it open. "Hmm. Go tell Augie I need to see him."

"Sure, Mister Dutch. Right away."

Minutes later, Augie stood before Dutch's tent.

"You wanted to see me, Dutchman?"

"I got a letter this morning. From your gal. Seems she's close by and wants to see you."

"No kiddin'?"

"Read it yourself," said Dutch, handing the note to Augie.

"Golly, Dutch. Ain't this swell? My girl's in town."

"Closer than that, Augie. She's stayin' at the farm down at the end of the lake."

"When can I go see her, Dutch?"

"Well, tomorrow's Saturday. We'll knock off work 'bout three o'clock. I'll send word to the farm that she can row up here if she wants. You and her can visit till suppertime."

"And Sunday? You did say she can come visit Sunday, right? Right, Dutch?"

"Sure, kid. In fact, you can walk into town with her and go to church if you've a mind to."

"Gosh, Dutch. You're a swell fella, puttin' such faith in me."

"Aw, don't think nothin' of it, kid. I trust you like I trust my own mother. Maybe more so."

Augie tossed and turned all night. Up before dawn, he helped Marvin prepare breakfast for the crew. Time seemed to drag on all

44

day, Augie eager to see his girl.

Three-thirty finally came and Augie rushed down to the dock, stripped to his waist and scrubbed his shirt and socks in the lake. Barefoot and bare-chested, he slid a bar of Lifebuoy soap into his hip pocket and dove off the dock. He scrubbed, splashed, and swam, then climbed onto the dock again in time to see a rowboat coming around the point. In it, a dark-haired, fair-skinned young woman pulled on the oars. He shouted, waved, and jumped into one of the warden's boats. Rowing toward her, his oars splashed, powered by a wild mix of passion and brute strength. Their boats nearly passed by each other before Augie turned. Both cedar strip rowboats met with a thump. Augie jumped from his, rocking hers and nearly sending both of them overboard. They fell to the bottom of her boat and embraced, laughing like the long-separate lovers they were.

An hour of catching up came next, Augie telling Delores of life in the camp and Delores relating news from back home.

"Oh, yes," said Delores, "I must tell you! I learned of a job prospect when you get out."

"What kind of job?" he replied.

"A fellow named Billy Moran is about to build a home on a lake near Hayward. Could be a good break for you."

"How'd you find out about this Moran and his building plans?"

"I met his nephew on the train. He was a cad, but it sounds like his uncle is loaded."

"Whaddaya mean, he was a cad?"

"Oh, nothing, really. Just tried to butter me up. Offered me a drink. Tried to charm me with his razzamatazz."

"Anybody ever as much as touches you and I'll break both his legs, Baby."

"I told him as much."

"You're *my* baby and mine alone, see?"

"You bet I do, Augie. Ain't nobody for me but you and nobody for you but me. Right?"

"You got it, Doll."

Side by side they drifted the afternoon away, listening to the loons calling from a distant bay. Toward evening, they parted, oars pulling them away from each other again. .

The next morning, Dutch and seven prison workers rowed to the farm and beached their boats. Delores met them near the shore. They walked the half-mile into town, Augie and Delores hand in hand, with church bells echoing from the nearby hills.

The afternoon sun found the lovebirds out on the lake again, exploring each little bay and cove until a sudden shower sent them ashore. Under the boughs of a tall balsam they hid from the raindrops. Lying on a thick bed of soft pine needles, they embraced, their passion pouring like the raindrops from above. When the rain ended, they brushed balsam needles from each other's bodies before climbing into the boat.

"Baby," said Augie as he rowed her back to the farm, "I've been thinkin'. Thinkin' 'bout you and me."

"That's all I ever do, Augie. I think about you and me day and night. Drives me crazy sometimes."

"I won't be locked up much longer. When I get out ..."

"Yes?"

"Baby, I got plans for you and me. Whaddaya say when I get out let's you and me get hitched?"

"Augie, are you proposing to me?"

"Proposin'? Well, yes. Yes! I'm proposin' we get hitched. Um ... married. You and me, see? Proper like. In a church. With a preacher. Your pa, my ma and pa, the grandmas, the grandpas, the whole ball of wax, see? Soon as I get out of the joint. Whaddaya say? Will you marry me, Baby? Will ya?"

"Oh, you bet I will, Augie Buelo. You bet I will!"

Chapter 8

Family concerns over Augie's twenty-two months in prison soured plans for a big wedding. The wife of the Fox Lake, Illinois, judge witnessed the Saturday afternoon rite. There was no ceremony. No guests attended. The lovebirds spent their wedding night in a resort cabin by the lake, then took the morning Greyhound bus back to Waukesha.

Augie found work painting trim for a Waukesha construction company. His six-bits-an-hour job, along with the thirty cents per hour plus tips Delores earned working at the Woolworth's lunch counter in Mukwonago, paid the rent and the grocery bill. And there was enough left over to save up for a car. Paging through the *Milwaukee Sentinel,* Augie came across a fixer-upper for fifty dollars—this time, a Ford Model A.

Within a few months, the Buelos were better off than many of their neighbors, most suffering from the Great Depression. Augie even had enough change in his pocket for a beer now and then. This began with stopping at a tavern one or two nights a week but soon stretched into drinking and cards after work every night.

As Augie prepared to leave for work one morning, Delores aired her feelings.

"Augie, please don't stop after work today. Thanksgiving is coming up and I'd like to have enough grocery money for a nice dinner. Maybe invite your folks."

"Aw, save up your tips for that. Eight, ten bucks should do."

"I don't make ten dollars in tips a month, Augie. You know that. And Christmas is coming. Wouldn't it be nice if we could do something special?"

"Like what?"

"I don't know, maybe spend a weekend in Chicago? Or save up for a radio. You know how much you love to listen to the football games. And I would like to hear the *Lux Hit Parade* now and then. We can't do much of anything with you wasting your pay at the tavern. Right now, I don't even know if we will be able to make next month's rent. Augie, honey, please don't stop tonight."

"Don't harp, Delores."

"You told me once that you'd like to have a son someday. A little boy to take fishing and camping up north. How do you expect to pay for that? How could we with you guzzling down your wages?"

"I said don't harp!"

"Look. I can't pay our way through life with what I make. You need to bring your paycheck home—*not* cash it at the bar."

"I'll do what I want."

"If that's the way it is, you can stop counting on me to put up with it. From now on, the food will be on the table at five-thirty. Be home by then or fix your own supper."

Augie glared at his wife. "Fine!"

Brow furled, Delores glared back. "And don't bother giving me your empty lunch bucket any more. Starting tomorrow, you can make your own sandwich and fill your own damn thermos *dear*."

"Fine!"

Augie slammed the door on his way out.

The monotony of painting trim all day offered the opportunity for his wife's words to sink in. She was right. That evening, he was home by five-thirty, a lunchbox in one hand, flowers in the other, and a gift—a Zenith Stratosphere radio in the back seat of the car.

Night after night, he and Delores dined together. Afterward, sitting side-by-side on the couch listening to the radio, they talked. One night, with the only light in the room coming from the glow of the radio dial, Delores asked a question. "Augie, I love this radio. The sound is so clear. And it looks so nice in our living room. Was it expensive?"

"Naw, not much. Besides, you're worth it, Baby."

"Really, Augie. How much did you pay for it?"

"Aw, I don't know. Not much."

"Did you buy it on the installment plan?"

"Naw, Baby. Might say I got it outright."

"At a pawn shop?"

"Hmm? Oh. Yeah, Yeah. Got it at a pawn shop."

"Here in town?"

"Um, no, um, Milwaukee. Don't remember just where."

"It wasn't from that office building where you're working?

Augie didn't answer.

"Aw, Augie honey. You didn't."

"They won't miss it."

"Honey, you swore to me that you'd go straight. Now this!" she said, turning on the light. She crossed the room, grabbed the radio's cord, and whipped the plug from the outlet.

"Why'd you go and do that?"

"Get rid of it."

"What?"

"I don't want something you swiped in our home. Get *rid* of it!"

"Get rid of it? You crazy, Doll? That Zenith is top a the line! Ninety-nine bucks at Monkey Wards!"

"And if your parole officer should stop by?"

"So what?"

"So what? The judge gave you three years. The parole board let you out in two if you promised to stay on the level. If your parole officer sees this expensive radio sitting on the floor in our living room, he's bound to wonder. And if he finds out one is missing from that building where you work ..."

"Nobody's gonna find out nothin'."

"What makes you so sure?"

"On accounta I took it from a pile of stuff that got moved into storage so as us painters could do our job. When they go to put stuff back, it will look like it got lost in the shuffle, Baby. To everybody in that building, one radio, that radio, don't no longer exist. But to us it's different. It's our pride and joy. And, Baby, it's paid for. Paid for free and clear."

"Is it worth going back to prison?"

"Don't sweat it, Baby. I ain't goin' back to prison—ever! This radio's ours now," he said plugging it in again. "Listen. Listen,

Baby. It's Bing Crosby singing my favorite tune, 'Brother, Can You Spare a Dime?'"

"A dime, Augie? Neither one of us will ever have a dime to spare if you go back to prison. You want that?"

"Don't harp on me, Delores. Listen to the crooner, will ya?"

"I'm going to bed. You sleep out here."

"Fine! Do that! What do I care? Now shut your yap so I can listen to my song."

The next night, Augie didn't come home for supper. Well after midnight, Delores woke to hear the kitchen door open and close. She looked at the alarm clock. Minutes later, her husband entered the bedroom and slipped under the covers.

"Augie, it's going on one in the morning."

"So what?"

"So, where've you been?"

"Out with the boys."

"*Just* the boys?"

"Yes, Delores. *Just* the boys."

"Got any money left?"

"For what?"

"Oh, I don't know, Augie. How about for Christmas? Or how about putting some aside for the future?"

"I got money, Baby. Won 'bout fifteen, twenty bucks at poker."

"Poker. You risked our grocery money playing poker?"

"Yes, poker."

"You know, honey, if we ever plan to have kids, if you ever want to take your little boy on a camping trip up north, you'll have to be more responsible. Can you do that? Can you be responsible?" She got out of bed, turned on the light, and went into the bathroom.

"Aw, can't you turn off the dang light, Delores? Hurts my eyes."

Moments later, she returned to find her husband out of bed. He stood before the mirror in his white boxer shorts, examining his face. "Look," he said, "all I did is take one night off to have some fun with the boys, see? Don't go fly off the handle, Delores. It ain't no big deal."

"So what's that cut on your chin about? And don't you dare say you ran into a door."

"Aw, I just got into a little scuffle, that's all."

"And what if you got thrown in jail for getting into a bar fight? Then what, Augie? What would I do?"

"Don't harp at me, Delores."

"No, dammit! You tell me, Augie. What would I do? How would I pay the rent? By going to the tavern and playing poker? Hanging around with the boys?"

"I said, *don't harp,* Delores!"

"All it would take is for one cop to haul you in and your parole officer would have you locked up again. You know it. You're a fool if you don't!"

Augie spun away from the mirror and struck Delores in the face, knocking her onto the bed.

"I warned you, Delores! Now look what ya made me go and do!"

She clutched her face with both hands, crying a muffled cry.

"Look, Baby, if you had even a lick of sense, you wouldn't harp on me. And don't you *ever* tell me you'd go to some tavern to play poker and such with the boys."

"Okay, Augie," she sobbed.

"Delores, I ain't gonna take it, see? I ain't gonna let you or no other skirt run my life! Now, quit your blubberin'."

Delores rolled to the far side of the bed, stood, and left the room, sobbing softly.

"Aw, I'm sorry, Baby. I didn't mean it. You know I didn't, Doll. Come back to bed, won'tcha? Let me make it up to you."

"No."

"Aw, c'mon, Baby. Please?"

"No, Augie," she wimpered, curling up on the couch.

"Fine!"

For the next three days, tension remained high between Augie and Delores. Each evening he stopped at the tavern, avoiding her, not wanting to see the bruise he left on her face. Then, one night after too many beers and several bad poker hands, Augie put all his money on the cards he held. In the flip of a ten of spades, he lost two week's pay. He guzzled his beer and left.

Outside, he noticed an odd smell, a moist, putrid smell—the smell of wet animal hides. It came from a truck parked ahead of his Ford. Curious, he pushed the tarp aside and looked into the back of the truck to see bales of muskrat pelts neatly stacked, front to back. Augie looked up the street, then down, then grabbed two bales, throwing them into the back seat of his car.

Heading home, a rear tire went flat three miles down National Avenue. He pulled onto the shoulder and jacked up the rear wheel. A police car pulled up, shining its headlights on Augie's car. Flashlight in hand, an officer stepped out.

"You picked a damn cold night to have a flat, buddy," said the patrolman.

"Never fails," replied Augie. "Bad weather brings bad luck."

"I hear ya. Seems every time we have a snowstorm or ice we deputies end up out in the midst of it. You know … tending to folks in trouble. Fender benders, falls, you name it. Say, can I give you a hand?"

"Naw, I can handle this." Augie cranked the lug wrench. "There," he said, tightening the last lug nut. "Got it." He lowered the jack, tossing it into the back seat through the open rear window.

The officer picked up the flat tire. "Where do you want this, pal?"

"Aw, just toss it into the back seat." He opened the door.

"Sheesh! What's that awful smell?"

"Rat skins."

"Come again?"

"I been doin' some trappin'."

"Really? Where'bouts?"

"Buddy, no trapper worth his salt tells where his traps lay."

"No, I suppose they don't. Okay, then. Well, looks like you're all set to go, buddy."

"I sure do 'preciate your help, officer. Awful nice of you. 'Specially on such a chilly night."

"Don't mention it."

Sunday, as Delores readied for church, she heard a knock.

"Sorry to bother you on a Sunday, ma'am," said the uniformed man. "I am with the Wisconsin Conservation Department. I'd like to speak to August Buelo."

"Conservation?"

"I'm a game warden, ma'am. Need a few words with the mister."

"Why?"

"Not for me to say outright. I need to speak with August, Mrs. Buelo."

"I don't know where he is."

A shout came from the bedroom. "Who is it, Baby?"

"Some game warden."

"Game warden? Tell him to go away."

"Mr. Buelo, I need to speak with you for a moment."

Augie came to the door, barefoot, fastening his belt. "What's this all about?"

"A local fur buyer reported some muskrat pelts were stolen. You know anything about that?"

"Why should I?"

"A Waukesha patrol officer said he helped you with a flat. Said you had some hides. You got a trapping license, do you?"

"Me? Uh, no. You got the wrong guy. I haven't had a flat tire since last summer."

"Really? Oh. Okay. I suppose the officer thought wrong."

"Yeah, he must've helped someone else out Tuesday night."

"Tuesday? I didn't say anything about Tuesday night."

"Sure you did. You heard him, right, Baby?"

"My hubby's right, Warden. That's what you said."

"Mister Buelo, tell me something. If I were to ask the fur buyers in the area, do you suppose sooner or later I would learn that you sold one of them ..."

"All right! All right! So, I found a couple bales of rat hides along the road up by Brookfield and I sold 'em. Sold 'em to to a guy I know up by 'Tosa. I got screwed over, too. Thirty bucks for a hundred prime pelts."

"You found these pelts?"

"Yeah. Like I said, buddy, up by Brookfield. Must've fallen off the poor sap's truck. He should be more careful. Why, he coulda caused a crash. Somebody might get hurt with him out there. You guys should thank me for helpin' you out."

"You didn't swipe those bales out of the back of a truck? Steal them down at the corner of West Main and Grand in Waukesha?"

"Nope. Found 'em on the road."

"What road was that?"

"Lemme think once. Watertown Plank, maybe. Can't say for sure. It was dark."

"And you sold these pelts to ..."

"Some fella in Wauwatosa."

"He have a name?"

"Don't recall. But when you find him, tell him he shouldn't stiff his trappers on the price."

The officer pulled a pen and pad from his pocket. "Mr. Buelo, I'm issuing you a citation."

"What? You can't fine me for finding something that fell off some truck."

"No, I can't, even when you and I know the real story—the truth about how you got those pelts. No, I'm citing you for transfer of ownership of animal pelts without a trapping license or a permit to buy and sell hides."

"Say, you can't do that!"

"Yes, Mr. Buelo, I can. And I'm sorry you got yourself into such a pickle. I suggest you call the clerk of courts first thing tomorrow. She will give you your court date."

"Court? Can't I just pay a fine?"

The warden handed the ticket to Augie, then turned to Delores. "Good morning, ma'am."

Twelve days later, Augie found himself in a familiar courtroom.

"All rise."

Judge Henry Broadmore strode from his chambers to the bench. He lowered his head to peer over his glasses at the defendant, then sat. "August Frederick Buelo, we meet again. It says here that you possessed and sold two bales of stolen muskrat pelts without a license or permit. Is that so, Gus?"

"Augie."

"What?"

"My friends call me Augie, Judge. You can, too."

"Oh, yes. Well, *Augie,* did you or did you not possess and sell those muskrat hides?"

"Well, sure, sure I did. But nobody got hurt in the deal. All I did was pick 'em up off the road so some chump wouldn't hit 'em and smash up his car. What's the harm in that?"

"Hmm. Yes. You claim they fell off the truck. You know, it seems I hear that line about every other day. So, is there anything else you want to say for yourself before I make my determination, Mister *Augie* Buelo?"

"Say?"

"Yes. Say on your behalf. Is there anything I should know about you?"

"Well, Judge, I got me a good wife. And I got me a good job painting the insides of office buildings and such."

"Anything else?"

"Well, Judge, this here is 'bout the only trouble I've been in since last time you seen me. And I hope you don't fine me too much 'cause me and Delores—that's my wife—we're savin' up to start a family."

"A family. Anything else?"

"Nope, I'd say that's about it, Judge."

"Well, son, you'll be pleased to hear that I won't slap you with a big fine, if that's what you're worried about."

"Whew! Jeez, thanks, Judge. That takes a load off."

"You're welcome, Augie. But it seems you have not yet learned your lesson. August Frederick Buelo, for the charge of selling peltries without a trapping license or a merchant's permit, I hereby sentence you to six months in the Waukesha County Jail, this sentence to commence ten days from today at nine o'clock in the morning."

"What? Six months for selling some dang muskrat hides?"

Judge Henry Broadmore smacked his gavel on the bench.

"Next case."

"Six months, Judge?"

Broadmore smacked his gavel again.

"Next case!"

Augie caught a bus home. Delores was waiting on the couch, listening to the radio.

"Pack your bags, Baby. We're leaving town."

"What?"

"Broadmore gave me six months. I ain't goin' back to jail. I ain't never gonna let them put me behind bars again no matter what. *Never!* You hear me? *Never!*"

"But, what will we ...?"

"You and me is pullin' out. We're leavin' tonight, Baby. Now go pack up."

"But, where ...?"

"West coast, Doll. Tacoma. I got me a friend out there who can set me up. We can start all over again. I got plans for you and me, Baby. Big plans."

Chapter 9

After dark, Augie crammed three suitcases, a stack of blankets and pillows, a box of pots, pans, and dishes, and the Zenith radio into the back seat of the Ford. He tied their small kitchen table to the roof, legs up. Two kitchen chairs came next, then a hall tree. Around midnight, they crossed the Illinois border. Augie breathed a sigh of relief as he cranked the wheel toward Rockford.

"Baby, I'm starvin'. Did you empty the icebox?"

"Aw, Jeez, Augie."

"You forgot?"

"I was in a hurry."

"Dammit, Delores!"

"So much stuff to pack. Don't be mad, Sweetie."

"There was a pound of ham and a quart of milk in there. And butter. And eggs. And my ma's blackberry jam!"

"I'm sorry. I did empty the cupboard, though. I put the pancake batter, spices, flour and such in a cardboard box."

"Wouldn't fit."

"What?"

"Wouldn't fit in the car. Left it on the porch."

"Jeez. We'll have to stop at a diner. Rockford can't be far."

"Diners cost money, Delores. We ain't got much and what we do got needs to go for gas."

"Did you pack my breadbox?"

"Nope."

"You didn't bring the breadbox my grandma gave us for a wedding gift?"

"No room."

"Jeez, Augie. You could have found a place for it. If your folks gave us that breadbox you would have found a place for it all right."

"Don't harp at me, Delores. You know better."

"Well, you could have at least brought that loaf of bread I baked yesterday. I don't see why you ..."

"I said, *don't harp*. I got enough on my mind already. Don't

57

need your harpin' to add to it, see?"

"That was a selfish thing to do."

"I'm warnin' ya," he said, raising his right hand from the wheel. "Just *one* more word!"

The Model A rolled down Highway 20, both passengers silent. A quarter-hour passed before Delores dared speak.

"How broke are we, Augie?"

"We ain't got enough dough to make Tacoma, that's for sure."

"How much do we have?"

"Between the cash in my wallet and what I found in the jar where you keep your tips, 'bout twenty-two bucks."

"Jeez. That won't get us far."

"Maybe I can find some work along the way."

"These days? Don't kid yourself."

"Aw, things'll work out, Baby. Things always do. You'll see."

"No, Augie, things *don't* always work out. Sometimes things go wrong. You know that a darn sight better than most. We need a plan. We need to lay out all our options, all our needs. We need to plot our trip town by town, choose the best route. If we're lucky enough to find work along the way, we might have to stay for a few weeks or a month in order to save up for the next leg of the trip."

"That's my gal! I'll do the drivin' whilst you plan and plot and so forth and so on. We'll make it. You'll see. You and me's on an adventure, Doll. Tacoma, Washington, here we come!"

Augie and Delores pulled into an all-night diner for coffee and eggs before rambling down the road again. Hours later, Delores woke as the first light of morning dimly revealed the eastern sky. Minutes later, heading into Iowa at Dubuque, their Model A Ford crossed a long bridge.

"Look, Sweetie!" said Delores, must be the Mississippi River. Oh, isn't it something?"

"Sure is. Mostly 'cuz it puts more real estate between us and Johnny Law."

"How you doing, Sweetie?" she asked.

"Oh, all right, I s'pose."

"You look drowsy."

"Huh? Oh, no, no. Just kinda bushed, that's all."

"You know, Sweetie, if some cop sees you weaving down the road, you'll get pulled over. That cop might make a call to the Wisconsin Highway Patrol. Before you know it, you'll be hauled back. And this time, you'll go straight to jail."

"I said I'm doin' fine, Delores."

"Let me drive a ways. It will give you a chance to catch up on your sleep."

"You don't have a license, Baby."

"That doesn't mean I don't know how to drive. I drove my pa's Chevy. Twice. This old Ford can't be much different."

"And what if *you* get pulled over?"

"Out here? In the middle of nowhere? There's not a cop around for miles."

"Listen, Doll. One thing I learned in the joint is that them dang screws are everywhere and they watch everything. Just 'cause you don't see them, don't mean they don't see you."

"Well, it's up to you, Augie. But I think our chance of getting stopped by some lawman is greater with you behind the wheel than me. Besides, *I* don't have a record. They can check all they want and my name won't come up."

"You think they don't got your name? Hardy har har, Delores. That's a good one. You're the wife of an ex-con who's still on parole for one conviction and now has another stretch to serve. Why they got your name, your grandma's name, your pa's, my folks' and 'most everybody we know. Why, them coppers prob'ly got the names and addresses of every little guppy in your cousin's fish bowl."

"But it's not likely any Iowa cop will be the least bit concerned about me, a young woman, taking her turn driving west to find work while her husband sleeps."

"All right! All right! You made your point, Doll. I'll pull over up ahead."

Delores drove the rest of the day. Augie counted the money in his wallet, watched the landscape pass by, then counted their money again. At a Texaco filling station in Sioux City, the attendant filled the gas tank, checked the oil, and topped off the radiator. From there, they drove north. Somewhere south of Sioux Falls, Delores noticed steam wafting from the radiator cap.

"Sweetie, I think Bessie needs a drink of water."

"Huh?"

"It's not supposed to steam like that, is it?"

Augie looked at the temperature gauge. "Should be okay for a while. Slow down some. Next town we come to, pull into a filling station, Doll."

"Looks like you got yourself a radiator leak, fella," said the station attendant.

"You got somethin' I can toss in that'll fix it?"

"Looks worse than that. Let me get our mechanic out here. He'll know best what to do."

A thin, clean-shaven man wearing grease-stained, blue work pants and a matching shirt ambled from the station. He slid under the front bumper, a flashlight in hand.

"Hmm. Don't look good, buddy," he muttered from below the car.

"Naw," said Augie. "Can't be more than a small leak."

"Wish I could agree with you, friend, But 'fraid she's a gonner."

"Naw, can't be," said Augie. "Can't we just throw somethin' in it to plug it up?"

"Nope. Nothin's gonna fix that crack. I've seen this before on these Fords. Radiator's cracked clear through. Gonna creep on you and keep on creepin'. Can't do nothin' but get worse. You'll need to replace it."

"How much?"

"Eight bucks for the radiator, buck-fifty to install it."

"That's more than I got. Can I put it on a tab?"

"Depends. You live someplace nearby?"

"Other side of Sioux City."

The mechanic glanced at the Wisconsin plates. "You got work here?"

"Not yet, but I 'spect to by middle of the week."

"Buddy, my boss would have my ass if I did this job on the cuff. You understand."

"Yeah, I s'pose. There any way I can work it off? Put in a day or two helpin' out?"

"Friend, there's a long line ahead of you. 'Round these parts, fellas outa work are like kernels on a corncob."

"You don't have a used one I can buy?"

"Say, I do. I can pull one from a Model A we're 'bout to junk out. Tell you what. I'll give it to you for five bucks plus two dollars labor."

"I'll give you four dollars flat and do the work myself. Plus you can keep my old radiator for scrap. Ought to be worth at least four bits. Deal?"

"Fella, you got yourself a deal."

Delores handed tools to Augie as he swapped radiators, then refilled the cooling system with water.

"Sweetie," she said, "I think we should try to find some work here. Once you pay this off and fill the gas tank, we'll be down to about twelve dollars."

"We can make it to Montana on twelve bucks."

"Sure we can. But then what? We'll be flat broke. Wouldn't it be better to find some work *before* we're busted? We should try to always keep ourselves at least ten dollars ahead of the game, don't you think?"

"I s'pose you're right. Okay. We'll see what we can do once I finish this up. Okay, Doll?"

Augie filled the radiator, paid the bill and drove, tapping his fingers on the wheel all the way through the city. When near the Nebraska border, he pulled into another station.

"Let's switch, Baby. You drive for a while, okay?"

"Sure, Sweetie. Sure."

Delores slid across the seat to the driver's side. Motor running, Augie watched the attendant top off the gas tank, then followed him inside. Seconds later, he ran out, clutching a fistful of cash. He jumped into the car, the station attendant, nose bleeding, running toward them.

"Step on it, Baby! Step on it!"

Delores sped off.

"Augie, what did you do back there?"

"Hmm? Oh, I just give us some breathin' room, that's all, Doll."

"You swiped the cash from that fella's till?"

"Yeah. 'Spose I did. So what?"

"So what? Jeez, Augie! The cops will be on us in no time at all!"

"Delores, we're half-a-mile from the Nebraska border. No Iowa cop is gonna cross the border for a two-bit gas station heist. Trust me. I know this. Three years in a state prison teaches you plenty."

"Boy, I hope you're right, Augie."

"Stick with me, Baby. I can teach you things you never dreamed possible. Now, step on it. Tacoma, here we come!"

Chapter 10

Late the next night, somewhere east of Missoula, Montana, the Buelo's Ford sat stranded along the highway. Delores held the flashlight while Augie set the jack and raised the left front wheel.

"Looks like we got a burnt out wheel bearing, Delores."

"Is that bad?"

"Bad? Well, I should say so. We're stuck here, miles from nowhere. I'd call that bad. Wouldn't you?"

"What are we going to do?"

Augie scratched his head. "Well, if I can't fix it, I s'pose we'll have to wait here for somebody to come along and give you a lift."

"Me? Give me a lift?"

"Well, somebody's gotta stay with the car. You wanna be left out here in the dark?"

"Jeez. You want me to ride with some stranger? Go into some strange town in the middle of the night and try to find help? And it could take hours to catch a ride. We haven't seen another car since we left Butte."

"Say, hand me that can of grease in my toolbox, will ya, Doll? Maybe I can pack enough in the hub to get us into town. If it works, you'll have to drive real slow so as not to grind it to shreds."

"Oh, I'll creep along slower than a snail if that's what it takes."

Thirty miles and three hours later, Delores pulled into a garage where a mechanic replaced the bad bearing. Augie studied the bill, then handed it to Delores.

He turned to the mechanic. "Nineteen dollars? Back home, I can get new wheel bearings for both left and right for half that much."

The mechanic grinned. "Well, buddy, I guess you ain't back home. Out here, in my garage, the price is nineteen dollars."

"Tell you what. I'll give you five."

"Who do you think you're dealin' with, fella? The bill is nineteen bucks. Take it or leave it."

"You can't be serious," said Delores.

"Hell, yes, I'm serious. Look, lady, I can take that new wheel bearing out just as fast as I put it in. Is that what you want, sweet cheeks?"

Augie moved in close. "Hey, watch your mouth. That's my wife you're talkin' to, hayseed. Show some respect."

"What'd you call me?"

Delores stepped between them. "It's all right, mister. My husband didn't mean anything by it. How about we pay you ten and call it a day?"

"Like hell!" said Augie. "No jerkwater grease monkey is gonna take me to the cleaners."

"That's it, buddy," said the mechanic, swinging his wrench at Augie.

Augie's reflexes were faster. His right fist struck the man under the left eye. His left hit the man's jaw, sending him sprawling across the floor. Augie grabbed him by the collar, lifted him up, and wound up for a third punch. The mechanic covered his face with both hands.

"Augie! Don't!" screamed Delores.

Augie held his fist high, waiting for a reason to bring it down onto the mechanic's face. "So, hayseed, did I hear you say five bucks?"

"Sure, sure. Five bucks. Just don't hit me no more."

"Delores, whaddaya say we give the hayseed a fiver?"

"Fine. But don't hit him again. Okay?"

He dropped the mechanic onto the concrete floor. "Sure, Baby. Whatever you say." Augie pulled a five-dollar bill from his wallet, crumpled it up, and tossed it at the mechanic. "Let's blow this two-bit grease pit."

"I'm with you."

Augie turned the key, hit the starter switch, and the engine stumbled to a start. Delores slammed her door and the Model A rolled out of the service bay and down the street.

"Sweetie, you think that man will call the police?"

"That's what I figure. Most likely he's on the phone right now."

"What are you going to do if the cops come after us?"

"Play it by ear."

"That's it? That's your plan? Play it by ear?"

"You got somethin' better in mind?"

"Maybe."

A single, far-away police siren caught their attention.

"Well, spit it out, Delores. You think we got all day?"

"Find the Woolworth's store."

"What?"

"Every city has one. It will be someplace downtown."

"That's your plan? Go shoppin' at some dime store?"

"I know how to get us out of this. You gotta trust me, Sweetie."

Augie cranked the wheel, bounced across some railroad tracks, and turned onto Main Street. Pedal to the floor, the Ford raced down the street. Another siren joined the first.

"There it is," shouted Delores. "A block ahead on the right. Drop me off at the main door and go around the block. I'll be waiting. Pick me up."

"You're nuts, Delores. You're gonna get us caught."

"No, I'm gonna get us out of this jam. Just do as I say."

Augie screeched to a stop before the Woolworth store. Delores jumped out and ran inside while he raced down the block and around the corner. Moments later, he rounded the corner to see Delores waiting at the curb. Behind her, a stream of shoppers and clerks poured out of the front door, chased by the loud ringing of a fire alarm. Augie pulled up. Delores jumped in and off they sped.

"Delores, what's goin' on?"

"Get off the main drag and slow down, Sweetie. All the fire trucks and all the cops in town will be here in a few minutes. They won't be interested in two guys in a fistfight in some garage. Right now they think their Woolworth's is on fire."

"What? How ..."

"Every Woolworth's in the country, including the one where I worked, installed fire alarms last year. And they're all hooked into the local fire departments. Now for Pete's sake, slow down and drive normal so you don't draw attention. We'll be out of town and across the state border before they realize what's going on."

"Well, if that don't beat all. We did it, Baby! We bamboozled them. Think about it—you and me snookering the cops and hightailing it out of town. We're just like Bonnie and Clyde."

"Don't you dare say that, Augie! We are not like Bonnie and Clyde! We are just a regular husband and wife trying to eke out a living and scrape by through life like almost every other couple. Don't you dare go getting any big ideas about taking on the law. You'll never win. Do you remember what happened to Bonnie and Clyde Barrow? You saw the papers. You saw the pictures. Massacred by G-Men. And Pretty Boy Floyd? And John Dillinger? And their gang members? All shot. Shot down in their tracks just like so many others who defied the law. They're all dead, Augie. You are not some hardboiled criminal. And don't you become one! I do not want to be the widow of another gun-downed gangster. Promise me, Augie! Promise me you'll stay straight. Promise me you'll keep out of trouble."

"It's not that easy, Baby. You think I go lookin' for trouble? Hell, I don't want to end up in court or prison again. Never! All I want is to have a nice little place for you and me to listen to our Zenith, raise a few kids, and go to ball games on warm summer nights and picnics in the park and decorate our own Christmas tree just like everybody else. But, it ain't that easy, Baby. I'm tellin' ya, I don't look for trouble. I don't have to—it finds me. And when it does, I'm like one of them Katzenjammer kids in a candy store—I can't say no."

"You have to. If you're not willing to say so long to trouble, then you'll have to say so long to me."

"You can't say that, Baby! Don't you see? You're all I got."

"Augie, I won't put up with it. I can't! I refuse to spend my nights wondering if you're lying in some ditch, bleeding to death from some G-man's bullet. And I sure as hell won't bring children into this world knowing the only time they will ever see their father is in prison or on some post office wanted poster. You have to choose, Augie."

"I know. I know."

"So? What's it gonna be? You have to choose. You have to choose right now. Right this minute."

"Okay, okay. You're right, Baby. Startin' today, I'm goin' straight. From here on out, I won't as much as jaywalk. You'll see."

"Promise me. Promise me, now!"

"Okay! For cryin' out loud, I'll stay on the straight and narrow."

"You promise?"

"I promise! Okay?"

Delores put her hand on his arm. "I love you, Sweetie. I will forever."

"Love you, too, Doll. You're everything to me. Say, look! There's the sign for the state line. We're almost in Idaho and not a single copper in sight. We did it! We got it made, Baby. Look out, Tacoma. Here we come."

Late the next day, the couple's Model A left Idaho and entered Washington. Hungry, low on both gas and money, they pulled into a ranch in the Spokane valley.

"What are we going to do, Augie?"

"You go knock on the back door, Baby. Maybe the owner of this joint could use some help in trade for some food or gas. You'd have a better chance of getting something than me."

"Jeez, Augie. I don't know."

"What's not to know? Just go knock on the dang door, Delores. Worse you can get is the boot."

As told, Delores knocked. The door opened. A dark, middle-aged man with a cigarette hanging from his lip looked at Delores, then beyond her at the Ford with its cargo tied on top.

"Whaddaya want?" he grumbled.

"Mister, I'm hoping you'd be willing to spare a bite to eat for a couple of hungry travelers. We can help out with chores, if you want."

"What makes you think I have food to spare?"

"Uh, well, I don't know that you do. But if you need some work done, my husband and I can help you out."

The owner stretched to look over her shoulder again. "You tell him to come here."

Delores waved. "Sweetie, come meet the gentleman."

Her brawny, six-foot-two husband climbed the porch steps. "Mister, this is my hubby, August Buelo. I'm Delores."

"Where you kids from?"

"Wiscon ..."

"Ohio," interrupted Augie. "Me and my gal, here, we been travelin' all week and it's gettin' on my nerves. Sure could use a meal and some good, hard work to break up the boredom."

"My hubby is quite the handyman. Surely there must be *something* we can do to help you out, Mister ..."

"Ralstin. Clyde Ralstin."

"You name it and I'll do it," Augie said.

"Well, don't just stand there, c'mon in and have a seat. I'll make some coffee. There's some chicken in the icebox. Fryin' pan's in the cupboard. You two can help make supper for the three of us. Bread's on the counter."

"That's very kind of you, sir. So, is there something we can do to help out?"

"Matter of fact, you can, son. There's some money in it for you, too." He opened his wallet. "Here's a ten-spot, August. You'll get another ten when we get back."

"Back from where?"

"Newport. It's up the road apiece."

"Yes," said Delores. "We just drove through there."

"August, I'm a detective with the Spokane Police Department. You're gonna help me with a case I'm workin' on."

"You're a police detective?" said Delores. "Jeez ..."

Augie smiled. "Aw, don't mind Delores, Clyde. She don't get out much. Prob'ly never seen a real detective before. And call me Augie for short. All my friends do."

"Mister Ralstin," said Delores, "are you sure you want Augie involved in your case? Shouldn't some other officer ...?"

"That's the problem. It seems some of our local police have dirt on their hands. I don't know who I can trust."

"This isn't dangerous, is it? I don't want my sweetie to ..."

"Don't you fret about it, Delores," said Augie. "I can handle myself fine."

"No," said Clyde. "there's nothin' dangerous about this. I just need to confiscate some stolen cheese and butter from a warehouse up in Newport, that's all. I was gonna do it myself but it's about half-a-ton and I could use the help. We'll take my truck, load it up, and be back by, oh, I'd say ten, maybe ten-thirty."

"That's fine by me, Clyde," said Augie. "Imagine that, Delores. Me, Augie Buelo, helpin' out the Spokane police. Now don't that take the cake?"

Chapter 11

Clyde Ralstin slid open the double doors of the Newport Creamery warehouse. Augie backed the truck in and Clyde closed the doors. It took less than five minutes for the two men to silently load twenty cases of cheese and butter onto the bed of the truck. As Clyde placed the last box on the bed, they heard a car pull up outside.

"Just keep quiet, kid," said Clyde, drawing his revolver. "Get behind the wheel and be ready to roll. I'll see who's out there."

A shout came from outside. "You in the warehouse, this is Marshal Conniff. Slide open that door and come out with your hands where I can see 'em."

"George?" shouted Clyde. "George, it's me, Clyde Ralstin of the Spokane police." He slid the door open.

The marshal trained his pistol on Ralstin. "Better explain yourself, Clyde."

"We're confiscating some stolen merchandise, here. I'd appreciate it if you'd keep this under your hat. Don't want word to get out. Seems someone in my department has been swipin' eggs from the henhouse."

"That wouldn't be you, now, would it Clyde? I've heard some talk about you and your moonlight excursions into the warehouse district."

"Me? No, George. You been hearin' wrong. Somebody's been spreadin' rumors. Probably tryin' to cover for their own monkeyshines. Now, point that pistol somewhere else. It makes me nervous." Clyde slid the doors wide. "Augie," he shouted over his shoulder, "I'll just be a minute. Go ahead and start up the truck." He walked outside with the marshal.

Augie turned the key and stepped on the starter switch. As the truck's engine roared to a start, he thought he heard gunshots.

Moments later, Clyde climbed into the front seat. "Okay, kid. We can go."

Augie pulled to a stop just outside the warehouse door, next to the marshal's car. "You want I should shut the door, Clyde?"

"Aw, don't bother. Marshal Conniff will shut it for us when he leaves."

"Was them gunshots I heard a minute ago?"

"Hmm? Oh, no. Sounded to me like backfire from some young fella's jalopy. Okay, Augie, turn left up ahead. It's a nice night for a drive. We'll take the long way back."

"Sure, Clyde. Sure. Say, that lawman back there. You don't s'pose he's gonna spill the beans on your investigation, do you?"

"George Conniff? Hell no. He's a square shooter. Won't say a word. Say, when you get to the bridge beyond that curve up ahead, pull over a minute. I gotta see a man about a horse."

"Sure thing, Clyde."

Augie slowed at the curve and stopped on the bridge over the Spokane River. Clyde pulled his revolver from his shoulder holster.

"So ... whatcha plannin' to do with that, Clyde?"

"Clyde stared into Augie's eyes for several seconds, then got out. Augie watched in the side mirror as his boss walked behind the truck and up to the guardrail, then tossed the pistol into the rapids below. Clyde unzipped his trousers. A minute later, he was back in the cab.

"Augie. Head back to my place. Soon as we unload, you and your wife are gonna hit the road."

"So soon? How come?"

"I didn't count on anyone showing up tonight. It would be best if you weren't around in the mornin' just in case somebody should start askin' questions. Far as I'm concerned, you were never there. In fact, you never met me, see?"

"Sure, Clyde. Whatever you say. Don't know that we'll make it out of town, though. My Ford's nearly outa gas."

"I got a fuel barrel outside my tractor shed. I'll help you top off your gas tank 'fore you go."

Clyde's truck sped down the highway, the only vehicle on the road that night. Augie turned into Ralstin's driveway and backed into the barn. Minutes later, Delores held the flashlight while Clyde filled the Model A's gas tank.

"Did everything go alright, tonight, fellas?" she asked.

"Smooth as silk," replied Ralstin. "I sure 'preciate you lendin' me your husband. It was good to have him along to keep me company. Say, Delores, I hope you don't mind me shooin' you two down the road in the middle of the night. But, well, I think it's for the best."

"We don't mind at all, Clyde. I did the dishes and cleaned up the kitchen a bit while you were gone. Wish we could do more in trade for your hospitality."

"Your husband did plenty. In fact, more than I ever expected of him."

The gas tank full, Augie replaced the cap. Clyde hung up the hose and reached for his wallet. "Gas is on me and here's that other ten-spot I promised. More than enough to get you kids to the coast."

"We don't deserve no twenty dollars, Clyde," said Augie. "You oughta take this ten back."

"No sir! A bargain is a bargain. Think of it like this. The first ten dollars was for helpin' me out. The second was for you two fogettin' all about tonight. You'll be helpin' me and the entire Spokane Police Department by keepin' this whole matter under your hat."

"And that's exactly what we will do, Mr. Ralstin," said Delores. "Mum's the word. We'll send you a postcard as soon as we reach Tacoma."

"No, you won't. Delores, we never met. Remember that."

Augie and Delores drove through the night, stopping at a diner in Connell for breakfast.

"Such a nice, generous man," said Delores, stirring a sugar cube into her coffee.

"Aw, thanks, Baby." Augie replied.

"Not you, Sweetie. Well, I mean yes, you're nice, too. But I was thinking about Clyde. Wasn't that thoughtful of him? I mean to give us twenty bucks? And a tank of gasoline and dinner besides."

"Who?"

"Clyde."

"Delores, you forget," said Augie in a hushed voice. "You and me, we never met nobody by the name of Clyde Ralstin. Heck, we never even stopped in Spokane! Remember? Just passed right through on our way out west."

"Why, you're serious, aren't you?"

"Look, Baby. I been around enough to know that when you get paid ten bucks to keep your yap shut, you keep your dang yap shut! Now wipe that name and everything that happened last night from your pretty little head, Doll."

"Sure, Sweetie, sure."

"Besides ...."

"Besides what?"

"Naw, I shouldn't say nothin'."

"Aw, you can tell me, Sweetie."

"Well ... somethin' went wrong last night."

"Like what?"

"A friend of Clyde's stumbled onto us. The city marshal. George something-or-other."

"So what? Can't a police detective have friends?"

"They talked for a bit outside the warehouse. That's when I thought I heard gunshots. Five, maybe six."

"Gunshots? Jeez! But maybe you imagined it, Sweetie. I mean, after all, didn't Clyde say it wouldn't be dangerous?"

"Look. Don't you think I've been tryin' to convince myself it wasn't gunfire? Problem is, Delores, I heard what I heard."

"Sometimes our imaginations get the best of us, Augie."

"Oh, that's only the start of it. When we left the creamery, the marshal's car was still there but he was no place to be seen."

"Oh, you're just jumping to conclusions. So you didn't see him. I'm sure nothing bad happened."

"Then Clyde told me to take a different way back to his place. And when we came to a bridge, he said he had to take a leak."

"I've seen you stop the car to go plenty of times."

"Sure, Delores. But how many of them times did I pull out a pistol and heave it off a bridge into the drink? Answer me that, will ya?"

"Clyde did that?"

"I seen him with my own two eyes in the side mirror, Delores."

"Jeez."

"Then he sends you and me off down the road in the middle of the night and tells us to keep our yaps shut about the whole dang deal."

"Jeez."

"See what I mean, Baby? Somethin' went wrong last night. Real wrong."

"Jeez, Ray. I see what you mean. Better finish your eggs. I think we better scram and right now!"

Throughout the day, the highway wound through beautiful scenery. But the beauty of the landscape could not stop Augie's mind from wandering back to the events of the previous night. Neither of them mentioned Clyde Ralstin's name. That evening, they took a room in a small hotel in Yakima. Augie signed the register using Delores's maiden name, Olson. For a first name, he chose Ray. As far as the desk clerk was concerned, it was Ray Olson who paid two dollars for the night.

"Thank you, Mr. and Mrs. Olson. You'll be in room 204. Top of the stairs, second door on the right. Can I carry your bags?"

"Thanks, but no thanks," said Ray with a wide grin. "Delores can carry hers and mine both."

"Very, very funny, Sweetie. You're a regular W. C. Fields. Just for that, you can carry them all up yourself, you big Palooka."

Ray stuffed one suitcase under his left arm, picked up the other with his left hand, then grabbed Delores around the waist and heaved her onto his shoulder.

"Jeez, Ray, put me down. Can't you see how this must look to these folks?" she said as he scaled the stairway two steps by two. "Raymond Olson, you put me down!"

They entered their room laughing like children. Delores jumped onto the bed. "Look, Sweetie, a real bed. First one in six days. And a radio. Oh, and a bathtub!"

"Baby, there's a tavern 'cross the street. I'm goin' over to get us some beer."

"You'll be back right away? I mean, you're not going to leave me alone up here while you drink up our travel money, are you?"

"Naw, them days is over, Doll. Over and done. I'm not that fella you used to know. I'm now Ray Olson, *respectable* Ray Olson. Walkin' the straight and narrow Ray Olson. See, Doll?"

"All right, respectable Ray Olson. Hurry back with that beer as fast as your feet can carry you. Don't dilly dally, Sweetie. I'll be waiting for you in the bathtub."

Ray rushed from the room.

"And don't forget to bring a church key!" she shouted through the door.

Delores could hear her husband tromp down the stairs as she turned on the radio next to the bed. Rotating the dial, she searched until she found soft music, then went into the bathroom to fill the tub. From the radio in the other room, she heard the news bulletin.

We interrupt tonight's broadcast with this newsflash. The body of Marshal George Conniff of Pend Oreilles County was found early this morning behind a Newport, Washington, creamery. The county coroner reported Conniff was shot four times in the chest with a .32 caliber pistol. The murder weapon has not yet been found. The Spokane Police Department reports the murder may have been linked to the theft of a supply of cheese and butter from the Newport Dairy. Detective Clyde Ralstin of the Spokane Police Department is leading the investigation and feels certain the murderer or murderers will soon be apprehended. Anyone with information on the death of Marshal George Conniff is asked to contact the City of Spokane Police Department. We now return you to your regular progam.

Delores sank back onto the bed, her pulse racing. Tears welled in her eyes. "Oh, dear God, why do you let trouble follow my man

76

wherever he goes? He's not a bad fellow. Why can't you give him a break? Just once, give him a fair shake." She heard footsteps on the stairway, again two by two.

The door swung open. Augie set a six-pack of Miller High Life on the table and held up the front page of the evening newspaper. NEWPORT MARSHAL MURDERED.

"We got trouble, Baby."

"I know. I just heard about it on the radio. But I think we're in the clear."

"In the clear? You nuts, Baby?"

"The radio said Clyde Ralstin is the detective leading the investigation. If he was going to give you up, we would have been in jail before sunrise. He can't say a word about you or me. He knows you'd tell your side of the story and he'd be the one on the hot seat."

"Hope you're right, Doll. I spent more than my share of time behind bars. Ain't no way Johnny Law's ever gonna put me in the slammer again."

"We have to stick to our story. We never stopped in Spokane. We never heard of Ralstin. Far as anyone knows, we're just an out-of-work husband and wife headed west, hoping to find a new life. Mister and Mrs. Ray Olson. Plain, respectable folks. Walking the straight and narrow. That's the lot of it."

"Your tub's about full, Mrs. Olson."

Delores jumped from the bed and ran into the bath. "Jeez! I forgot all about it."

Ray grabbed the beer. "Hey, Baby. Wait for me!"

Chapter 12

After breakfast, the Olsons were on the road again. Highway 12 wound through the mountains before beginning its descent to the coast. Motoring down a hill on Pacific Avenue, Delores and Ray first viewed their new home—Tacoma, Washington. Lit by filtered sunlight, the city's downtown buildings glowed against the dark blue background of Commencement Bay.

"Wake up, Baby," said Ray. "Take a gander at our new home."

"Oh, Ray, isn't it beautiful? What a perfect place to live! I just know everything will work out for us now, Sweetie. We'll find a nice little bungalow and be in seventh heaven before you know it."

"Hope we can afford the rent, Doll. I'm down to about fourteen bucks. Ain't hardly enough for a month's rent if we want to eat, besides."

"Who's that fellow who you said might be able to help us out?"

"Sam Campbell. I did some masonry work with him once. Sam told me if I ever come to Tacoma to look him up. Said he could set me up with a legit job."

"You got an address, Ray?"

"Don't need one. Sam said to mention his name at any downtown pool hall and they'll know where to find him."

"So, is this guy on the level?"

"Sam? Why, sure, Baby! Sam's an upstanding citizen out here. Told me he knows people who can get me work—good work."

"Long as it's honest work. We can't risk you getting into trouble again. Not with that murder in Newport and a jail term hanging over your head back in Wisconsin."

"Not hangin' over *my* head, Doll. I'm just a regular fella named Ray Olson. Those suckers are waiting for some Joe named Augie Buelo."

Sam Campbell looked up from the poker table. "Well, I'll be a monkey's uncle! Augie Buelo! If this don't beat all. You found your way out to the coast!"

"I think you're mistakin' me for somebody else. Name's Ray.

79

Ray Olson. Me and my wife just blew in from St. Louis. We don't know anybody named Augie Buelo."

Sam laughed. "Fellas, meet my old pal, Ray Olson. Ray, this here is Ernie Bellagotti and Tiny McClure. Let's say they're ... associates of mine."

Ray eyed the other two players at the table. Ernie, a dark handsome man with a thin moustache, wore a sharp, black suit with a large diamond stick pin precisely centered on his tie. He pushed his chair back, stood, and nodded hello. The clean-shaven, obese man across the card table sat with his shirt sleeves rolled up and held with garters. "Ernie, Tiny, good to meetcha. This here's my wife, Delores."

Ernie stood, taking her hand. "I am quite pleased to make your acquaintance, Mrs. Olson. Oh, and that of your husband, as well." He shook Ray's hand. "Please have a seat. Here, take mine."

"Good idea," said Sam. "Ray, Delores, take a load off. I've got a bottle of Canadian in the back. It's been sittin' there all mornin' waitin' for me to find a reason to pop the cork. Let's have a drink to your arrival in the Evergreen State."

"Yeah, evergreen," said Tiny, with a raspy chuckle. "Got da name from da color a all da easy money out here."

Sam placed five glasses on the table and filled four. Delores put her hand over hers. "Not for me, Sam. But thanks anyway."

"Aw, Baby," said Ray, "go ahead and have a snort to toast meetin' our new friends, our *Tacoma* friends."

"All right. But, not much," she replied. "Just enough for a toast."

Sam filled the glass. "Aw, don't worry 'bout it," he said. "Tiny will finish up what you leave. Nothing goes to waste around here, right Tiny?"

"'At's right, Sammy. You said a mouthful." He raised his glass. "Here's ta our friends just in from who-knows-where and let's us keep it dat way!"

Five glasses met above the center of the table. Delores had the only glass not empty when they returned to the table.

"Sam," said Ray, "I'm here to take you up on your offer."

"Offer?"

"You said when I get outa the joint that I should look you up—that you could help me and Delores get settled down out here."

"Oh, sure thing, buddy. Yeah. Seems that rings a bell. I said I would help you find work. Well, Ray, a promise is a promise. Me, Tiny, and Ernesto, here, we can always use someone like you in our businesses."

"Youse both can be on the job tomorrow, if you're up to it," said Tiny. "I got dis truckload of car parts due in from Frisco tonight that needs to be sorted and priced and such."

Delores interrupted. "Ray needs an *honest* job. Nothing that will raise some cop's eyebrow."

"Hey, little lady, I got me a legit store. I buy from used parts dealers down the coast and sell 'em ta upstandin' folks. What's not legit about dat?"

"What Tiny means," said Sam, "is that you don't need to worry your pretty little head over it, Delores. Tacoma's a good place to do business. Out here, the cops, the D.A. and even the judges know who's their friends and who ain't. And we keep it that way, see? We don't just grease a palm here and grease a palm there like they do in Milwaukee and St. Paul. We got a system, see? We take care of them and they take care of us. Everybody shares the wealth from the gamblin', the girls, the graft, you name it."

"Even the used car parts trade," said Tiny.

"That's fine. But, still, Ray wants nothing to do with the cops."

"I'll handle it, Delores," said Ray. "Sam, is there any construction work to be had out here?"

"Naw. Nobody's buildin' these days. 'Sides, you'd have to first get a union card and that'd run ya a bundle."

"How about the WPA?" said Ernie. "Seems Mr. Roosevelt is always looking for men, though he don't pay worth a damn."

"Naw," said Ray. "I don't want the fed's in my life—our life, right Delores?"

She smiled and nodded.

"I need to steer clear of both the cops and the government," said Ray. "Sam, I'm good with tools. I can fix 'most anything there is to fix. Must be some call for that, even in these times."

"I know a fella who's got a little fix-it shop near here. Seems like he's always griping about too much work pilin' up and how he can't find somebody to hire on accounta because nobody knows how to fix things anymore. I done him a favor once. Maybe you and me we should pay him a visit, eh?"

"Gee, that'd be swell, Sam!" said Delores. "Hear that, Sweetie? Sam might be able to get you a job—an honest job."

"Right now, Baby, I'll take any job I can get."

"Great!" said Sam. "This calls for a celebration." He filled the glasses again. "I'll tell you what. I'll show the two of you around the city tonight. We're gonna celebrate your arrival—do it up in style. And, Roy? I'm buyin'!"

"That's Ray. Ray and Delores Olson. From St. Louis, see?"

"Whatever you say, pal. Whatever you say."

That evening, Delores, Ray, Sam, and an attractive bleach blond in a tight, red dress shared a table in a swank, downtown restaurant overlooking Commencement Bay.

"Delores, Ray," said Sam. "You go ahead and order what you want. I'm buyin'. I'll order for me and my tomata." He turned to the blonde. "What's your name again, muffin?"

"Don't be a pill, Sam." She turned to Ray and Delores. "I'm Vera and I am pleased to make your acquaintance. Don't let this wise guy string you along. Sam and I have been sharing the same bedroom for more than six months, now. Ain't that right, Sam?"

"Aw, I was just foolin' with them. Ever since I got out of the joint, Vera and me, we been like this," said Sam, waving two crossed fingers. "Peas in a pod packed tighter than sardines."

"Well," said Ray, "you sure picked a winner, Sam. A regular Jean Harlow."

Vera primped here hair. "Oh, you think so, Ray? You really think I take after Harlow?"

Delores eyed Ray as he answered. "Heck, you could take Harlow's place on Clark Gable's lap and nobody would know the difference. Not even Gable."

"Hear that, Sam? Ray thinks I got movie-star quality!"

"Sure, Vera," said Sam. "In fact, your latest movie is showin' downtown right now."

"All right, wisenheimer," she scoffed. "What's the punchline?"

"Oh, ain't you heard? It's called King Kong—and you're playin' the lead role and it ain't Faye Wray. Get it?"

Both men laughed. Vera and Delores shook their heads.

"Oh, I get it all right," said Vera. "I get it but I don't want it. Sam, if I really want a good laugh, I'll look for you in the Sunday funny papers."

"Now, see that, Ray?" said Sam, "Just tryin' to make a little joke and that's what I get. When it comes to dames, seems like I can't win for losin'."

Vera grabbed Ray's arm. "Ray, I know you wouldn't make a crude joke like that about Delores. You got class, which is more than I can say for Sam." She squeezed his forearm. "Ooh, and you're so strong!"

"Say, what a beautiful ring, Vera!" Delores said, pulling Vera's hand from her husband's arm. "Did Sam give it to you?"

"This old thing? No, I got it on my eighteenth birth ..."

"Sam," interrupted Delores, "Ray and I are looking for a nice little house to rent. You got any ideas?"

Sam scratched his head. "There's a bungalow for rent down the street from me. South M Street. Nice neighborhood."

"What's a place rent for out here?" asked Ray.

"Small place like that? Oh, twenty, maybe thirty a month."

"That much, huh? Way too rich for my blood."

"Well, you two should swing by and take a look at it. If you like it and the price is too high, you let me know. I can help."

"Help?" asked Delores.

"Maybe I can have Ernie talk with them about the importance of insurance. Ernie can be very convincing."

"Insurance? How would that help us?"

"See, my pally, Ernesto, would say a few words, the landlord would listen, then the two of them would agree on a reasonable price for the rent."

"I don't understand," said Vera. "What makes you think this landlord would pay any attention to some dago in a cheap suit?"

"Well, it's like this, muffin. Ernie would mention that Ray is a good friend and having the Olsons as renters would be in the landlord's best interest. Ray and Delores could look out for the place, see? Then, Ernie would ask what value that might have to the guy and suggest he reduce the monthly rent by that much."

"Don't make no sense."

"See, muffin, if they come to a mutual agreement, so be it. If not, well, the landlord might be faced with other expenses."

"Such as?"

"Oh, maybe medical expenses. Or maybe he'd have to worry about a fire. Who knows? But nobody likes to worry, see? He'd come around. Ernie would see to it Delores and Ray get a fair price on the rent, that's all."

"Sounds good to me," said Ray.

"Sounds like a shakedown to me," said Vera.

Sam shot her a look. "Nothin' wrong with negotiations, muffin. And Ernie knows the ropes, knows how to encourage others to be fair. He knows how to convince them it's in their best interest to be reasonable. You know, that's the trouble nowadays. Seems like nobody knows the meaning of fair and reasonable no more. Ernie reminds them, that's all. It's totally legit."

"Well," said Ray, "if it gets us a nice place to live and nobody's the worse for wear, I'd say it's copasetic. And awful nice of Ernie, don'tcha think, Delores?"

"I don't know how we'd ever pay him back."

"Pay him back?" Vera laughed. "Ernie Bellagotti? Don't kid yourself, sister. He'll find a way."

84

Chapter 13

A week later, the Olsons were in their new home, a one-bedroom bungalow with a white picket fence, a garage, and a small yard. With Ray working at the fix-it shop three days a week, they could afford the ten-dollar-a-month rent, but little more. Then, Saturday morning, Sam knocked on the door.

"Ray, I got some more work for you. I got two of my slot machines in the back seat," he said, nodding toward his car. "They been jammin' up on me and irritatin' my customers. I can't afford nobody gettin' irritated, pal. Not good for business. See what you can do."

Ray spent the rest of his day in his garage, door closed, slot machine parts spread across the workbench.

Sunday, after he and Delores returned from church, he went back to work on them. By two o'clock, every nickel dropped in the slot worked as it should. At three, he dropped one more nickel, this time in the slot of the payphone on the corner.

"Sammy's Pool Hall, Buddy speakin'."

"Say, Buddy, this here is Ray Olson. Get Sammy on the horn for me, will ya?"

"Sure thing, Ray."

Ray waited. And waited. Then, "Ray?"

"Yeah?"

"Sam's busy. Can't come to the phone right now."

"Didja tell him it's me?"

"Well, see, Sam's upstairs right now. You follow?"

"Oh. Gotcha, Buddy. Don't bother him, okay?"

"I can tell him to call you back."

"Nope. Won't work. I ain't got no phone, yet. You just tell Sam to come over to my place and pick up his kids. Okay, Buddy?"

"Kids? Sam ain't got no ..."

"Just tell him, Bud. He'll know."

Sam Campbell pulled up after dark. They met in Ray's garage.

"See, Ray," he said, "I knew you'd be able to figure these

things out. What was the problem, anyhow?"

"Well, one machine is just plain too old to cut the mustard, Sammy. I tightened things up where I could and greased the rollers, but I can't say how long it's good for. For all I know, it'll give up the ghost within a few months."

"A few months?" Sam laughed. "A slot machine can collect plenty in a few months. How 'bout the other one?"

"Well, that's a horse of a different color."

"Like what, for instance?"

"Sam, do you got somebody hangin' around the back room that don't like you?"

"Come again?"

"You know, somebody what don't cater much to the idea of you havin' slots in the neighborhood?

"What makes you ask that?"

Ray held out three nickels stuck together with chewing gum. "This."

"Well, I'll be," said Sam, taking the sticky nickels. "Looks like ... gum?"

"It's a wonder that machine worked at all, Sam."

"I s'pose some mug got his gum on a nickel somehow and then put it in anyhow. I s'pose that's the way the ball bounces. Accidents happen."

"But this weren't no accident. I pulled 'bout half-a-pack of gum from that machine."

"Half-a-pack?"

"Juicy Fruit. Wrigley's Juicy Fruit. Sammy, you got some chump what chews Juicy Fruit playin' your slots?"

"Hell if I know."

"I'd say you might want to find out, buddy. Took me two hours to get that old, worn-out slot back in shape. But I spent six, maybe seven hours cleaning the gum outa this one. How many slots you got in that back room of yours?"

"Eight."

"My guess is that you'll be bringin' me another one, soon. If I was you, I'd be watchin' who sits in front of what slot and what one gets jammed up next. Get my drift?"

"I get it, buddy. I'll keep an eye out." Sam pulled out his wallet. "Here's for your trouble, Ray."

Ray looked at the twenty in Sam's hand. "Aw, I can't take that from you, Sammy. I mean, look at all you done for me and my gal already. No, you keep it."

"Raymond, I insist. If you won't take it in payment for the work you did on my machines, then take it as a retainer for more work. Soon as I nail this bum who's jammin' up my slots, I plan to bring you each machine I own for a tune-up, see? And I got friends in the business. They'll think ten bucks a machine is a bargain. So you just take this double sawbuck on account, hear?"

"On account?" Ray took the twenty, stuffing it into a shirt pocket. "I take it on accounta Delores could use a night on the town. Or maybe I'll buy her a new dress and some curtains for the bedroom. But don't you never try to pay me for fixin' your slots, again, my friend. If somebody else wants to trade a ten-spot for a tune-up, so be it. For you, buddy, it's gratis."

"Thanks, Ray. I'll get the word out."

Two days later at Rhode's Department Store, Ray paged through the *Tacoma News Tribune* while Delores tried on dresses. In the police and fire report on page twelve, a paragraph told of a small-time Seattle hood, Willie Briggs, in a coma after being victim of a hit-and-run near the Tacoma waterfront. The police had no leads other than his pockets were full of nickels and Wrigley's Juicy Fruit gum.

Delores stepped from the fitting room.

"Say, now!" said Ray, as his wife modeled the dress for him. "That's a doozy of a dress, Baby. There ain't a twist on the coast who could hold a candle to you in that outfit. Do they have it in red?"

"You don't like me in blue, Ray?"

"Hey, don't get me wrong. I like the blue one just fine. But try on a red one, just to see. One like Vera had on the other night. Okay, Doll?"

"So, you got a thing for Vera?"

"Vera? Naw. But I got a thing about seein' you in a red dress, Doll. Go ahead. Try it on for me, will ya?"

"Sure, Ray. Sure."

Back at their bungalow, Ray pulled into the driveway. Delores carried the box containing her new blue dress up the walk and into the house as Ray opened the garage door. There, in a row, stood four slot machines. A note on one read, *Two from me, two from Benny D. Fix Benny's first. S.C.*

Ray rushed into the house. "Delores, I got good news. C'mon."

"C'mon where?"

"Hop in the car. I'll tell ya on the way."

"On the way where?"

"We're headin' back to the store."

"What? Why?"

"Why, to get you that other dress, Baby. I gotta feelin' things are about to look up."

Within a month, Ray's job at the fix-it shop and his clandestine repair service brought more money into the Olson home than ever before. Delores had a new winter coat. Bell Telephone had installed one of the latest table-top telephones, and Ray was looking at a car—a 1933 Ford sedan with a flat-head, eight-cylinder motor.

"Now *there's* a car, Baby. She'll outrun anything else on the road. Not a cop in the west can keep up."

"Is that important, Sweetie?"

"What?"

"Do we need a car fast enough to outrun the law?"

"Well, no, not right now. Not today. But, who knows?"

"Remember what you told me? Remember how you promised you'd stay out of trouble? Stay clear of the law? Stay out of jail?"

"Well, sure I remember, Baby. But that don't mean we can't drive a nice car, does it?"

"Look, Sweetie. I know Sam's been a good friend. Ernie and

Tiny, too. But, face it. You've fallen in with pals who are over the edge when it comes to the law. Sooner or later, they're going to lead you over that edge. You know I'm right, Ray."

"So, what am I supposed to do? Give up the best job I ever had? Baby, I got a good thing goin'. I'm makin' good money—real good money. People look up to me."

"Are they the right kind of people? Will they look up to you after the state gambling commission knocks on the door? Or after some judge lands you back in jail?"

"That won't happen. Sam says the fix is in. I got protection. We're in Pierce County, see? Sam tells me that in Pierce, Kitsap, and King Counties, every last public official gets a piece of the gamblin' action."

"It's still a crime."

"But it's a crime that don't hurt nobody, see? And nobody but nobody will come knockin', Delores."

"Maybe not today, maybe not tomorrow, but sooner or later you'll be in trouble again. Worse trouble than you ..."

"Don't you harp at me, Delores. I ain't givin' up the best job I ever had. And I'm buyin' that Ford with the flathead eight. End of discussion."

Ray was right. No one knocked except owners of gambling rooms, taverns, and strip clubs wanting slot machines repaired. At their request, Ray soon began visiting their businesses to inspect machines for wear and rebuild worn parts. Word of his services spread from Olympia to Seattle. Within months, Ray was in demand, his wallet bulged, and a shiny, new Ford sedan occupied the Olson garage along with spare slot machine parts.

Ray's circle of friends quickly grew. He often lingered in the clubs after his repairs were done, drinking and playing cards with his new pals. One night, on the way home, he heard a siren and saw a flashing red light in the rearview mirror. He pulled over and opened the door. The headlights of the car behind blinded him as the red light stopped blinking and two large men go out.

"You Ray Olson?" one asked.

Ray squinted, shielding the glare from their headlights with his arm. "Yeah. What'd I do, officer?"

The men came forward. "You the Ray Olson who works on slot machines?"

"Me? Uh … no. You got the wrong Ray Olson. I work in a two-bit fix-it shop."

One of the men shined a flashlight into Ray's face. "Naw, you're him alright. My boss wants to talk with you. He's in the car."

"Then, you ain't cops?"

One of the men laughed. "Me and Lloyd? Cops?" He turned to his partner. "Didja hear that, Lloyd?"

"Cops ain't the only ones who can buy a red light, pally," said Lloyd. "Come with me."

Ray hesitated.

"Let's go, buddy. The boss ain't got all night."

The rear door of the Mercury sedan swung open, sending the smell of cigar smoke into the air.

"Entrare," came a voice from within. "Join me, Ray Olson. Please."

"How 'bout instead you join me out here?" said Ray.

He felt a shove on his shoulder from behind. "Don't get wise, pal," said Lloyd. "Just do as you're told."

Ray obeyed. Lloyd closed the door. Inside, in the glow of the headlights, he saw a man with a cigar, probably in his twenties, and wearing a white suit and a white fedora with a black hatband.

The man drew on the cigar then exhaled, filling the car with smoke. "My name is Valentino. Giovanni Valentino. You heard of me?"

"I've heard the name."

"My friends call me Geno. You should call me that, too, for I am your *paesano*."

"Gee, thanks."

"You care for a cigar, Raymond?"

90

"Sure. I'll smoke one of your stogies. Why not?"

"Here," Geno said, reaching into an inside pocket, "take several. I import them by the case. They're made up *especial in la città dove sono nato*, How you say? Eh ... my place of birth. *Siracusa*."

"You from New York, then? Syracuse?"

"No, no. *Siracusa*. In Sicily. S*iracusa. Mi urbano. Mi dove sono nato. Capiche*?"

"Yeah, I capiche, Geno. Your home town is in Sicily. But you didn't order them two mugs out there to pull me over in the dark just to tell me where you're from and give me a pocketful of panetellas."

"No. No, I suppose I didn't."

"So, what's all this about?"

"I've heard you *are altamente qualificato ... esparto* ... eh ... an expert with the machines. I am told you have helped many of my friends with their machines. For this, I thank you, paesano."

"Why, that's nice of you. Real nice. But they thank me plenty enough with their greenbacks, Geno."

"Yes. I suppose they do. Still, I am sure a man like you, a man who has become so skilled at his craft, enjoys hearing his skills are *gradito* ...eh ... appreciated. No?"

"Sure, Geno. Sure. But you could have mailed me a thank you card and said the same thing instead of havin' your gorillas pull me over on a dark night. So, what's this all about?"

"I employ many people here. *Esparti*. Experts with skills in many areas. Smart people like you. And now I would like to add your name, the name of Raymond Olson to the list of others on my payroll."

"You want me to fix your slots? Is that what this is about?"

"No. Not for me. Not my slots. I want you to work on slots owned by others. You can do that for me?"

"Geno, it don't matter to me what machines I work on. Long as I get paid. I get ...uh ... fifteen bucks for each machine."

"Raymond, Raymond. You think I don't know that you make

ten, maybe twelve dollars for each machine you fix? Do not insult me. I know everything about this business. Everything about this town."

"You got me, Geno. Okay. Twelve bucks."

"No. I don't give you ten, twelve bucks. I give you twenty. What you say?"

"Twenty?"

"Si. Twenty. What you say?"

"I say, what gives, Geno?"

"I love how Yanks talk. What gives. Only in America would someone ask what gives. Okay. Here is what gives. Raymondo, have you ever noticed a red heart painted on the inside of a slot machine?"

"Sure. Plenty of times."

"Those are my machines."

"I know better. Those machines are scattered all over. Why, half the machines I fix have them hearts inside."

"Yes. but you see, *I* provided them to the owners of the business establishments who then brought them to you when they needed care. I get a small commission, a few pennies, maybe a few nickels every day from each one of those machines. You see, paesano, a penny here and a penny there, it can soon add up. That's where you come in, Raymond."

"I get it. You want me to lower the odds on your machines so you get more money out of the pockets of the players. That's it, ain't it? You're out to skin the players. Sure, I can change the odds. No sweat!"

"Paesano! No, no. You misunderstand. I do not want you to change the odds on *my* machines. No, I want those good people who put a nickel or a dime in one of my machines to have a good chance to win. Raymond, what I need you to do is lower the odds on my competitor's machines. Make their machines ... *ostile* ... unfriendly to the fellow with a pocketful of silver to throw away. Put the odds against that player winning on my competitors' slot machines. Make it a bit worse—not much—but enough that after a few pulls, the player walks out the door to another joint, walks up to one of my machines. Capiche?"

"Capiche, Geno. But, do you really think that will work?"

"Si. It works for me in San Francisco, San Diego, many other places. You will do this for me?"

"How much do you want the odds changed?"

Valentino leaned back in his seat. "Raymond, give me your hand."

"Come again?"

"Hold out your hand."

Ray did. Valentino flicked the ash from his cigar into Ray's upturned palm. Ray didn't flinch.

"Raymondo, you ask me how much I want the odds against winning lowered on my competitors' machines? The answer, paesano, is one-tenth the weight of the ashes you hold."

"You don't ask much, Geno."

"It's like this. Even though a drop of water is small and means nothing by itself, enough drops, in time, can fill an ocean. The owners of the machines will not notice a small change. But the man with the nickel, he will notice. I want those who play *my* machines to enjoy one, maybe two percent better odds. No more."

"And for that you'll pay me a double sawbuck for each machine?"

"Si. For tending to my machines like they are your own bambinos and for telling nobody—nobody about our arrangement. Twenty dollars for each machine. That is my offer. Capiche?"

"Oh, I capiche, Geno Valentino. And how."

Valentino rapped on the window. The door opened. Ray stepped out, then turned back. "Geno," he said, "your boys 'bout scared the Shinola outa me with that red light a theirs. Next time, just call me up. The operator has my number. Capiche?"

"Capiche, paesano. Capiche," came the reply and a laugh. "Buona Notte, Raymondo."

Chapter 14

Ray held the phone's receiver tight to his ear. "Hello? Is that you, Ma?"

. . .

"No. It's me, Augie."

. . .

"Huh? No. Augie. Your son. Can you hear me okay?"

. . .

"No, Ma, nothin's wrong. Me and Delores are just callin' to say happy Thanksgivin'."

. . .

"No, I ain't in trouble again."

. . .

"What? No, Ma. I said I ain't in trouble."

. . .

"Oh, for Pete's sake, listen. I got me a good job. Me and Delores have a nice house with a yard and everything. We're doin' good, Ma. We just wanted to see how you and Pa are gettin' along, see? So, how are you?"

. . .

"Whaddaya mean, worried? There's nothin' for you and Pa to worry yourselves about. I'm tellin' ya, me and Delores are doin' just fine."

. . .

"The State Patrol?"

. . .

"They came to the house? Oh, I see. Yeah, I suppose they would want to ask you about me. Well, don't you go losin' no sleep about the cops, Ma. Me and Delores are long gone, see? Where we are the Wisconsin law won't never touch us."

. . .

"Where? Out on the coast. The west coast."

. . .

"Well, I'd just not say right now. You understand, don't you Ma? We got us a nice place in a nice town, that's all I can say."

...

"What? Oh, that's fine, Ma. Say, you havin' the family over for Thanksgivin'?"

...

"Aw, I sure wish we could, Ma. But it just ain't in the cards. And it ain't the first Thanksgivin' dinner I missed, you know."

...

"Yeah, someday, Ma. Say, maybe next summer you and Pa could come out here for a visit."

...

"Aw, don't you worry 'bout how much for the train. I can pay for your tickets. I got me a good job and plenty a dough. You could take the Great Northern through the Rocky Mountains. Pa would love to see them. Maybe stop at Yellowstone Park. Maybe Delores and me could meet you there. We could see all the sights, and visit, and catch up on things.

...

"What's 'at?"

...

"Yeah, that *would* be nice. Yeah, I miss you and Pa plenty. Delores does, too."

...

"Okay, well, I better go, Ma. When Pa gets off from work, you tell him I called. Make sure you tell him I got me a good job."

...

"What?"

...

"No, I'm a mechanic. I fix machines."

...

"Cars? No. Just regular machines. The pay's good and there's plenty of work for me. You be sure to tell Pa, okay?"

...

"Yeah, Delores and me, we love you too, Ma. Love you to pieces. She told me to say happy Thanksgivin' to you and Pa. Sorry we can't be there. Maybe someday."

...

"Okay, Ma. I will."

...

"Yes, I'll stay clear of trouble. I promise."

...

"Love you, too, Ma. Goodbye."

Ray hung up the phone, tears welling in his eyes. Delores put her arms around him.

"Oh, Sweetie, I know how much you miss your folks. But, they'll be all right. They'll have a nice Thanksgiving and everything will work out."

"She's so worried 'bout us. Runnin' from the law and everything."

"Mothers always worry about their children. Always have, always will."

"I know it. But, Baby, it's just that I feel so bad that I let you and Ma and everybody down. I wish I woulda stayed there and served out my dang six months. Then we could come and go as we please."

"Too late for wishes, Ray. You go back now and that six months might turn into six years, for all we know."

"Aw, how I miss bein' home."

"Ray, we *are* home. *This* is our home." She turned on the radio to hear *Stardust,* then turned it up.

"Dance with me, Ray Olson," she whispered. "Dance your cares away. C'mon."

"Sure, Baby."

They waltzed to the the Zenith's soft sounds.

Sometimes I wonder why I spend the lonely night dreaming of a song.

"Ma said she didn't have a turkey in the oven. Pa got cut back on his work and they're pinchin' their pennies."

"Oh, jeez. I'm so sorry for your folks, Sweetie."

The melody haunts my reverie, and I am once again with you.

"And I can't even send them some dough without worryin' 'bout the coppers findin' out where we are."

When our love was new, and each kiss an inspiration.

"I know. But that's just the way things are right now. I haven't written home, either. Your folks and mine can muddle through and so can we."

But that was long ago. Now my consolation is in the stardust of a song.

"Ray, someday, things will change. Everything changes with time. You watch. In time, this will all be so far in the past that nobody will remember. Nobody will care what some guy named Augie Buelo did when he was just a kid—just a dumbbell."

Beside a garden wall, when stars are bright, you are in my arms.

"Hey! Watch who you're callin' a dumbbell," he said with a laugh.

The nightingale tells his fairy tale. Of paradise where roses bloom.

"Oh, you know what I mean. The trouble you've been in is the result of the adventuresome nature of young men. Boys who want to be seen as bold risk-takers. Daring. Carefree. Courageous soldiers of fortune. Pirates. High-stakes gamblers. That's you to a tee, Sweetie."

Though I dream in vain. In my heart, it always will remain. My stardust melody—the memory of love's refrain.

"You'll laugh when I tell you this."

"What? Tell me, Ray."

"When I was a kid, I always wanted to be a cop."

"A cop? You?"

"Now, don't that paint a pretty picture, Baby? Me with a badge and a gun?"

"Well, some say that crooks make the best cops."

"You think I should shed these duds and put on a cop's uniform?"

"You know, Ray? I think you could. Why, you're a good man—a person who cares about others. And let's face it, you know the ropes. You'd be able to see things comin' better than most cops, I'd bet. If crooks make the best cops, you'd be terrific!"

"Yeah? Well, I've also heard that cops make the worst crooks, too. That a badge is all you need to get away with 'most anything."

"I suppose there is temptation in a job like that."

"Delores, you give a crook a badge and he has a big edge over every other guy out there. He has the law on his side, see? I don't never wanna be up against some crook with a badge. They can get away with murder and then sweep it all under the judge's rug. I'm tellin' ya, Baby, if I ever run up against a lawbreaker that's a lawman, I'm hightailin' it like Lou Gehrig stealin' second."

"That's good, Sweetie. As long as you stay clear of the cops, I think we'll be fine."

"Well, we're sittin' on a rainbow now, Doll, even if we can't sit down to a nice Thanksgivin' dinner with our folks this year. Better times are sure to come. I just know it."

"I know it, too, Ray. Like Crosby says, we got the world on a string."

Chapter 15

Saturday afternoon, Ray pulled up behind a strip club on the outskirts of Seattle. He grabbed his toolbox from the back seat and ran through the rain, entering the club through the back door. Big Bill O'Banion, the owner of the club got up from a back room card game. He showed Ray six machines needing maintenance. All but one were Valentino machines. After servicing each, Ray made a note of the machine numbers in a small book kept in his hip pocket.

He approached O'Banion. "That'll be a hundred fifteen, Bill."

Bill looked up from the table. "Last time, I paid you ten bucks per. So, what gives?"

"Five of them slots are Valentino's. He pays twenty. Other one ain't, so it's fifteen."

"Fifteen? Twenty? Since when?"

"Call Valentino. He'll square up with you."

"Naw," he said, pulling several bills from his winnings. "I don't like talkin' to that wop. I know better than to go up against the dagos in this town. Christ, how's a fella s'posed to make an honest livin' with them tappin' your till?"

"Tell you what," said Ray, "deal me in and I'll give you a chance to win your money back."

"You're on, buddy. Name of the game is five card stud."

"Fine by me."

"Ante up five bucks, fellas."

Each man laid a five on the table. O'Banion dealt each player one card down and one up.

Ray looked at his hole card and the King he was dealt, then tossed a dollar into the pot. "I bet a buck on my kings, boys."

Each man matched the bet. O'Banion sent another card to each. "King bets," he said.

Ray looked at the Queen and King before him, peeked at his hole card again, then slapped another five onto the table. "I'll go five more on the old man and his dame."

Again the bet was matched. Again O'Banion sent cards around. "Still your bet, Mr.Fix-it."

Ray studied the cards and the eyes of each player, then bet five more. The man to his left folded. The next matched his five and raised five. O'Banion tossed a ten-dollar bill onto the pile. Ray laid a twenty on the stack and pulled out fifteen. "I call your raise, Bill."

O'Banion dealt the fifth and last card, again face up. Ray now had a King, a Queen, a Jack, and a ten showing. He peeked at his hole card again. "Fellas, it's gonna cost you a double sawbuck to see my hand," he said with a grin.

"Naw, can't be," said the man to his left. "I don't figure you got an ace or a nine. Not a chance."

"Cost you twenty to see for sure, friend," said Ray.

The man studied his cards, then Ray's, then folded.

O'Banion scooped up his cards and tossed them down. "Looks like you got Lady Luck on your side, Ray. Pot's yours."

The second hand, a smaller pot, went to O'Banion. The third, fourth, and fifth, to Ray, bluffing his way through each. The man to his left bowed out, leaving the table. Three players remained.

Ray's confidence showed as he dealt the sixth hand. Five cards later, the next man left the table saying, "You're too damn lucky, buddy. I ain't wastin' one more dime on you."

"Just you and me, Ray," said O'Banion, dealing Ray a card down and an ace up. "Your ace bets."

Ray peeked at his hole card, then looked at Big Bill's seven of hearts. "Ten to you, Bill."

Bill tossed a twenty on the board. "Ten back to ya," he said.

Ray slapped down thirty dollars. "Raise you twenty."

"See your twenty and I'll go twenty more, pal."

Ray called the bet. He studied O'Banion's eyes as the next cards came around. O'Banion's was another seven. Ray's, a deuce.

"My pair of sevens bets fifty bucks, Mr. Fix-it. Looks like I might get some of my money back, after all."

"Maybe so. Here's your fifty and fifty more."

O'Banion silently slid a fifty into the pot, rapped his knuckles on the table, and dealt two more cards up—Ray a deuce, Bill the four of diamonds.

"Fifty to you, Mr. Fix-it."

Ray studied the cards, then pulled two fifties from his wallet. "Y'know, Bill? My little lady could use a nice fur coat. Looks like tonight's her night."

Bill met the raise, rapped his knuckles on the table, and dealt each a fifth card, again face up. "My sevens still bet," he said, laying a hundred-dollar bill on the table. "No sense in hollerin' whoa in a horse race, right Ray?"

"Nope," said Ray as he matched the bet and raised another hundred.

O'Banion stared at the fifth card Ray had been dealt, another ace. "So, Ray, the way I see it, you got a pair of bullets and a pair of deuces up," he said. "And, the way you been raisin', a fella might figure you could have a third ace in the hole. Or maybe another deuce. Either hand would beat my three sevens."

"I 'spose, Bill."

"Of course, my three sevens would take the pot if all you got is two pair. Hmm. Should I believe you have a third ace? Or maybe a third deuce? My, my, my. But the big question, my friend, is should I follow my hunch that you're bluffin'? That you been bluffin' your way through just about every hand we've played here tonight?"

"Yep, I 'spose that's the big question, all right. Maybe I been bluffin'. Or maybe not. Who knows? Maybe it's my lucky night."

"Yes, it seems the cards have been on your side."

"They surely have."

"But a good string of luck can't last forever, Ray."

"But it might last through this hand, Bill."

O'Banion slapped two hundred-dollar bills on the table. "Two C-notes to you, my friend."

Ray leaned back in his chair, considering the bet and his cards. Searching through his winnings, he pulled out six twenties, four tens, and eight fives. "I'm callin' your two hundred and raisin' you two more."

O'Banion smiled, then met the raise and raised another two hundred.

Ray pulled four bills from his wallet. "Two hundred more, Bill."

"My sevens see your raise and I'll go you two-fifty more."

"I'll see your two-fifty and go another two," Ray said, laying four-fifty on the table.

"Here's your two hundred, Mr. Fix-it. And here's a grand more."

Ray froze. He couldn't cover the bet. "Bill, I'm short on cash. Can you spot me seven hundred?"

"Seven hundred? That's quite a roll. You good for it?"

"I'd never run out on a friend what borrowed money to me, Bill."

"Okay, Ray, I'll spot you seven hundred. Payable one week from today or it doubles."

"Fine by me. I call. I got me two pair," Ray said, flipping his hole card, a seven of spades. "You got that last seven?"

Bill smiled, then turned up his card, the seven of hearts. "And you thought you could bluff me with your two measly pair, Ray? Too bad for you, buddy. My sevens take this pot, hands down."

"I'll say this much for you, O'Banion, you sure got guts."

"Some say it's courage. Others say I know a pushover when I see one."

Ray shoved his chair back. Grabbing his tool box, he headed toward the door.

O'Banion lit a cigar. "One week, Ray Olson. I want to see that money in seven days if not sooner."

"Bank on it," Ray answered, slamming the door.

The other two players sat at the table again. O'Banion handed each a hundred-dollar bill. "This'll cover your losses and then some, boys." He reached into his coat pocket, pulling out two aces and two deuces, then slid them back into the deck and shuffled the cards. "I tell ya boys, there's a sucker born every minute."

Chapter 16

Ray headed south to Tacoma, but didn't go home. Instead, he drove north, crossing the narrows by ferry. Three miles later, he parked under a sign flashing *Foxie's - Foxie's - Foxie's* in red neon. He entered the busy Gig Harbor roadhouse, this time without his tool box. Foxie Miller, the red-headed, high-heeled owner of the club, saw him, filled two glasses with ice, then topped them both with bourbon, leaving the bottle on the bar. She lit two cigarettes, gave Ray one, then came around the end of the bar.

"Ray, you seem a little down. Why so glum, chum?"

"Aw, it's nothin', Foxie. But you'll have to put this drink on the tab. I'm short of cash."

"You? Short on cash? You're kidding me, right?"

"Don't I wish."

"What's going on?"

"I had some unexpected expenses, that's all."

"It happens, hon." She put her hand on his, squeezing it gently. "Don't worry, you'll survive."

"Yeah, I know, I know. But it's the first time since I moved out here that I been broke. I forgot what it's like, see? One minute I'm king of the hill and the next I'm in the gutter."

"You and 'most everybody else these days. So, do you want to tell Foxie what happened?"

"Aw, you don't need to hear my troubles."

"Oh, go ahead, hon. Get it off your chest. And, drink up. I'm buying tonight."

"I got carried away in a poker game on what I thought was a pat hand that's all. Bet more than I should. Now I owe Big Bill O'Banion seven hundred that I don't got."

"Oh, my."

"Aw, it's only seven hundred. I'll make it up."

"It's not that, Ray." She filled their glasses again.

"Huh?"

"It's O'Banion."

"What?"

105

"He's a slippery one."

"Huh?"

"With the cards."

"Whaddaya mean?"

"Oh, I shouldn't say …"

"Spit it out, Foxie. What's the deal?"

"That's just it, Ray. The deal."

"Aw, for chrissake, Foxie, stop beatin' around the dang bush."

"Who was dealing when you lost that hand?"

"O'Banion."

"I figured."

Ray sipped his bourbon. "You think he cheated me?"

"I'd put money on it."

"What makes you think so?"

"It's what he does. And he's good. Real good."

"Naw, he wouldn't dare. I played poker plenty before. I can spot a cheat a mile away. "

"Don't take my word for it. Ask anybody who knows him." She turned, shouting to her bartender, "Hey, Johnny, I hear Big Bill might drop in for a poker game tomorrow night. You want in?"

"O'Banion?" replied Johnny. "I might just as well flush my paycheck down the crapper."

Foxie turned back to Ray, putting her arm around him. "See what I mean? Ask anyone and they'll tell you the same."

"So, maybe I shouldn't pay off what I owe him? Is that what you're sayin'?"

"Oh, I wouldn't dare run out on a debt to Big Bill. He's a mean one. Better to pay him off and chalk it up to experience." Foxie topped off his glass.

"I ain't worried. What could he do?"

"Oh, I don't know. Maybe shoot you full of holes and dump you in the Columbia River."

"After *he* cheated *me*?"

"If I were you, Ray, I'd just pay off what you owe and stay as far away from O'Banion as possible. He's trouble with a capital T."

"That don't sit well with me, Foxie."

"Don't go up against him, hon. He's mean and he's got friends who are meaner. I'm telling you, pay him off and get as far away from him as you can. Bill is dangerous." She leaned in close, rubbing his thigh. "Ray, you're a swell guy. I'd hate to see you get hurt. Besides, who'd take care of my slots? Do us both a favor, pay off the jerk and let go of it."

As Foxie reached for the bottle again, the front door swung open. Four uniformed policemen rushed in.

"This is a raid," said one. "Hands in the air and keep them there." Five more officers followed, heading toward the back room."

"Say, what is this?" said Foxie.

"You'll have to ask the captain, ma'am."

Police Captain Ralph Stone entered the bar with a press photographer. "That's her at the end of the bar, Mike," he said to the newsman.

"Ralph, what's the meaning of this?" demanded Foxie.

"Oh, you know how it is, Foxie," he said, reaching for his handcuffs. He turned to the photographer. "Get in real tight on me and Foxie, now, Mike."

As the handcuffs clicked, the press camera flashed. "Got it, Captain," said Mike.

"No, Ralph, I don't know how it is. What the hell do you think you're doing?"

"Mayor Strand is looking for some good news coverage just before Christmas. Thinks it makes him look good in the public eye."

"But, why me, Ralph? You know very well that I pay you guys every month so this sort of thing won't happen. You think I want my picture in the paper wearing handcuffs?"

"Somebody down at city hall decided it was your turn, Foxie. Don't worry" he said, taking the handcuffs off, "we'll be out of your way in no time. And just look at all the free publicity you'll get. Why, you'll make plenty more dough than you'll lose."

"Jesus, Ralph. You coulda at least given me a heads up. There's some folks in here who don't need their name in the paper."

"And I know just who they are. I'll see to it they slip out the back door." He turned to Ray. "And who might this be, Foxie?"

"This is my maintenance man, Ray Olson. No need to bother with him."

"No? Well, he's goin' downtown in the paddy wagon with the rest."

"Like hell I am."

"What'd you say?"

"I didn't do anything wrong."

"What you did wrong, sonny, is you picked this here illegal gambling joint over twenty-some others in these parts. Don't sweat it. We'll give you a free ride to the station, book you, and you'll pay a five-dollar fine, that's all. You'll be out of the slammer before closing time."

"What gives you the right to ...?"

"This badge, sonny. And a nightstick if the need arises."

Ray downed the rest of his drink. "And you call yourself a cop. You're no more than a flunky for a crooked mayor."

"Watch your mouth, sonny."

"Ray," said Foxie, "just go along with it."

"Look, Captain, my wife's at home waiting for me," Ray said, slurring now. "You say the word and I'll be gone out the same back door as those others."

"You're goin' downtown, sonny," said the captain, grabbing Ray by the collar.

Instinctively, Ray's arm came up, breaking the officer's grip. His elbow struck the man's chin, throwing him into the bar. Ray's fist came up for the next blow.

"Ray, don't!" shouted Foxie. The captain cowered, slumped against the bar. "It's not worth it. Just go with them. I'll cover the fine."

Two policemen grabbed Ray from behind, wrestling him to the floor. Captain Stone stood, rubbing his jaw.

"Say, sonny. You got some spunk there. But you got more brawn than brains. That little move is gonna cost you seven days in the slammer."

"Aw, let him go, Ralph," begged Foxie. "Ray's had a bum streak of luck today."

"That's his problem, not mine. Nobody hits me and gets away with it, see? Nobody."

"You're the one who belongs in jail," said Ray. "Nothin' but a dang, two-bit, crook who whores for the mayor and the other thugs what run this town."

"Make that ten days!"

"So, now you're the judge, too?"

"No. That would be my brother."

Eleven days later, Ray sat across the table from Big Bill O'Banion.

"Bill, I got the seven hundred I owed you."

"Seven?" O'Banion counted the money, then stuffed the bills into a shirt pocket. "You got a short memory. It's fourteen hundred. That was the deal then, Olson. That's still the deal now."

"I woulda got it to you sooner but some damn cop tossed me in the cooler."

"You don't say."

"I had to sell my Ford just to get you the seven hundred."

"Problem is, you owe me fourteen hundred so you're seven short and it doubles again in three days."

"I can't cover it that quick."

"Tell me something I don't already know."

"So, what's next? You gonna have a couple of your goons work me over?"

"I could. But I got an out for you. A way for you to square up."

"I'm listenin'."

"I need a favor."

"What kind of favor?"

"I want you to pick somebody up for me."

"At the depot?"

"No. At his house. A ten-year-old nephew of mine. Pick him up tonight and bring him to me."

"That's it? Pick up your nephew?"

"You can't let anyone see you or talk to you."

"And why's that?"

"You don't need to ask any questions, either."

Ray looked at O'Banion. "So, why don't you just pick him up yourself?"

"I told you, you don't need to ask any questions. Just pick up the kid where and when I say and you and me are square, see?"

"All right. All right. I'll do it. I'll need a car and directions to the place."

"No, you don't. Be at the corner of Second and Grand at five-o'clock sharp. I'll have a driver pick you up. He'll know where to go. Parents won't be home. You'll need a mask."

"A mask? Why?"

"Because I'm calling the shots. Pay me another seven hundred or be ready at five. You in or not?"

Ray stared at O'Banion. "Tell your driver to be there on time."

That December 27, 1936, evening, a black Buick sedan pulled along the railroad tracks near Commencement Bay. Ray pulled his hat down and his collar up before climbing the hill to a large, opulent, stone home with a patio overlooking the bay. He crossed the yard to a pair of French doors, tied a bandanna around his face, then forced the doors open. He stepped into the room and stood, listening to the sound of children playing somewhere down the hall. Silently, he crossed to the next door and peered from the darkness at two girls and two boys playing pick-up-sticks near a Christmas tree. The oldest, a boy in his teens, froze when he looked up to see a man in a mask. Ray rushed in, seizing the younger boy by the wrist. He jerked the boy from the floor. All four children screamed.

"Shut your yaps! Shut up!" shouted Ray. "Are you Charlie?" he asked the younger boy. "Charlie Mattson?"

"Leave me alone," the boy screamed, kicking and thrashing.

110

"Settle down! I asked you a question. Are you Charlie Mattson?"

"Yes. Now leave me alone!"

Ray tightened his grip on the boy's wrist. "You're pa sent me here to take you to see your uncle."

"I don't got no uncle," said the boy as he swung at Ray, pulling the mask down.

"All right! Now you done it," said Ray as he slapped the boy in the face. "I'm warnin' you, settle down or else! And you other kids, you get over there against the wall. Now, I'm takin' Charlie to see his uncle. If you call the cops or anybody else, you're gonna be in for it, see?"

"Where are you taking our brother?" demanded the older girl.

"None of your business. You just remember what I said. If anybody tells the cops, little Charlie and all the rest of you are gonna be in for it. Understand?"

No child answered.

"I asked you a question! *Do you understand?*"

"Yes!" said the older boy. "We are not to call anybody. You go with him, Charlie. Dad will find you and bring you back home. Go with him, Charlie."

"There," said Ray, "that's usin' your noggin, boy." He handed him an envelope. "This here's from Charlie's uncle. You give it to your pa when he gets home. Me and Charlie are leavin' now. You kids stay right here in this room until your ma and pa get back and remember, don't you call nobody. If I find out you did, you'll be sorry."

Pulling Charlie by the wrist, Ray crossed the back yard and followed the trail down the hill to the Buick waiting near the railroad track. The driver opened the trunk and stuffed ten-year-old Charlie Mattson inside.

"Now, you listen to me, kid," said the driver. "If I hear as much as a peep out of you, just one sound, I'll give you a thrashin' you'll never forget. Now you behave or else." He slammed the trunk lid.

In the cold, December night, the Buick rolled down the gravel road along the tracks, then out onto Seventy Avenue before the driver turned on the headlights.

"So, I take it Charlie's not Big Bill's nephew?" Ray asked.

"That's not your concern."

"What's gonna happen to the kid?"

"Look. You did your job and your off the hook with the boss."

"You dang well better see to it that kid don't get hurt."

"Hurt him? Why that kid's a gold mine. His old man is loaded. If he's smart, he'll pay up and have the kid home in no time."

Minutes later, the Buick turned onto M Street and pulled up in front of the Olson bungalow.

"You just make sure the kid don't get hurt," Ray said, stepping from the car. He watched as O'Banion's man drove off with Charlie Mattson still in the trunk. Behind him, a lamp glowed beyond the living room window.

On the couch, nervously flipping page after page through a magazine, Delores heard her husband come into the kitchen. She watched him untie the bandanna, pulling it from his neck.

"Where have you been, Ray?" she asked.

He opened a cabinet and grabbed a near-empty liquor bottle. Trembling, he pulled the cork and tipped the bottle up, guzzling the remains.

"Where, Ray? With that woman again? That tramp, Foxie? I've told you …"

"I squared up with O'Banion for what I owed him."

"So, you were able to sell the car?"

"I didn't get what I paid for it."

"Why are you shaking?"

"I'm cold."

"I know you, Ray. Something is wrong. What is it?"

"Baby, I did a terrible thing tonight. I ..."

"Tell me."

"O'Banion said he'd let me off easy—tear up my marker—save me seven bills if I did a job for him."

"What job?"

"Said I should pick up his nephew. Said that would square us up. But, well, when I went to the house to get him, it didn't turn out the way I figured it would."

"What do you mean?"

"The kid wasn't his nephew, Delores. I just got hoodwinked into snatchin' a little boy from some rich fella. It's just like those bums who kidnapped the Weyerhaeuser kid and the Lindbergh baby."

"Jeez, Ray. How could you get yourself mixed up with ...?"

"I don't know, Baby. It just happened. It *always* just happens."

"Anybody asks me I'll swear you were home with me all night. We ate supper and listened to Jack Benny and Fibber MaGee and Molly. Then we played a few hands of gin rummy and ..."

"They saw me."

"What?"

"The kid pulled off my mask and the other three kids there saw me, Delores."

"Oh, jeez, Ray." She hugged him, feeling the cold dampness of his coat through her blouse. "What do we do, now?"

"Baby, I gotta get out of here tonight. Them kids know what I look like. And kids got good memories. If their pa goes to the cops, they'll be after me by mornin'. Maybe sooner. I gotta go."

"You sold our car, Ray. How are we supposed to ...?"

"I got some money left over. I'll hop the first Greyhound out of town. You stay here, pack up what you can, and catch a bus back

113

home to Wisconsin—to your pa's place. Wait there until you hear from me."

"You'll call me?"

"Too risky. I'll put an ad in the classifides with my pa's first name and a phone number. *Milwaukee Sentinal*. Watch for it. When you see it, call me up from some pay phone, see?"

"Okay."

Ray pulled out his wallet. "Here's a couple C-notes. That should get you back home just fine. Don't forget to take the Zenith. And my tool kit. Make sure you bring my tool kit, Baby."

She stared at the two bills. "Ray, do you have enough? Shouldn't you take another hundred?"

"I got me enough to make it out of the state. That's all I care about right now. After that, what dough I need I'll just have to dig up on my own."

"Oh, jeez, Ray. Please try to stay out of trouble. Promise me you'll stay out of trouble."

"No promises this time, Baby. I'll stay clear of the law as best I can. Gimme a kiss, Doll. I gotta go."

Trembling, Delores Olson watched her husband walk beyond the white gate of their Tacoma bungalow and vanish into the dark, cold, December drizzle.

Ten-year-old Charlie Mattson went missing that night. An hour later, so did Ray Olson.

Chapter 17

Charlie Mattson's older brother called the Tacoma police. Within minutes, the Point Defiance neighborhood was teeming with squad cars and police officers. In the living room of the Mattson home, Captain Ralph Stone unfolded a note printed in colored ink with a child's toy printing set. He read it to Dr. William Mattson and his wife, Hazel, as both fought back tears.

*"Get eighteen thousand dollars, five and ten dollar old bills, numbers not to run consecutively. Get ten thousand in fifty dollar old bills, numbers not to run consecutively. This amount will double each week. The boy is safe. When you are ready, insert in personal column in Seattle Times, 'Mabel, what is your address? Ann.' Disregard any notes received by you unless this type and this color ink is used and signed Tim. Use an old Ford car. Tim."**

"Our poor, poor Charlie," sobbed Hazel. "He must be frightened to death. Captain Stone, isn't there some way to…?"

"Mrs. Mattson, I have the whole force out looking for your little boy. Right now my men are knocking on every door in the area, looking for any witness who might have heard or seen something—anything. And the Seattle police are on the lookout, too. And the Washington State Patrol. Every effort will be made to bring Charlie back home as soon as possible."

A uniformed officer entered the room. "Captain," he said, "we followed the footprints down the hill. It looks like there was a car waiting for them. Tracks in the snow tell us there were two men involved."

Dr. Mattson embraced his wife as she burst into tears. "Isn't there more you can do, Captain?"

"The state police are setting up roadblocks as we speak."

"Roadblocks? But, won't that put our son at risk?" asked Dr. Mattson.

*Precise wording of the ransom note left at the scene of the 1936 Mattson kidnapping.

"There's no telling what these criminals have in mind. Best if we can catch him quick and get Charlie back home."

"No!" said Hazel. "We can't risk making those men angry. We have to cooperate with them in every way. We want to pay. Bill, you agree, don't you?"

"My wife is right. Charlie's safety is at stake. We must cooperate with them. I can borrow the money. I insist you call off the roadblocks."

"We'll get the money together just as the note says," said Hazel. "Bill, we can place the ad in the paper tomorrow."

Stone rubbed his chin. "Well, if that's what you want to do. But I won't take any responsibility."

"Captain, you don't have to," said Dr. Mattson. "It's our decision. Charlie's not your little boy. He's ours."

"Then I'll see to it right away. Meanwhile, Dr. Mattson, Mrs. Mattson, I want you to know that every police officer in the State of Washington will be on the lookout for your son. We're going to get him back home safe and sound. You can count on that."

An hour later, Captain Stone's unmarked car pulled up to a strip club on the outskirts of Seattle. He entered through the back door where Big Bill O'Banion waited.

"Bill, they're gonna pay up, just like I said they would."

"Good." O'Banion, reached for a bottle of Scotch. "When?"

"Soon as they can. Tomorrow, I'd say."

"Like takin' candy from a baby."

"You just make dang sure your man doesn't harm the boy."

"Bennie? He won't touch a hair on the kid's head."

"You're sure about that, Stone?"

"If I know Bennie, he has the kid eatin' ice cream and readin' comic books by now. But ..."

"But what?"

"Well, there's a hitch. A problem."

"Well, let's have it, Stone."

"Olson's mask came off when the kid took a swipe at him. Bill, the other three kids saw his face."

"Oh, that's just swell! If Ray Olson gets nabbed, how long before the feds start lookin' at me? They'll find out he owed me and couldn't pay up."

"Yeah? Well, I'm on the front burner, too. Remember, I'm the one who threw him in jail for you."

"Find him, Stone. Find him and take care of him before he can finger us."

"Ten to one he's already out of the state."

"What?"

"Look. Olson's been around. Knows the score. Knows that those other kids can identify him. And he knows a kidnapping conviction would land him in the joint for life. You can bet Olson bugged out as soon as Bennie dropped him off."

"Look, Stone. You said this would go like clockwork. That we could grab the kid, the doc would pay up without involving the police, and the whole thing would get swept under the rug in a day or two. Now you say because some kids saw Olson's face, that ..."

"There's another way out."

"How?"

"I can alibi him. Far as anyone else is concerned, Ray Olson was with me tonight."

"You? Why would he be with you?"

"Look, Bill. He was released from jail this morning, right?"

"So what?"

"Far as anyone else is concerned, I picked him up again. You know, to set him straight. To let him know I've got his number. Nobody will question it. If those kids finger Olson, he'll have the tightest alibi out there. I'll see to it."

"You think the FBI will go along with it?"

"The feds can go lay an egg for all I care. Nobody's gonna suspect me, a twenty-year captain on the force, for givin' a jailbird some counseling on the day he's released."

"You sure?"

"Positive."

"All right. But, if Olson comes back, you damn well better make sure he disappears for keeps."

"Bill, nobody but nobody will see him in the State of Washington again." Stone lifted his glass. "Here's to our chump, Ray Olson."

Ray had no intention of returning to Washington. The Greyhound he boarded took him through Oregon and into California. He stepped off the bus in downtown San Francisco. A sign above the door to a diner near the Folsom Street bus station read, *TUNA SANDWICH & COFFEE – 25¢*. As he crossed the street a man approached him. He froze.

"Say, pal, I see you're headed for the diner. I haven't eaten in two days. I'd be grateful if you could spare two bits for a meal."

Ray studied the man's face, clothes, and worn shoes.

"Aw, c'mon, buddy. Spot me enough for a sandwich. Okay?"

"Look, pal. I'm down to my last three bucks."

"You got three bucks? Last time I had three bucks was … Aw, please. Just two bits. It'll be like a steak dinner to a guy like me."

118

"All right. All right, pal. If a sandwich and a cup a joe will shut you up, then your supper's on me."

Ray laid a silver dollar on the counter. "Give us two of them tuna sandwich specials," he said to the waitress.

"Boy, I sure do appreciate this, buddy."

"Well, it ain't like I never been in your shoes."

"They call me Johnny. Jamestown Johnny. You?"

"Ray."

The waitress put two mugs of coffee on the counter.

"Where from, Ray?" asked Johnny, pouring sugar and cream into his coffee.

"Nowhere special."

"Where you headed?"

"Same place."

Johnny sipped his coffee, then added more cream and sugar. He looked at Ray. "On the lam, huh?"

"Where'd you get that notion? What are you drivin' at?"

"Oh, don't mind me. Sometimes I ask too many questions."

"I'm workin' my way back east, that's all."

"By Greyhound?" Johnny added more cream and sugar and stirred again. The waitress brought the sandwiches. "Say, missy, you're out of cream here," he complained.

"Greyhound? If only. No money left for bus fare. Like I said, I'm down to my last …"

"I'm headed back east, too. Georgia, Florida, somewhere warm. You're welcome to tag along."

Ray looked at him. "You gonna sprout wings and fly, pal?"

"Nope. Overland express."

"Come again?"

"Train travel is my preference. The modern day American railway industry is a marvel to behold. And quite inexpensive if a fellow is willing to forego first class."

"Still more than I can afford."

"Oh, the fare might surprise you."

"Like … how much?"

119

"I can have you on an express headed east by eight o'clock tonight at no cost. That is, if you're willing to jump on with me."

"Jump on? I ain't never jumped even a freight, much less an express train."

"I can show you the ropes ... if you got the gumption."

"Say, I got plenty of gumption, pal. Plenty."

"I don't doubt that for a minute, Ray. And you look like you might be tough enough for the road."

"I'm plenty tough. Tough and full of gumption."

"All right. My friend, I've been on the road near to six years. I know the ins and outs." Johnny added more cream and sugar. "And I know how to steer clear of the railroad constables in just about every big or little railroad stop you never heard of."

"Aw, sez you."

"Yes, sez me. And says any 'bo and any railroad crewman and most every one of those small town constables out there. In fact, I can introduce you to most of them ... if you got the gumption."

"You on the level?"

"I'm not prone to exaggeration, if that's what you're getting at. So, are you in?"

"You're askin' me if I want to hop on a train? An eastbound overland express?"

"Why, you catch on pretty quick, buddy. You in?"

"And this ain't some sort of con?"

"Nope. Consider it repayment for this gourmet dinner you're throwing for me. So, are you in?"

"Jamestown Johnny, I'm in."

The men finished their sandwiches. Johnny poured more cream and sugar into his cup, gulping it down. He turned to the waitress. "Say, missy, if I were to forego the coffee, do you suppose you could make me another tuna sandwich for, say, fifteen cents?"

"Say, what is this?" asked Ray. "I ain't buyin' you another sandwich, bud."

"Oh my, no," Johnny replied. "I'll get this one, if this pretty waitress here will oblige."

"Sure, mister. I can do that for you. But keep it under your hat. Wouldn't want my boss to get drift of it. Hard to find work nowadays."

"Aw, that's swell of you, missy, It'll be our little secret. Now, don't skimp on the tuna. And throw on some extra mayonnaise, Okay? And a slice of onion. And a pickle. Don't forget the pickle."

"Yeah, yeah, you got it, mister."

"Oh, and would you mind very much if I asked you to cut it down the middle and wrap each half in wax paper? Could you do that for me, missy?"

"Will do."

As the waitress made the sandwich, Johnny slipped the teaspoon into his pocket, then pulled out two dimes.

The girl put the sandwich on the counter. "That'll be fif ...."

"Here you go," said Johnny, handing her both dimes and Ray one of the sandwich halves. "Keep the change, missy."

"Gee, thanks, mister. Stop in again. Anytime."

"Oh, I'll be in again, though I can't say just when."

The men slid off their stools and headed for the door.

Walking down Fremont toward the railyard, Ray had to ask. "So, Johnny, I thought you said you were broke."

"Lesson number one for anyone planning a life on the road. When you're on the bum, you *never* let the other fella know what you have and what you don't. There's more than one stiff out there who will dent your skull for that change in your pocket. Never tip your hand, Ray. Never let on."

"And the spoon?"

"Oh, yes. Your lucky teaspoon." Johnny handed the spoon to Ray. "Here you are, buddy. I have my own."

"So, what's lucky about a spoon?"

"Lucky for you if you have one."

"How so?"

"You want to have a spoon handy just in case you stumble into some hobo jungle where they are cooking up a Mulligan stew. Hard to eat stew with your fingers, not that I haven't done it in a pinch.

That's lesson number two. Take my word for it. You'll soon know every trick in the book, everything you need to master in order to travel this land free as a jaybird."

"Free as a jaybird. I like that. Just as long as there's no *L* in it."

"Come again?"

"Jaybird is fine. Jailbird ain't," said Ray.

"Buddy, you stick close to Jamestown Johnny and you won't need to fret about the coppers."

"That's music to my ears, pal. I'll stick closer to you than bark on a maple tree."

Chapter 18

That night, in the light of a half moon, Johnny and Ray waited a quarter mile down the line from the San Francisco train station. Each carried his bindle, a small bag secured with a rope that looped over the shoulder. In it, tightly packed, were all of his belongings. Two long whistles from the locomotive told them the train was about to leave the station.

"Okay, Ray. Here she comes. We'll jump on between the tender and the next car."

"Tender?

"Railroad lingo for a coal car."

"Why not jump into an open boxcar?"

"Odds of finding one are slim. Besides, when looking for tramps, the bulls always check the open boxcars first."

"Bulls?"

"Railroad company constables."

"Huh?"

"Consta-bulls, my friend."

"Very clever. So, after the tender, we go for the ladder?"

"Right. We jump on while she's gaining speed. You'll have to run like the dickens until you reach the ladder, then swing yourself up and hold on tight with both hands till you have your bearings. Next, you swing around between the cars and plant your feet on the platform."

"You sure about this?"

"I've done it hundreds of times and will do it hundreds more. But, buddy, pay attention to what you're doing. There's plenty of stiffs who lost an arm or a leg or both or worse. One slip might be your last."

Ray watched as the locomotive chugged by. He looked up at the engineer and fireman in the cab, then at Johnny. As the tender passed, Johnny took off like a racehorse at the bell with Ray right behind. Matching their speed to that of the train, each man, in turn, reached for the ladder then maneuvered onto the narrow platforms between the cars.

"See? What'd I say? Nothing to it. Buddy, once you get the hang of this, you'll be riding the rails wherever and whenever you choose to roam. The railroad tycoons hate us for it on account of they don't get their four cents a mile. But do we give a dang? I should say not!"

"Well, it's not like ridin' in coach, but I gotta say this is a far sight better than hoofin' it."

The two men leaned back against their bindles, staring into the darkness as the night rolled by. Now and then the light from an occasional farmhouse broke their trance. Mile after mile passed before the train slowed to take on water.

"Okay. Now follow my lead," said Johnny. "Take off your hat and stuff it inside your coat."

"What?"

"So you don't lose it when we jump off, buddy."

"Jump off? Why give up a good seat?"

"'Because the company bull will be checking cars. You coming?"

"You're the professor."

As the train slowed, Johnny sprang from the far side of the car, beyond sight of anyone at the water tower. He landed with his feet forward. His legs outstretched, the momentum of his body brought him upright. He ran as fast as he could until his feet caught up with the rest of him. He turned to see Ray on the ladder.

"Keep your feet out in front, Ray!"

Ray jumped, feet straight down. His shoes struck the ground below and he rolled like tumbleweed in a windstorm.

Johnny caught his bindle. "C'mon! We have another ride to catch."

Ray scrambled to his feet, shaking off dirt and humiliation. "You call this a good way to travel?"

"Follow me," said Johnny, leading Ray up the line.

They waited for the whistle. Far behind, two lanterns bobbed along the right-of-way.

"Ray," he said. "You see those two men walking the grade?"

"What about 'em?"

"Railroad bulls. Looking for stiffs like us."

"Stiffs?"

"Hobos. You know. Lucky stiffs."

"Yeah. Real lucky."

"Around here, the bulls get a twenty-five cent bonus from the city for every collar."

"Why in blazes would the city spend two bits on a tramp?"

"Oh, the city makes out just fine. Fellas who can't pay the twenty-dollar fine get thirty days on the chain gain, digging ditches or fixing roads. Our job is to deny the bulls that extra two bits."

"I'm all for that, pal."

The whistle blew. As the train approached, both men crouched in the brush.

"Ready, Ray?"

"Right behind you, pal."

Suddenly, "Bull coming!" shouted Johnny. "Run for it!"

The two raced up the railroad grade, leaping onto the third car. Out of breath, both held tight.

Then, masked by the roar of the locomotive, the railroad constable bounded onto the same platform. As he grabbed Ray's sleeve, Johnny slammed him back against the brake wheel, shouting, "Jump, Ray!"

Both tramps tumbled down the bank. Two cars passed before they found their footing. The train gaining speed, they saw the railroad constable lean out, grinning and waving the cuff from Ray's coat.

"That was a close one, Johnny," said Ray, staring at his torn sleeve.

More cars passed.

"He figures he ditched us. Get ready."

More cars passed.

"Now, Ray!"

Both men vaulted onto the twelfth car.

Johnny peeked ahead. "Gol dang it! He's onto us!"

"How in blazes …?"

"He's good, that's how."

"So, what now?"

"We are going to show him what it means to be king of the road, my friend."

Johnny watched as the constable jumped onto the shoulder ahead, waiting to snag the oncoming pair of tramps. The train rumbled ahead faster and faster.

"C'mon!" said Johnny, jumping off the far side.

Ray followed, this time staying upright. They ran like wolf-chased deer up the grade, passing the sixth, fifth, and fourth cars before swinging onto the platform behind the third.

"And that's how you give a bull the slip," said Johnny, peeking back down the line.

The constable looked up and down the row of cars, then roared, "Jamestown Johnny, you're one son of a toad!"

"I'll look for you on the return run," Rosco Stubbs." Johnny shouted. "Kiss the wife for me!" He reached into his coat pocket, pulling out a hipflask. "You know, Ray, sometimes I regret denying the bulls their bonus. But that's how the ball bounces. If the bulls were smarter, their kids would eat better.

"Well, here's to the road!" he said, tipping the flask up. He handed it to Ray. "Have a snort, buddy. A few more lessons and you'll be a first class tramp!"

"If I live that long," Ray said, taking a drink. "That was way too close for comfort. But I'll give you this much, Johnny from Jamestown, this ain't no boring way to get from here to there."

Weeks later, Johnny and Ray lost track of each other in a Savannah rainstorm. But by then, Ray knew the way of the road. He knew that carved near every water tower was the tramps' code that told who would and wouldn't offer a hand out. He knew "EZ" carved near some house meant the owner might invite a fellow on the bum inside for a meal. He knew what towns to avoid in order to

126

stay out of jail. He knew which railroad lines let tramps sleep in the roundhouse during cold weather, rather than find them frozen stiff outside the next day. And he knew that no hobo cared who you were, what you did, or why you were on the road.

Ray missed Delores more and more each day. When he could find them, he followed the papers, watching for any news from his  old home town. Then, in a week-old copy of the Louisville Courier-Journal, he ran across an article about a boy who'd been kidnapped in Tacoma. The police sketch in the paper resembled him more than he liked. He found the same picture in a Cleveland paper and realized the same news item had probably appeared in every paper across the country. The article said the parents of young Charlie Mattson had followed the kidnappers' instructions to the letter, even trying unsuccessfully to deliver the ransom money during a snowstorm one night.

Days later, Ray saw a front page story in the Chicago Times. It said the boy had been found by a hunter. The body of little Charlie Mattson was left in a willow thicket outside of Seattle, apparently bludgeoned and left to die in the cold. Tears welled in Ray's eyes. This couldn't be the same boy. And yet, it had to be. And now he read that President Franklin Roosevelt made a statement about the crime, vowing that the government would intervene. He read, too, that J. Edgar Hoover himself had sent flowers for the funeral service along with forty-two FBI agents. And he read that a $10,000 reward would be given to the person who turned him in. And the governor was confident the kidnapper would be captured, convicted, and the penalty would be as harsh as the law would allow. Ray vomited into the newspaper, threw it onto the ground, then looked for a train—any train—to anywhere.

For the next two months he rode city to city, haunted by the newspaper story. Hoping to appear less like the man in the police sketch, he let his beard grow and traded coats with another tramp.

*Actual Tacoma P.D. sketch

127

He found an old watch cap in a boxcar and tossed his hat away. Then, one night on a train bound for Toronto, he saw in the shadow of a water tower, the silhouette of a man he thought could be his rail-riding mentor, Jamestown Johnny. His train flew by too fast to tell for sure. He ditched at the next stop and waited for a southbound. But when it pulled up to the same water tower, the man was gone. Ray lost his chance to speak with his old pal.

Weeks later, in an overcast Cincinnati, he again thought he saw Johnny, this time stepping out of the rain and into the city library. He followed.

"Say, buddy" said Ray, "can you spare a quarter for a tuna sandwich?"

"And a cup of joe?" replied Johnny, turning around with a grin.

"Jamestown Johnny! I wondered when I might stumble onto you. Thought maybe you found a job someplace or another."

"Me? A job? Why would I go and do a fool thing like that when I still have more country to see?"

"Naw, I s'pose I knew better. No king of the road can keep his crown by sittin' still. So, which way you headin' now?"

"Not sure. Maybe I'll give the northeast a try again. Seems I left a young woman waiting there long ago. Maybe I'll look her up. And you?"

"I've been thinkin' along the same lines. Y'know? On all those rambles we had, all those weeks we spent together ... well, I kept something under my hat. Johnny, I never told you, but I got me a wife. A dang good wife, too. Delores. Pretty as lilacs in the springtime. A regular Hedy Lamarr."

"Sounds to me like you have had enough of life on the road, buddy."

"Maybe so."

"Might be time for you to get back home. Back to that gal of yours."

"She's the best thing that ever happened to me."

"You could find some work. Settle down."

"I admit I could stand a pair of trousers with a full set of

128

buttons."

"And remember this—just because you're not on the road doesn't mean it isn't there waiting for you another day. I know some tramps who only ride the rails now and then. Anytime they get the urge."

"Yeah?"

"And you know the ropes better than most, Ray. Why, you can jump on an express whenever you want."

"Yes. You're right. I can. There's always gonna be a train a-comin' or a-goin' someplace or another. By golly, I'll do it, Johnny. I'll go find Delores. Who knows? Maybe the two of us can tramp around the country together."

"Say, pal," said Johnny, "I've … ah … I've seen the papers."

"Oh?"

"Ray, whether you had a hand in it or not, I don't know. What I do know is that, deep down, you're a good person."

"I got no clue what you're talkin' about, Johnny."

"Can't say as I blame you for playing dumb."

"Dumb? You know better. I can out-think the lot of 'em. The bulls, the coppers, the feds, all of 'em. By God, I can out-run 'em, too."

"I have to agree—on all counts. You sure had no trouble keeping up with me. You've shown plenty of nerve, too. More than most who claim to be king of the road."

"So, how 'bout that tuna sandwich?"

"I'll go you one better, Ray. If you'll follow me to my hotel, I'll buy you a steak dinner."

"Your … hotel?"

"It's not far. Just down the block."

"Sleepin' in the basement, are you?"

"Penthouse."

"Penthouse my foot!"

"Remember back in Frisco when I told you not to tip your hand to the next stiff? To never let on what you have and you don't?"

"Yeah. Sure I do, but …"

"Well, you're not the only one who can keep something under his hat."

"What are you drivin' at?"

"Ray, when I say my hotel, well …"

"Spit it out, already."

"I really *mean* my hotel. You see, I own it."

"Aw, you're pullin' my leg."

"Not this time. In fact, I own six hotels. Nice hotels. My grandfather willed them to me."

"C'mon, pal. I said I ain't dumb."

"Ray, my real name is Pierpont. John Pierpont. Of the Jamestown Pierponts."

"What?"

"John Jacob Pierpont the fourth, to be precise."

"Baloney!"

"'Fraid so, chum. Your pal, Jamestown Johnny, is heir to the Pierpont fortune."

"You? A vagabond? A hobo?"

"That's me alright. A blue-blooded, devil-may-care tramp."

"Are you sayin' …?"

"Some fellas climb mountains, others sail the seas. Me? Well, I just love riding the rails."

"So, the road is … ?"

"Merely a hobby."

"Well, run me through the wringer and hang me up to dry if I ain't been trampin' around with a millionaire tycoon!"

"Ready for that steak dinner, buddy?"

"I got my lucky spoon."

"Come again?"

"Just in case Jamestown Johnny's steak dinner turns out to be Mulligan stew."

Chapter 19

As she had done every morning since leaving the coast, the young, pretty, brunette waitress at Woolworth's lunch counter in Waukesha, Wisconsin, pawed through the *Milwaukee Sentinel* classifieds. Disappointed once again, she closed the paper, then whipped it open when she realized what she nearly missed seeing.

Emil: See you soon. Call me 9 AM Sat. at Walnut 3221. R.

Delores pulled a pad from her apron pocket, jotting the phone number on the back of a guest check. She tore the slip from the pad, folded it twice, then slid it back into her pocket. Heart racing, she fumbled with the newspaper, trying to put it in order, then quickly laid it on the counter as her supervisor came in.

"Miss Olson!" snapped her boss. "Just because we don't have any customers right now doesn't mean you can stand idle. This is not a library. Make yourself useful."

"Yes, Mrs. Geary."

"This counter looks a mess. Grab a sponge and wipe it down. Then dish up some apple squares for the lunchtime rush. Chop chop!"

"Right away, ma'am."

"Mercy! You young people these days. No idea the value of having a job—especially a job where you get tips."

Delores held her tongue, thinking of the twenty-seven cents in tips she'd received after serving thirty diners during the breakfast rush. She squeezed the sponge into the sink before wiping down the counter.

"Something funny, Delores?"

"What, ma'am?"

"Why, you're grinning like the Cheshire Cat."

"I am? Oh, yes. I suppose I am. It's just that I got some good news today."

"Which is ...?"

"Hmm? Oh, nothing, really."

"Come on, Delores. Share your news with me."

"Oh, you wouldn't be interested."

"Sure I would."

Delores rinsed the sponge, knowing she couldn't tell the truth and wondering what to say.

"Some friends are coming over for cards tonight, that's all."

"That's it? *That's* your good news?"

"Yes, Mrs. Geary."

"Well, it sure doesn't take much to cheer you up."

"No, ma'am. Not much at all."

"That husband of yours ever show up?"

"No, not for a while, now."

"Well, what kind of a cad is he? The man doesn't come home to his wife for months!"

"He can't, Mrs. Geary. Ray is ... on assignment. He works quite a ways from here."

A uniformed policeman came through the front door, walked past a cardboard stand of five-cent paper kites, and straight toward Delores. He plopped onto a counter stool. Delores pulled her pad and pencil from her apron again. As she did, the folded slip fell onto the counter.

"What'll you have, Officer Andrews?"

"Oh, I suppose the same old thing, Delores. Cup of coffee and a piece of cheesecake."

"Comin' right up."

Delores poured his coffee and set the cheesecake before him, then picked up her sponge.

"Morning, Peter," said Mrs. Geary."

Pete tipped his hat. "Gladys."

"Delores, here, says her husband hasn't been home now for ages. Can you beat that?"

Pete glanced at Delores as he sipped his coffee.

Mrs. Geary picked up the slip of paper from the counter, scowled at Delores, then continued. "Well, don't you think that's just terrible of him, Peter? I mean ..."

"Mrs. Geary," Delores interrupted, staring at the paper in her supervisor's hand. "I told you he's on assignment working far from

132

here and can't come home every night like most men." She turned to the officer. "You understand. Right, Officer Anderson?"

"Sure I do, Delores."

"Well, I think a man's place is at home," said Gladys.

"Gladys," said the officer, "these days, there's plenty of men who can't find a job at all, much less near their homes. Pretty common for a fellow to work someplace else."

"There! See?" Delores said. "What'd I tell you?"

Gladys huffed. "Well, I still say …"

Delores threw her sponge in the sink. "And I think you would do well to mind your own damn business!" She ripped the guest check from her boss's hand, crushed it, and tossed it into the trash can.

"Well!" snorted Gladys. She stomped to the end of the counter and into the office.

"That old busy-body," said Delores. "Always sticking her nose where it doesn't belong."

"Oh, don't let it bother you. Some people are like that, Delores. Just keep calm and let Gladys be the one to make a fool of herself."

"Well, that stuffy, old battle-axe struts around here like she thinks she's the queen bee. Pete, I swear that someday I am going to give old *Glad-ass* Geary a piece of my mind and put that fat-faced old broad in her rightful place, dammit."

Peter grinned. "Well, I don't blame you. But you better hold your tongue, Delores. You don't want to lose your job for sassing your boss."

"I don't care. I'm not sticking around much longer."

"No?"

"Won't be long before I find a new place to hang my hat. And far, far away from here."

"A girl can get in trouble going off on her own."

"Oh, I won't be alone."

"No?"

"Ready for a warm-up?"

"Sure."

Delores refilled his cup, considering what she'd said. "Aw, I'm just spouting off steam, I guess. Sure, I'd like to take off, travel around some, maybe find a better life. But I'm nearly dead broke and back living with my pa. I couldn't go anywhere if I wanted to. You're right, Pete. I'd better just take the old bag's guff and be happy I've got work." Delores fished the wrinkled guest check from the trash and stuffed it into her pocket.

"Good for you, Delores." The officer took the last bite of his cheesecake. "Say, how about you and me go out to the movies tonight?"

"Movies? Oh, I don't know. My hubby would object."

"Nothing wrong with two friends seeing a movie now and then, is there?"

"Pete, you're a sweet fella, but you'd be better off finding somebody else to take to the movies."

"Well, I just thought I'd offer, that's all. Life must be lonely for you not having your husband around."

"I've been able to get along."

"Listen, Delores. If you ever change your mind, ever want to go out for a bite or to the movies or even for an evening walk, just say the word." He laid a dollar on the counter. "Here you go, kid. Keep the change."

Three-hundred miles northwest, in a downtown St. Paul train station, Ray fished a scrap of paper from a trash can. On it, he printed "Out of Order" in pencil, then stuck a wad of chewing gum on the back. He posted the sign on the end phone in a row of payphones across from the ticket windows. From the same trash, Ray pulled a copy of the *St. Paul Pioneer Press,* then sat on a nearby bench, paging through the comics.

The depot was quiet for Saturday morning. A man crossed from one of the ten boarding platforms to the ticket window. As he did, the sound of his hard, leather heels striking polished marble echoed from the vaulted ceiling. Two custodians, each wearing a matching red hat and vest, pushed wide, shaggy brooms across the floor.

A distant train whistle told Ray the room would soon be busy. He paged through the paper as a middle-aged woman in a long, dark, wool coat dropped a coin in the phone next to the one with the note. Ray looked up at the large clock on the end wall as the clock struck nine times. The woman talked on, slipping nickels into the slot every few minutes. The end phone rang. She stared at it, but went on talking. Ray didn't move. It stopped after eight rings. A minute later, it rang again. The woman, finished with her call, said "goodbye," and hung up. As she reached for the ringing phone, Ray jumped to his feet.

"Hey, that's for me," he blurted, snatching the receiver from her hand.

"Well!" snapped the woman. "Land sakes! How *some* people act these days."

"Aw, don't worry about it, lady." Then, speaking into the phone, "Hello? Mother?"

"Ray, is that you, Sweetie?" asked Delores.

"Why, yes, Mother, it is."

The woman stood there, listening. "Young man, you would do well to ask your mother to teach you some manners."

"Mother, can you hold on for a second?" He turned to the woman. "Lady, you can go now. This ain't for you."

The woman didn't leave.

"Mother, I've missed you," Ray continued into the phone. "How are you?" With a pronounced sneer, he stared at the woman.

"Ray," said Delores, "I've missed you, too. I've worried so. Where have you been all these months?"

"Yes, mother, I know."

The woman remained.

"I can't really talk right now."

135

"Why, Ray? What is the matter?"

The woman leaned in, trying to hear both conversations.

Ray turned, sneering at her again. "Lady, do you mind? I'd like to talk with my mother in private."

"Me? Mind?" she said. "Why, I don't mind at all. But I don't see any reason to be more courteous to you than you've been to me. Therefore, I intend to remain right here, if you please."

"What is it?" asked Delores. "Ray, what's going on?"

"What's goin' on? I'll tell you what's goin' on, Mother. You see, I've come down with a terrible case of tuberculosis. Very bad, contagious tuberculosis." He suddenly turned, coughing violently into the face of the eavesdropping woman.

Gasping, she turned and ran across the marble floor. Her wool coat flapping behind. The clip-clop-clip-clop of her two-inch heels echoed throughout the lobby.

"Ray, darling?" said Delores. "Are you going to be alright?"

"Me? Oh, sure, Baby. I'm fine."

"What about the TB? Have you seen a doctor?"

"Oh that? Naw, I don't have TB. Heck, I'm fit as a fiddle. But the lady who was buttin' in on me just a second ago, I'll bet she is headed straight for the hospital right now."

"What the dickens are you talking about?"

"I'll explain it all to you when we meet up, Doll."

"Meet? Oh, that's wonderful, Ray! I can't wait."

"Me neither, Doll."

A man's monotone voice came through the speakers. *"Now arriving gate four from Chi-ca-go, Mil-wau-kee, Mad-i-son, La-Crosse, and Red-Wing."*

"Where are you?"

"St. Paul Union Depot. It's where you're gonna be, too, as soon as you can get up here."

"St. Paul?"

"Yes. When can you leave?"

"It's not that easy, Sweetie. You see, I got my old job back at the Woolworth's lunch counter. If I miss work, my boss will fire

136

me. I know she will. I won't have a job waiting when I come back."

"Baby, you won't be comin' back."

"What?"

"Your home is with me, Delores. Pack up your things and come to St. Paul. We can start over, you and me. I know where I can find work in a place so far out of the way that nobody will ever bother us again. Ever."

A rush of people poured in through gate four.

"Really Ray?"

"I'll tell you all about it when you get here. I'll be waitin' at the station near gate number ten."

The depot's bank of phones quickly filled with callers, some two and three-deep in line. Two men waited behind Ray.

"It's gettin' noisy in here, Doll. I'll be waitin' at gate number ten. Got it?"

"Gate number ten. All right, I'll do it. I'll come. I'll pack up and catch the first train I can. Oh, Ray! I'm so excited. I love you and I've missed you so much. Oh, this is wonderful, Sweetie. I can't wait to see you."

"What? It's louder in here than all get out. You'll have to speak up."

"I love you, Ray Olson!" shouted Delores.

"Ditto for me, Doll. Say, don't forget the Zenith."

"What?"

"Bring the Zenith!"

Chapter 20

Ray pushed his way across the lobby through the throngs of travelers. A thin veil of coal smoke from the engines in the railyard blended with the odor of cigar and cigarette smoke. Near the main entrance, a woman pushed a child in a stroller while struggling with two suitcases. Ray held the door for her.

"Oh, thank you, dear," said the woman. "I'd completely forgotten what it's like to fight these crowds. My little grandson thanks you, too. He's visiting me for the weekend." Then, "oops!" as she dropped her purse, the contents spilling onto the sidewalk.

"Here, let me help you with that," said Ray, stuffing items back into the purse. He handed it to her, then grabbed both suitcases, carrying them to the curb.

"Want me to whistle up a taxi for you, ma'am?"

"Oh, you are such a dear. Yes. That would be nice." She tucked the blanket around the child in the stroller. "Your wife is so lucky to have a courteous man like you around."

"Actually, I'm waitin' for my wife right now." Ray stuck two fingers between his teeth and made a shrill whistle, then waved. Down the block, a cab pulled from the curb. "She's comin' in by train tonight. We haven't seen each other for eight months and four days. You see, I've been on the road a lot."

"And tonight is your reunion? How romantic! But, you can't possibly meet your wife looking like that."

"Huh? What do you mean?"

"That coat of yours is a mess. And your shoes. And shirt. And your beard needs a trim." She dug into her purse. "Here," she said, handing him a twenty-dollar bill, "you helped me and now I'm about to help you. Go get yourself a new outfit and a shave."

"I don't know what to say," he replied as he snatched the bill from her fingers. "You're so kind." He folded the twenty and stuffed it into his pocket. "I really shouldn't take this from you."

"Now, now. Tit for tat, I always say. Back when my hubby was around, he wouldn't let me help out a body in need. Not a nickel. He always said he worked for his money and others must, too.

"He made millions, that man. But he worked so hard it killed him. Nowadays, I get a big charge out of giving away his booty." She pulled another bill from her purse. "Here, take this, too," she ordered, handing Ray a two-dollar bill. "This is for a bouquet of flowers for your sweetheart. She'll appreciate it. Take my word."

The cab driver put the stroller and suitcases in the trunk. Ray held the door as the woman and child slid into the back seat. "Thank you for your kindness, young man," she said. "I envy your wife. I can just tell that you and she will have a marvelous future, a long, happy life together. And you can tell her that."

"Lady, it's me who should be doin' all the thankin'. But I'll be sure to tell Delores what you said."

"Oh, do. Well, toodaloo."

Ray strolled down the street to the first tavern and cashed his two-dollar bill for four quarters, nine dimes, and a schooner of beer. "Say, bud, where can a fella find a fair slot machine around here?" he asked the bartender.

"Aw, they're all rigged." came the reply. "Don't waste your money, fella."

"Well, if I was gonna waste my money on a slot, where would be a good place to find one?"

"All right," said the bartender. "If you're dead set on blowing your dough, you might try a joint called the Y-Go-By Bar on Wabasha. Joey Klein owns it and treats people pretty fair. Beer's a nickel-a-glass and I'm guessing that his slots are fair, too, though there's no such thing as gettin' an even break when it comes to slot machines."

That afternoon, a clean-shaven, well-dressed Ray Olson entered the smoky back room of the Y-Go-By Bar. Twenty slot machines waited there in two rows. Six players sat on stools, stuffing in coins, pulling levers, mesmerized by the spinning wheels. Occasionally, the sound of a winning pull and falling coins clattered throughout the room. Ray checked out each machine before dropping his first coin in the slot. Peering through the glass, past the wheels, and inside, he read the number of each machine, then settled on the last in the row of twenty. It stood seven stools from the nearest player. He pulled a single dime from his pocket, inserted it in the slot, and pulled the handle, listening carefully.

The three rollers inside spun and spun, before the first one stopped on a cherry. The next stopped on a plum, the third on a cherry. The machine spit out two dimes.

Ray leaned his stool against the slot machine and walked down the row to an elderly man who slipped quarters in the slot of his machine. The gambler pulled the lever with one hand, holding a lit Lucky Strike with the other.

"Say, pop," Ray said, "I wonder if I could bum a smoke. I'm fresh out."

The old man looked Ray over, then shook a cigarette from the pack, saying, "Sure, kid. Knock yourself out."

"Thanks, friend," said Ray, peering past the wheels at the number inside his machine.

He returned to the end machine, investing another dime. The rollers spun and spun then stopped with no payout. Ray lit his Lucky and waited, watching the others. He finished his cigarette before dropping his third dime in the slot. He studied the machine, then looked down the row at the other players again, then looked back at his machine.

"Say, kid," said the old man seven stools down, "you sure do take your time, there. You got some system up your sleeve? You know something I don't?"

"No. No tricks. I just know that the faster I play, the faster I lose my dough, that's all. I enjoy the dream of winning while I still have a dime left to burn. Might as well make the dream last."

"I suppose you have a point, there, kid. Me? Well, I'd rather play fast and get it over with"

"You and dang near everybody else who feeds these one-arm-bandits, pop."

Ray sat before the end machine, watching the other six until, near the far end, the only woman in the room shrieked when three plums appeared. Everyone but Ray looked her way to see coins spill into the tray. Everyone but Ray heard the sound of coins dropping. Everyone but Ray cheered for the woman who, laughing, scrambled to stuff her winnings into her purse.

Taking advantage of the distraction, Ray gave the handle a hard pull, then wrapped his arms around the machine. He lifted it several inches from the counter and dropped it hard on the right front corner. He glanced down the row of players. No one noticed, all focused on the woman's winnings.

The wheels inside his machine spun and spun and spun. The woman at the end was still laughing when the first wheel on Ray's machine clicked to a stop on a cherry. The second wheel clicked to a stop, again on a cherry.

"Hey, fellas," shouted the woman, "I'll buy it if you'll drink it!"

Ray listened to the cheers of the other players as the third wheel spun and spun, then stopped on a third cherry. Coins clanked and clattered into the tray below. Ten, twenty, thirty dollars in dimes.

"Jackpot, kid!" shouted the old man seven stools down. "Looks like your slow-but-steady system is a winner. As for me, I'm tapped out. I'm gonna take Maggie up on her offer for a drink before she comes to her senses."

"I'll join you in a minute, pops," said Ray.

The others in the back room left for the bar, some leaning their stools against their machines. Pockets bulging with dimes, Ray moved to the old man's machine. He dropped a quarter into the slot, pulled the handle, lifted the machine, slammed it down on the right front corner, and watched as three cherries again fell into place. Before the machine could spit out the first quarter, he stuffed his new felt fedora into the payout tray. The sound of two-hundred-eighty quarters slowly spilling into his hat brought a wide grin. Ray hauled the coins into the barroom.

"Maggie's good luck must've rubbed off on me," he said, dumping the coins onto the bar. "I wonder if I could trade these in for something a bit easier to tote around."

After buying a round for the house, Ray strolled back toward the railroad station, stopping at a florist. An hour later, he sat on a park bench a block from the Union Depot. The warm afternoon sun added to the pleasure of the day—a day he began flat broke, looking like a bum, and without his girl. Now, here he sat, looking dapper, pockets full of cash, and holding a bouquet in the warm, spring air. As he soaked in the sunlight, he saw a black Plymouth coupe pull up to the curb across the street. An elderly woman got out with an envelope in one hand and a small suitcase in the other. A man in a brown, tweed suit met her on the sidewalk.

From his bench across the street, Ray watched as they talked. The man opened the envelope, looked at a paper inside, folded it, and returned it to the lady before leaving. She appeared upset as she plopped her suitcase onto the park bench across from Ray. She sat, staring at the envelope. Within minutes, she was in tears. Ray crossed the street.

"Say, lady," he said, "is there something I can do?"

The woman looked up with a start. "Oh! No. I don't suppose anyone can help me now," she said. "I'm in a terrible way. Just terrible. I could just curl up and die. Who would care?"

"Now, now, mother. Don't talk that way. I've been down before. Plenty of times. But now look at me. Everything is as rosy as rosy can be."

"Well, I'm happy for you, mister. But nothing is rosy in my world. Nothing!"

"Aw, look at it this way. When you're on the very bottom, the only way you can go is up. Now tell me what the problem is. Maybe old Ray can lend a hand."

"I got evicted from my apartment, like you would care. How you gonna help with that?"

"Oh, evicted. I see. Is there somebody who can take you in till you're back on your feet?"

"You must be a mind reader. I was on my way to New Orleans to live with my son. My neighbor was supposed to buy my Plymouth so I'd have ticket money. He backed out just a few minutes ago. Now, here I sit. Not only don't I have the train fare to New Orleans, but I have this car and no place to keep it. Mister, I need to leave today and I don't know what to do with my car or what to do for train fare. Oh, don't you see? I'm in a terrible way. Just terrible," the woman sobbed.

"How much is the ticket?"

"What?"

"To New Orleans. How much?"

"One-way fare in coach is sixty-two dollars. Why?"

"And you were gonna sell your car for that much?"

"Yes. But that's out the window, now. I just don't know what to do. I'd be better off dead."

"I'll tell you what, lady. I will give you sixty-five bucks for the car. How's that?"

"You will? Oh, you are too kind."

"If it will help you out, I'll be happy to take the car off your hands."

"Well, yes. I'll sell you my car." She handed Ray the envelope. "You can see for yourself that the title is signed, license plates are paid up, and my trusty little Plymouth is ready to go. I'm afraid there isn't much gasoline in it. It will cost you another dollar fifty to fill up the fuel tank."

Ray pulled a roll of bills from his pocket and peeled off sixty-five dollars. "There you go, mother. Now, you have a wonderful train ride to New Orleans. And always remember, when you're on the very bottom, the only way to go is up."

The old woman licked her thumb and counted the cash, then stuffed it into her purse. "I left the keys in the ignition," she said as she walked away.

"Wait! Your suitcase!" shouted Ray, grabbing it from the bench.

"Oh, dear! I am so happy that you helped me, I guess I just plain forgot."

Ray hefted the suitcase. "Boy, you sure travel light."

"Oh, I had most of my belongings sent on ahead," she said taking it from him. "I'd better go now. Train to catch, y'know." The woman walked down the block, then turned the corner, walking away from the train station.

Ray climbed into his car and turned the key, starting the motor. It purred like a kitten. "Wait till my baby sees this!" he said. "Not bad for sixty-five bucks."

A well-dressed Ray Olson met his wife at the station, gate ten, just as planned. The Plymouth coupe rolled up Highway 35 late that night, Ray at the wheel.

"So, whaddaya think about our new car, Doll?"

"Pretty snazzy, Ray. When did you get it?"

"This afternoon. I bought it from a sweet, little old lady for sixty-five bucks. I figure it's worth a hundred."

"So, you have a job?"

"Not hardly. Haven't had the desire to work since I learned to bum me a livin'. But I'm done with all that now."

"You were a bum? A tramp?"

"Along with thousands of other nameless fellas out of work. I'll tell you all about it someday."

"Then, how could you afford the car?"

"Hmm? Oh, I came into some easy dough today."

"Honest money?"

"Huh?"

"Did you come by the money honestly?"

"More or less."

"More, Ray? Or less?"

"Let's just say there's an East Bank tavern owner who wouldn't appreciate the way I played his slots."

"Sweetie, you know you have to stay clear of the law."

"I was careful. Besides, I knew he wouldn't call the cops."

"Just don't take any chances."

"You got it, Doll."

"So, where we headed?"

"An honest day's labor for good pay."

"What, Sweetie?"

"A fellow told me that long ago. 'An honest day's labor for good pay.'"

"Who?"

"I didn't catch his name. He's a resort owner. Westview Resort, I think. Me and Dutch Kowalski met him when I was up north with Oscar Lee's work party. He said he could put me to work."

"In Wisconsin? What about the jail term you skipped out on?"

"That wasn't me. Remember? That was some stiff named Augie Buelo. As long as I keep my head down and stay clear of Johnny Law, me and you will be fine, Doll."

"You think the job is still there for you after all this time?"

"Only one way to find out. Wisconsin, here we come!"

Chapter 21

In the early morning twilight, Ray pulled off Highway 77 at the sign reading Peterson's Westview Resort. With his wife fast asleep beside him, he drove down the dusty town road and parked near the resort's main lodge.

The mirror-like surface of the water reflected the far shore. Ray stepped out, stretched, and stared, watching the sun creep up over the treetops across the lake. The distant call of a loon welcomed him back to northern Wisconsin. Ray strolled down the shore. The grounds lay cluttered with leaves, pine needles, and dead branches. The cabins looked run down. The boats needed bailing. He returned to the car.

"Delores, we're here. Wake up. Wake up."

"Hmm?"

"C'mon. Wake up, Doll. Get a load of this beautiful lake. Ain't it somethin'?"

"Where are we?"

"Wisconsin. Round Lake. Westview Resort. This is the place I was tellin' you 'bout. Where the owner offered me a job once. From the looks of it, he has plenty of work for me. Plenty! Ain't it great?"

Two fishermen carried tackle boxes, fishing rods, and a large net to one of the boats tied to the dock.

"Boy, oh boy, Delores. Just think. In a few days, that could be you and me goin' out to catch our dinner."

"And where am I supposed to cook our dinner?"

"Don't worry, Baby. I'm goin' to find work and a place to stay. Just you wait. You'll see. C'mon. Let's see what's for breakfast. I'm starvin'."

They entered the main lodge. In the dining room, the woman poured their coffee.

"Toast and eggs, sunny side up," said Ray. He turned to his wife. "How 'bout you, Doll?"

"Make mine over easy. And could you bring some jam for the toast?"

"Sure, hon."

"Say, is the owner around?" asked Ray.

"My hubby? Well, I should hope so. He's your cook."

"The owner?"

"Yeah, I know what you're thinking. But times are tough these days. A lot of our regular guests don't come up any more. Nobody has a dime to spare. And never mind trying to attract new tourists. No, we've had to cut back. Way back."

"Jeez, that's too bad," said Delores. "Ray and I were hoping we might find work here."

"Here?" She laughed. "Jobs are awful scarce nowadays."

"Jeez."

"Oh, I'm sure you'll find something. I'll ask George. Maybe he'll have a suggestion."

Minutes later, George Peterson placed two plates of eggs and toast before Ray and Delores. Mrs. Peterson refilled their cups and filled another for her husband.

"Remember me, sir?" said Ray.

"Didn't you rent a cabin a while back?"

"Nope. Me and you met out front two years ago. I was in a state truck with fieldstones in the back. You said you were lookin' to hire. An honest day's work for good pay. That's what you said, word for word. It's been runnin' through my mind ever since."

"Oh, yes. You stopped in for a bottle of soda pop, right?"

"Yep. That was me, all right. Ray Olson. This here is Delores, my wife. So, does the offer still stand?"

"Offer? You mean the job?"

"I can start today."

"Boy, I'd give anything to hire you, Ray. But here we are in our summer season and not half our rooms are filled. I can't pay for work with money I don't have. Until things pick up, I'm afraid ..."

"We can help," said Delores.

"How?" asked Ray.

"Sweetie, didn't you hear what this nice man said? He said he'd give anything to hire us. We need a place to stay. This nice man has empty rooms and needs some work done around the resort. Mister Peterson, would you be willing to trade a room for some work around the place?"

"Gee, I ... I don't know."

"Now, George, just hold your horses," said Mrs. Peterson. She turned to Delores. "Hon, have you ever waited tables?"

"I used to work the lunch counter at a Woolworth's five and dime. Does that count?"

"Close enough," she said, removing her apron. "George, we're putting these folks up. That's all there is to it."

"Well, you're the boss. Ray, Delores, you kids can take the last room at the top of the stairs."

"Nonsense," said his wife. "These kids need some privacy. We're putting them up in cabin number four. Delores, as soon as you're done with your breakfast, I'll show you the ropes. George will put Ray to work outside. By the way, you can call me Nora."

"Swell!" said Ray. "Um, I'll still have to find a job someplace. But I'll give you two full days a week in trade."

"And I will wait tables all week just for the tips, Mrs. Peter ... er, Nora."

"By golly, it's a deal," said George. "Welcome to Westview!"

Two days later, as Ray pushed a mower across the front lawn in the midday heat, George approached.

"Ray, I talked to John Bluesky at the filling station this morning. He's got a job setting fence posts at the Richardson farm. John said he could use some help. He can't find anyone willing to work outside in this heat."

"Fence posts, eh? Hard work."

"Bluesky says old man Richardson pays two bits a post."

"Two bits? I'm all for that!"

"If you want, I'll show you where the place is as soon as you finish up here."

"Thanks, Mr. Peterson. I 'preciate it."

For the next two days, Ray and John Bluesky set tamarack fence posts, dawn to dusk. As they were finishing the job in the midday heat on the third day, Amos Richardson joined them in the field. Stoop-shouldered and gray, he stood at the corner and eyeballed the row of wooden posts.

"Not very straight," he grumbled.

Ray looked down the line. "Might want to clean your glasses, Amos. Straight as a frozen rope."

"Eighty-eight posts," said John. "Twenty-two dollars. We'd like our pay now."

Richardson looked at him and the tall hulk of Ray Olson standing behind. "Bluesky, I told you I'd pay you twenty-five cents a post. I didn't say nothin' about payin' nobody else. Who is this fella, anyway?"

"Friend. Name is Ray."

"You from around here?"

"Nope," said Ray. "Naperville."

"Where?"

"Down by Chicago."

"Hmph. I shoulda known. Bluesky, I'll pay you your eleven dollars for setting your half of them posts. But I ain't paying this city fella more than five dollars flat."

"Eighty-eight posts," said John. "Twenty-two dollars."

"Nope. Not paying you more than sixteen."

Ray wrapped his arms around the corner post and gave a heave, pulling it from the ground. "You're short six dollars, Amos. I can pull two dozen posts out and make it right, if that's what you want."

150

Richardson pulled some bills from his wallet. Here's eleven for you, John. And a five for your helper. Take it or leave it."

As John took the sixteen dollars, Ray's big hand shot out, snatching the wallet. "You don't want word gettin' around that you're a cheapskate, do you, Amos?" He fished out a five and a one, then tossed the wallet on the ground at Richardson's feet. "There. See, John? Amos kept his word after all."

"If I had a telephone, I'd report you two bums to the sheriff."

"We're the ones who should be callin' the coppers," said Ray. He reached in his pocket. "Here's a quarter for that last post. Set it yourself. Have a good time."

"All right. All right. Keep your two-bits and set that post." I can't take this heat."

Ray slammed the post into the hole and walked toward his car.

"Hey!" yelled Richardson. "That post is crooked!"

Ray laughed. "Not as crooked as the owner, Amos. Hope you remember that each and every time you see it!"

"I'll pay you a quarter to straighten it."

"C'mon, Johnny. I'll buy you a cold beer."

Downtown, Ray parked his Plymouth in front of Angler's Bar. A sign outside read, "Bowling — 10¢." Another, "Ice Cold Beer." Inside, he ordered two beers and two pickled eggs. "Here ya go, Johnny. This'll hold you over till suppertime."

"Ain't never had one before."

"You never ate a pickled egg?"

"Nope."

"You'll like it."

"Smells funny."

"Go ahead. Take a bite. It'll put hair on your chest."

"Why would I want hair on my chest?"

"Aw, never mind. Eat your dang egg."

John took a bite, scowled, then slugged down some beer.

"Well?"

"Different."

Ray laughed. "That's it? First time bitin' into a pickled egg and all you got to say is, 'different?'"

"Kinda ... good ... sort of."

"Well, there you go. See? I told you you'd like it." Ray popped his into his mouth whole, chewed, then chugged his beer, slamming the empty can on the bar. "That's how you eat a pickled egg, John. Now finish yours up and I'll buy you another."

"Nope."

"You don't want another egg? I thought you said it was good."

"One was good. Two? Maybe not that good."

"Say, bartender. Bartender!"

The man washing beer glasses behind the bar dried his hands. "Name's Cullie."

"Cullie, give us two more Old Styles and some of them pickled pigs' feet in the other jar, there."

"Sure thing, mister ..."

"Olson. Ray Olson."

"Pigs' feet comin' right up, Ray."

"Now, Johnny, pickled eggs is one thing, but don't you go tellin' me you never had pickled pigs' feet."

"Nope."

"What?"

"Never."

"Don't your old lady ever let you outa the house?"

"Keeps me tied to the bed."

"Well, John Bluesky, you stick with me and I'll show you how to paint the town red."

"You and your missus should come to my house. My wife cooks good."

"Yeah? Delores will be tickled to death. You just say when and we'll be there."

Cullie Johnson laid a plate heaped with pickled pigs' feet on the bar. Ray grabbed one and chewed away.

John stared at them, then at his friend. "Ray, you want more work?"

"Like what?"

"Building a dock."

"Who for?"

"Deerfoot."

"Who's Deerfoot?"

"Deerfoot Lodge. Big Chip."

"What?"

"Besides pickled eggs and pigs' feet, you don't know much."

"Huh?"

"Deerfoot Lodge. On the Chippewa Flowage. Big Chip."

"Oh. When?"

"Next week?"

"Sounds good."

"You show up Monday. Early."

"Will do. Say, you gonna eat your pigs' feet?"

"Be my guest."

"Johnny Bluesky, you don't know what yer missin'."

Chapter 22

Undersheriff Jim Berard met Cullie Johnson at the Moose Café for breakfast one April morning. They didn't notice Ray at the next table.

"Cullie," said Berard, "can you spare a couple of hours today? There's a five-spot in it for you."

"Sure, Jim. What's going on?"

Berard lowered his voice. "The game warden called. He said he's been watching some poachers out at Round Lake."

Ray strained to hear the conversation behind him.

"He said there's a fish camp on the east shore. Nine guys. They've been spearing walleyes. They pack the fillets in dry ice and ship them to some Chicago restaurant. Leon plans to pinch them but thinks it wouldn't be wise to go in alone. Sheriff Seehuetter, Jim Hamblin, and I are going to back him up. I'd like you and a couple of others to come along. Merely a show of force, mind you. We don't expect any trouble."

"I'm your man, Jim. As always."

"I knew I could count on you, Cullie."

"When and where?"

"These guys eat lunch at Westview every day. Leon figures on raiding their camp, then joining them for lunch, if you get my drift. I'll pick you up at the bar. Eleven sharp."

"I'll be ready."

Ray finished his coffee, laid a dime on the table, and walked out of the restaurant.

Two hours later, Ray drove down the dusty road leading from the Westview Resort. In town, he parked his Plymouth behind the railroad depot and set two, ice-cold wooden crates on the shipping dock. He paid the clerk, then drove off.

Later, Game Warden Leon Plante and five others stood outside the fishing camp they'd come to raid.

"I don't get it," said Plante. "I've been watching these guys all week. They spear every night, then pack their fish in dry ice. Next day, after lunch, they take their catch to the depot. Why, I figured I'd have them cold—as cold as those damn fillets."

"Nothing here," said Sheriff Seehuetter. "No fish. No spears. Nothing but a pile of beer cans out back and a deck of cards left on the breakfast table."

"They're over at Westview right now," said Berard. "Want to have a talk with them?"

"Naw. No point," replied the warden. "Somehow, these guys found out I had them in my sights and they cleaned up the place. There's no way they will spill their guts. These bastards are having a good laugh at my expense."

"You could still teach them a lesson," said Cullie.

"What?"

"They have some fishing rods in the boat. Bait a couple of hooks, throw them in the lake and wait for these guys to come back. Pinch them for having unattended lines."

"Not my style, Cullie. If I pinch someone, it means I caught 'em red-handed, not because I set them up."

"Leon's right," said Berard. "These guys know they came damn close to getting fined and their names in the paper. I doubt they will try this again. Leon, I think we should chalk this up to experience."

In the Westview Resort dining room, nine men celebrated their week-long fishing success.

"Say, Delores," said one. "Bring us a round of beers, including one for Ray. We're buying him lunch."

"Aw, no need to do that," he said, returning from the depot.

"Nonsense! If not for you, we'd all be up the creek without a paddle."

"What I'd give to see the look on that warden's face!" said another man. "Boy! I bet he was miffed."

"He's a tough one," said Ray. "I run into him before. He ain't never pinched me, but he's come awful close. I have a secret method, see?"

"What method is that?"

"I call it my one-step-ahead-of-the-law method. Works good."

"Sometimes," said Delores as she set a tray of Hamm's beer bottles on the table. "But not always. Not often enough."

"Say, speakin' of the law," said Ray, "if I were you guys, I'd keep to the straight and narrow for a while. You just hoodwinked the game warden and embarrassed him in front of the sheriff and his friends. Deputy Hamblin's a square shooter. But Berard and Seehuetter? Let's just say they ain't known for their sense of humor. First time you roll through a stop sign or cross the center line, you'll have a siren behind you screamin' away. My advice is to lay low. Keep your heads down."

"Sounds like you know what you're talking about."

"Oh, I know. Don't I, Doll?"

"Oh, yes. Ray knows. Let me tell you."

"Delores," said one of the men, "seeing as how we won't be paying the county judge, you can bring us ten T-bone steaks with all the fixin's."

"Make it eleven if you can join us," said another. "And keep the beers coming, young lady. The party's about to begin!"

The next morning, a fat man in a rumpled, blue suit waddled through the front door of the resort. He plopped down near a window overlooking the lake. Delores came to take his order.

"You Delores Olson?"

The question startled her.

"That depends on who's asking."

He studied her, then said, "I'll have a hot beef sandwich, mashed potatoes and gravy."

"Coffee with that, mister?"

"Is Ray your husband?"

"Who?"

"Ray. Is he around someplace?"

"Haven't seen him. Why?"

"That's between me and him. Yes. Coffee. You expect him soon?"

157

"Ray? Oh, you just never know with him."

"See if you can find your husband. I need to talk to him."

"What about?"

"I told you, that is between *me* and *him*."

"Are you a lawman?"

"Me? That's a good one."

"I'll give your order to the cook, mister. Then I'll look around for Ray."

Delores found Ray splitting firewood behind the lodge.

"Sweetie, some goon just came in. Wants to talk to you. He's waiting for you in the dining room."

"Cop?"

"He doesn't fit the mold."

"Go ask him who he is. What he wants."

"I tried. He won't tell me anything. He's dead set on talking to you."

"Okay. Tell him to keep his shirt on. I'll be there in a jiffy."

Ray walked around the building to the parking lot. He laid his hand on the hood of each car until he found one still hot. Illinois plates. An open box of cookies lay on the seat. Candy wrappers cluttered the floor. Ashtray full of cigar butts. A leather suitcase lay on the back seat.

In the restaurant, Delores set the hot beef sandwich plate in front of the fat man.

"You find your husband?" He squeezed his napkin between his neck and collar and attacked the sandwich with knife and fork.

"He'll be here in a minute."

Stuffing a large forkful of gravy-soaked bread and meat into his mouth, he uttered, "A minute?" Like a hungry bulldog, he swallowed, then stuffed more in his mouth as Ray approached.

"Delores says you wanna talk to me?"

The fat man looked up, chewing as he spoke. "I do if you're Ray Olson."

"I'm him."

"Then I got a deal for you."

"What kinda deal?"

"You know of a fella named Valentino?"

"Who don't? We listen to him on our Zenith all the time. Say, are you're tryin' to sell me another radio?"

"Radio?" He laughed, still chewing. "No. You got the wrong Valentino. I'm talking about Giovanni Valentino. From out west. Portland. Seattle. Frisco."

"Yeah, maybe I've heard of him. So what?"

"This Valentino says you can be trusted."

"What's that got to do with the price of tea in China?"

"Huh?"

"Giovanni Valentino trusts me. So what?"

"He knows my boss."

"Who's your boss?"

"Just never mind that. Look, if you want, I can set you up with a couple dozen slots. New ones. Top of the line. You get them around to the resorts. You know, for the tourists. You take care of them, see?"

"What's in it for me?"

"The resort owner gets a cut. You get a cut. My boss gets the leftovers. You interested?"

"Maybe. Soon as you tell me who's your boss."

"Ray, that's for me to know and you not to know. Far as you're concerned, I'm your boss. I'm the one you'll call if you need more slots. I'm the one who'll pick up the money twice a month. And I'm the one who will arrange to have both your legs broke if you try to skim from the top which I know you won't do because Giovanni Valentino said you can be trusted, capiche?"

"How do I know you're not some cop tryin' to set me up?"

The fat man stuffed mashed potatoes into his mouth. "How do ya figure I know about Valentino?"

"S'pose you tell me."

"It's a family affair."

"What?"

159

"Valentino married my boss's sister."

"So, Chicago mob. I shoulda known."

"Hey, you want the job or not?"

"Yeah, sure. I'll take the job. I could use a few extra bucks. Besides, I owe Valentino."

"I'll tell my boss the good news. Plan on picking up your slots at the depot tomorrow. They'll be in twelve orange crates shipped to the Westview Resort."

"Say, wait just a minute, pal. Nobody but nobody knows where I am. Not my folks, not the cops, nobody. How did your boss find me?"

"How?" The fat man stuffed the rest of his potatoes in his mouth. "You can lay low from the cops, hide from your family, stay out of the newspapers. It don't matter." He used part of a dinner roll to swab up the rest of the gravy. He licked his fingers, then looked Ray in the eye. "Raymond, the family's got more men, more connections than the damn FBI. When we want to find you, you will be found. You can bet your life on it."

By the end of the month, Ray had placed all of the new slot machines in resorts and taverns. Some of his sat next to machines owned by competitors. Ray knew of two ways to beat the competition. He could increase the odds of winning on his machines, knowing that, in time, they would be played more. Or, he could use another method—a more direct approach he'd seen used in Seattle—a homemade, coin-sized lead slug, bent and slipped in the coin slot, would jam a competitor's machine.

A week later in Angler's lower bar, the owner, Cullie Johnson, noticed a tall, dark figure playing the slots. He watched as the man moved from one machine to the next, then headed for the door.

"Any luck, buddy?" asked Cullie before the man could leave.

"Naw. The slots in this joint are rigged for the house."

"Rigged? Why, I've never had a rigged machine. They work just fine. Payout is good, too."

"I can get you better ones. Machines that keep folks interested. Keep 'em playin'."

"Say, don't I know you?"

Ray looked the man over. "Maybe you were tendin' bar when I stopped in with John Bluesky last summer."

"Oh, sure. Olson, isn't it? Ray Olson? You and your wife work out at Westview, right? "

"So, you want some good slot machines? I can set you up."

"My slots *are* good. Nobody but you ever complained."

"Wait till tomorrow."

"What?"

"Aw, forget it."

"Tell me you didn't monkey with my slot machines."

"My pop taught me never to lie."

Cullie grabbed Ray's sleeve. "Did you tamper with ...?"

"So what if I did?" said Ray, pulling away and clenching his fists. "What are you gonna do about it?"

"Listen, Olson. And listen good. Any trouble from you and, so help me, your wife will be a young widow. You get my drift?"

Ray laughed. "You try anything—*anything*—and you better bring friends. You'll need 'em to take you to the hospital. You get *my* drift, Johnson?"

"Get out of my bar, Olson. And stay out."

"With pleasure!"

Chapter 23

A black '32 Plymouth coupe motored west between the lakes of northwest Wisconsin on a bright, Thursday morning, June 15, 1939. Behind the wheel, tall, broad-shouldered Ray Olson sat beside his young wife, Delores. Ray saw the patrol car in the rearview mirror. As he pulled up to the Round Lake Resort where Delores worked the morning shift, the patrol car followed, blocking Ray's Plymouth. Ray recognized the officer as they stepped out.

"Mornin' Jim," said Ray. "Something wrong?"

"Your license plates," replied Officer James Hamblin. "Can you tell me where you got them?"

"Came with the car. Why?"

"The number is a match for some plates stolen up in Duluth."

"Can't be. I'm tellin' ya, they came with the car." Ray walked to the rear of the Plymouth. "Hey, these ain't my plates!"

"Where'd they come from?"

"How the hell should I know, Jim? I ain't never seen 'em before."

"You didn't put these plates on your car?"

"Like I said, I ain't never seen them plates."

"Then, suppose you explain to me how they got there."

"I ... I can't. I got no idea how."

"Well, we can sort this all out in the sheriff's office."

"What? Me and Delores have to get to work."

"Not today you don't."

"Say, what's the deal, Hamblin? Did Cullie Johnson put you up to this? Is that the score?"

Hamblin didn't reply.

"Is that it? You workin' for Cullie now? Is he that sore about last week? Is that what this is all about?"

Still no reply.

"Look, Jim, just 'cuz me and Johnson had a little misunderstanding over some slot machines don't make this right. You got no call to haul me downtown."

"I have to take you in, Ray."

"I had nothing to do with his damaged slots."

"None of that matters to me."

"And what happens when we get to the station? I get worked over? I get framed? Charged for stealin' some plates I never seen before so Cullie Johnson can watch me get sent up the river? Is that it?"

"Ray, I have to take you in. That's all there is to it."

"Aw, have a heart, Jim. Just because somebody switched plates on me ain't no reason to …"

Hamblin interrupted. "Delores, you will ride in the back seat of my car. Ray, you drive your car ahead of me. You're going to lead us through town to the sheriff's office. It's in the building next to the courthouse."

"I know where it is."

Driving the Plymouth, Ray headed west, taking County Trunk B and Highway 27 into the city of Hayward. The Ford patrol car followed close behind with the deputy driving and Delores in the back seat.

"Jim, please don't do this to Ray," she pleaded. "He's a good guy just trying his best to keep the wolf from the door. He works hard and does his best to stay on the straight and narrow. You know that. I know you do. And Ray didn't steal those license plates. You know that, too."

"I have to bring him in, Delores. I have no choice."

"Look, Jim. You and your wife have known Ray and me for six, maybe seven months. When has my husband ever done anything that would make you treat him like this? When?"

"You don't understand. It's not up to me. Sheriff Seehuetter would have my hide if I didn't bring him in."

"Ray doesn't deserve this. If he's rubbing somebody the wrong way, you tell me what the problem is and I'll straighten it all out. Please, Jim. Give him a break. I beg you."

"Sorry, kid. I'm taking him in. Look, if like you say there's nothing to this, you'll both be free to go."

Nearing downtown, Ray pulled up to the Highway 27 stop sign across from the Moccasin Bar. Hamblin stopped close behind. Ray signaled a right turn. Hamblin did the same. The Plymouth did not pull out. Hamblin honked. Ray remained at the stop sign. To his left, a truck heavy with logs ambled toward them, heading north on Highway 63. It was followed by a long string of cars. Hamblin sounded his horn again. Ray waited.

"What the hell is he up to?" Hamblin asked his passenger.

"My husband is a very courteous driver," replied Delores, watching the truck draw near.

"Too courteous. He's up to something."

With the approaching truck mere yards away, Ray stomped on the gas pedal, turning right with smoke pouring from the squealing tires. The driver of the truck slammed on his brakes, narrowly missing the Plymouth, then continued ahead, blocking the deputy's patrol car. The truck rolled on by, followed by eight impatient motorists. Helpless, Hamblin watched as Ray raced north.

"Dammit! I knew it! I knew he was up to something." He flipped on his siren and red light, but couldn't pull out until the slow-moving string of vehicles passed by.

"Might as well give up right now," said Delores. "You'll never catch him."

"The hell I won't," replied the officer, finally pulling out. Flooring it, the sound of the roaring Ford engine soon merged with the scream of the siren.

Ray, a quarter-mile ahead and out of Hamblin's sight, swerved east onto Highway 77 toward Clam Lake.

Not seeing the Plymouth north on Highway 63, Hamblin did the same.

Olson raced on, but the six-cylinder Plymouth was no match for the Ford with its flathead eight. Sixty, seventy, eighty-five miles an hour and Hamblin quickly closed in.

Ray glanced at his rearview mirror to see the patrol car close behind. "I'll show you, copper," Ray said, jerking the wheel to the right. The Plymouth bounced across the shoulder and flew down the bank into the brush. Ray forced the door open and scrambled off into the thick woods along the Namekagon River.

Hamblin pulled over, silenced the siren, and stepped out.

"You got no place to go, Ray!" Hamblin screamed into the woods. "We've got your wife. C'mon, Olson. Give up."

Delores laughed. "Ray has hunted and trapped this country over a year. He knows it like the back of his hand. You'll never see him again."

"Don't be too sure. He's not the only fella who knows the woods around here. Meanwhile, you're coming with me to the station."

Sheriff George Seehuetter sat across the desk from Delores Olson. The clock said 9:30. Ray had been on the run for over an hour. In front of the sheriff lay the deputy's report and a pack of Camels. He offered her one. She refused.

"What do you have against my husband?" she asked.

"Stolen license plates."

"He didn't steal those plates. You know that as well as I do. This whole thing was cooked up because your buddy, Cullie Johnson, doesn't like Ray. Doesn't like it that my husband handles a few slots for Cullie's competition."

"I don't know anything about slot machines. We don't allow them in this county."

Delores laughed. "You know very well that just about every bar and resort has at least one slot machine somewhere."

"Don't tell me what I know and what I don't. I'm bringing Ray in, that's all."

"He won't give up. Not without a fight. And what happens to him if you can catch him?"

"*If* we can catch him? Oh, we'll catch him, all right."

"Or so you think. My Ray is like a fox running downwind from his hunters. You'll never get him."

The sheriff studied her, then Jim Hamblin's report. "Says here that you and Ray rent a cabin on Round Lake. Is that true?"

"Don't bother looking there. If I know Ray, he's already been there and left."

"That's a good eight miles from where he ditched the car."

"Shorter as the crow flies, Sheriff. Like I told Hamblin, Ray knows the woods like ..."

"Like the back of his hand. I know. But there's no way on God's green earth that he could ..."

"Don't be so sure. Ray's smart. And he's got friends."

"What friends? Who?"

"Why, everybody he knows, Sheriff. He has a lot more friends than you have deputies, I'll tell you that much. Ray is a good guy. He helps folks out."

"You mean the Indians?"

"Color doesn't matter to Ray. Friendship does. And trust."

"Where do you think your husband is now?"

"By now he's probably hitched a ride out of the county."

"Where to?"

"What makes you think I would tell you?"

"You mean to say he'd skip town knowing you're in custody?"

"Look. I've done nothing wrong. You can't hold me. I know it, you know it, Ray knows it."

"Were you involved when Ray broke into those two Moose Lake cabins last week?"

"Moose Lake? I don't know what you're talking about."

"We know it was Ray. Were you there with him?"

"You're barking up the wrong tree."

"Two cabins ransacked on the same night. Some fishing rods and tackle boxes missing. Ring a bell?"

"Ransacked? That's not my Ray. Like I told Hamblin, my husband's on the straight and narrow. Now, if you don't have anything else, I have tables to wait on today."

Officer Hamblin entered, handing the sheriff a sheet of paper. Seehuetter read it, then looked at his deputy. "You sure about this?"

"I just got off the horn with the St. Paul Police Department. They confirmed it."

Seehuetter smiled, then looked at Delores. "You won't be waiting on any tourists today, honey."

"Like hell I won't. I'm clean as rainwater and you know it."

"It says here that the Plymouth you and Ray have been joyriding in around here was stolen in St. Paul over a year ago."

"My husband bought that car from some old lady. She was moving and couldn't afford to keep it. Heck, he did her a favor."

"Delores, I'm holding you on a charge of accessory to grand theft auto pending investigation."

"What about my job? How am I supposed to pay our bills?"

"Not my problem. You'll be our guest until we nab your husband."

"Something tells me I'll be here for a long, long time."

"Sheriff," said Hamblin, "we got a tip that Olson might head for Deerfoot Lodge. Him and John Bluesky were supposed to repair one of their docks.

The sheriff turned back to Delores. "Is that true?"

"I doubt Ray will be going to work today, Sheriff."

"Is it true he works with Bluesky?"

"They have been helping out at some of the resorts. Nothing wrong with that, is there?"

"Hamblin, go find John Bluesky. Let's see what he knows."

Delores laughed. "John doesn't trust you cops any more than Ray does. He won't help you."

"We'll see about that. Meanwhile, we have you. If we can't get to Ray, maybe Ray will come to us."

Finding John Bluesky wasn't easy. Then, late the next evening, the sheriff's phone rang. Deputy Hamblin took the call, an anonymous tip. Two hours later, John Bluesky sat before the sheriff.

"You know why you're here, John? Why I had you picked up?"

Bluesky didn't answer.

"Where's Ray Olson?"

"Who?"

"Did you see him today? Give him a ride?"

"Don't have a car."

"Where is Olson?"

"Don't know."

"Olson is in big trouble. Stolen license plates. Stolen car. That's a felony. Anyone who helps him will be in big trouble, too. Probably go to prison. John, you don't want to go to prison just to protect a car thief, do you?"

Bluesky didn't answer.

"John?"

"Don't know what you're talking about."

"Do you know where he is?"

"I didn't help him."

"Where is he?"

"Can't say."

"Why? Why can't you say, John?"

"Don't know."

"You're covering for him. I know you are. Why?"

"Maybe he thinks you're planning to kill him."

"Did he tell you that?"

Bluesky didn't answer.

"Look, John. Your buddy is wanted for auto theft. A felony. Anyone helping him will go to jail. Understand?"

"You planning to kill him?"

"What? No. I want to bring him in. That's all. Where is he?"

"Can't say."

"Then you'll sit in jail until you can say."

"I did nothing wrong."

"It's for your own good. You won't be tempted to help Olson as long as you're in here."

"You can't keep me here."

"Tell me where Olson is and you're free to go."

"Don't know."

"Deputy, take this man to his cell."

That evening, the sheriff's phone rang again. A car had been stolen from the Meier Resort on Round Lake. And later, another call. A game warden had spotted the car as it raced down a gravel road near the Chippewa Flowage—with Olson at the wheel.

Seehuetter phoned his undersheriff, James Berard, at home.

"Jim, I think I know where we can find Olson. Leon Plante called. Said he saw him not far from the Bluesky place. Hamblin checked it out earlier today. Nobody there. At least, nobody he could see. Olson might think it's safe to hide there now that it's been checked out."

"You heading there now, George?"

"Tonight? No. Not in the dark. He could give us the slip again. We'll wait till daylight. See if you can round up five or six men to back us up. Have them meet us in town at eight o'clock sharp."

"Will do."

"And, Jim, tell each man to bring a gun."

Chapter 24

On Saturday, June 17, 1939, nine armed men in two cars sped down County Highway B near the Chippewa Flowage. Riding with the sheriff and Fred Sieh, Hayward's Chief of Police, were Burt Bruckman, Wilbur Hanson, and owner of the Twin Gables Restaurant, Fred Scott. Jim Berard drove the second patrol car. With him were Deputy Hamblin, Frank Symington, and Carl "Cullie" Johnson, co-owner of Angler's Bar.

Turning onto North River Road near the Bluesky cabin, Seehuetter signaled the car behind to stop. The undersheriff and Seehuetter's seven deputies synchronized their watches, checked their weapons, and listened as the sheriff used a stick to draw a map in the sand.

"I want three men to drop back into the woods and circle the Bluesky place from the right. Three more from the left. Spread out and pussyfoot toward the yard, but keep out of sight. Hamblin, Johnson, and I will stay here for now. At exactly eight forty-five, the three of us will move in from the front. The rest of you just watch the place. If he makes a run for it, don't let him get past you. But remember, your guns are only for your defense. Olson hasn't been convicted of anything. Technically, he's not a criminal. Nobody shoots unless I give the order."

The three teams of three took their positions and waited until time came for the circle to tighten. They'd only moved a few feet when Cullie spotted the car stolen from Meier's Resort. Sneaking from tree to tree, he approached it, then quietly opened the hood and yanked the coil wire from the distributor. Olson wouldn't escape using this car.

Johnson hid near the car while Hamblin and Seehuetter crept past two outbuildings, a woodshed, and an outhouse to the cabin door. With one hand on the butt of his holstered revolver, the sheriff knocked.

The door swung open and a woman stared through the screen, her black hair in braids, skin the color of old shoe leather, and eyes narrowed. "Who are you?" she demanded.

"Sawyer County Sheriff. Can I come in?"

"Why? What do you want?"

"I'm here for Ray Olson."

"Not here." She opened the screen door. "See for yourself."

Cautiously, Seehuetter entered the log cabin. Its neat interior suggested a simple life. The furniture, cupboard, and bed frame were hand-carved pine. On the floor, a bear rug. From floor to ceiling, the interior was immaculate. A deer rifle and a shotgun hung over the fireplace. A single coffee cup sat on the table, half full.

"Where is Olson?" asked the sheriff.

The woman didn't answer.

"Look, Ray Olson is in trouble. A lot of trouble. Tell me where he is or you and John will be in trouble, too."

"Where is John?"

"Never mind that. Do you know where Olson is?"

"First, where is John?"

"In Hayward. He is safe there."

"He is safe here. Why is he in Hayward?"

"Because I'm trying to keep him out of trouble."

"Is he in your jail?"

"Yes, but only as my guest. Help me find Ray Olson and I'll let John go. Tell me where Ray is."

"He owes my John thirty-two dollars."

"Where is he?"

"You will get me the money?"

"Yes. I'll get your money. Where is he?"

Her dark eyes shifted toward a small, tarpaper shack across the yard. "Sleep shack," she said. "Him and Blackie."

"Who's Blackie?"

"His dog."

"Does Olson have a gun?"

"She pointed at the fireplace. "Both John's guns are there."

Seehuetter and Hamblin moved away from the log cabin now. The sheriff signaled to the others, then pointed at the small shack.

172

Less concerned that Olson would be armed, he motioned for Cullie to join them. They approached the only door in the shanty.

"Ray Olson, this is the sheriff. Come out with your hands up."

No response.

"Give up, Olson. There's no way out."

Again, nothing.

"I know you're in there, Ray. I don't want any trouble. Come out with your hands up."

Still no reply.

Hamblin tried the door, finding it locked. Johnson grabbed a shovel leaning against the wall. With one swing, he broke the make-shift latch. Seehuetter pulled the door open. Inside, Blackie growled. A screen door came next, hooked on the inside. The men stared through the screen, seeing only the large, black dog, growling with teeth bared.

"Ray," said Hamblin. "This is your last chance. Come on out or we're comin' in."

Still no response.

The sheriff nodded to Johnson who forced the shovel between the door and jamb and gave a twist, then kicked the door open. Seehuetter, Hamblin, and Johnson peered in. There, with one foot on the bed, the other on a wooden crate, loomed the figure of Ray Olson aiming a single-barrel shotgun at them.

Each man felt his blood run cold upon hearing the click of the hammer being cocked.

174

Chapter 25

The blinding blast from the shotgun sent Cullie Johnson to the ground. Hamblin and the sheriff dove into the brush, fearing the next shotgun blast. Shot in the head, Cullie died instantly. Near him, in the dirt, lay his .38 caliber Colt revolver.

Inside, Ray ejected the shell and jammed another in the chamber.

Outside, the sheriff shouted, "Open fire!"

Olson jumped from the bed to the rafters, the shotgun clutched in one hand.

All four law officers leveled their weapons at the cabin and fired. The remaining four deputized volunteers followed suit, firing at will, chest high.

Ray shielded his head with one arm and waited, wondering if the next bullet would rip through him.

Lead slugs tore through all four walls of the flimsy tarpaper-clad shack, ricocheting and whizzing out the opposite side. Fragments of pine and tarpaper flew into the air and littered the ground. Round after round blasted through one wall of the shed and smashed out the other, destroying the bed and chair, and killing the dog.

A fog of acrid gunsmoke soon hung low over the backwoods battleground. Each man outside shot round after round until most weapons emptied, bringing a lull in the shooting.

Out of shells, Fred Scott took a chance. He raced across the yard through the gunsmoke toward his car for more ammunition. He heard the blast from the shotgun and felt lead tear into his left shoulder and through his chest. Fred lurched, spun, then stumbled toward the shack and fell. "I'm hit!" were the last words anyone would hear from him.

Two bodies now lay before the shack as silence overtook the murder scene.

"Who fired that shot?" shouted Hamblin.

No man answered.

"Who fired?" he repeated.

"There he is!" someone yelled. "In the door!"

"Shoot him!" screamed Seehuetter. "Shoot!"

Olson vaulted through the open doorway and reached down for Cullie Johnson's Colt .38.

"Open fire!" shouted the sheriff. "Get him!"

No man could. Ray tore across the open ground, dove into the brush, and vanished from sight.

Too low on ammunition to pursue the fugitive through the thick woods, the seven remaining men stood over the bodies of their friends, Cullie and Fred.

"All this over a stolen car?" said Berard. "It makes no sense!"

"Sheriff," said Hamblin, "the Bluesky woman told you that Olson didn't have a gun. I heard her."

"How could she know?" replied Seehuetter. "How could I know? Jesus! All Olson did was steal a car. There's no reason to kill someone over something like that."

"Unless …," added Hamblin.

"Unless what?"

"Unless he thought it was either him or us."

"What are you talking about?"

"Back in the station, Bluesky asked you a question? He said, 'Maybe Olson thinks you're planning to kill him.'"

"What are you driving at?"

"When I picked Olson up Thursday, he asked if he was being set up for a fall."

"Even so, why murder someone?"

"What if Olson saw us coming? Saw what he thought was a mob planning to snuff him out? Put yourself in his shoes. Nine men with guns surrounding you. What would you do?"

"Look, Hamblin, what's done is done. We have two dead men here. Murdered in cold blood. Nothing else matters. Olson is a fugitive wanted for murder, and, by God, I'm going to get him."

Olson raced through the hot, thick forest, heading for the West Fork of the Chippewa River. Reaching it, he slogged northeast through a swampy river bottom, running as fast as the tangles of tag alders allowed. Wood ticks crawled below his clothes while clouds of mosquitoes swarmed around him, attacking exposed skin. And on he ran.

On he ran, Colt tucked under his belt, shotgun in hand, not knowing who might be mere seconds behind—or seconds ahead. Visions of Cullie and Fred lying dead, lying in pools of blood near John Bluesky's sleep shack, haunted Ray.

"Why in the name of God did I get myself into such a jam?" he said aloud. Everybody will be after me! *Everybody!* They'll grab the nearest gun and come for me. I gotta move. Move fast. Go find Delores and get far away from here."

Ray knew the area and the men who hunted there. He knew it would only be a matter of time before they drove him out of the woods and into a hail of bullets like a whitetail buck caught in a November deer drive. His sole chance for escape was to quickly put distance between him and the crime scene. On he ran. Then, ahead—the Highway B bridge over the West Fork of the Chippewa River. And underneath the bridge, a perfect place to rest and plan his next step.

At the crime scene, Sheriff Seehuetter also made plans.

"Men, there's more ammo and a couple of shotguns in my car. I want you all to load up."

"We goin' after him?" asked Hamblin.

"Too risky trying to stalk him through the brush. Not enough firepower. Too few men. Olson knows these woods. He has friends here, too. Friends who don't know he stole a car and can't know he just murdered Cullie and Fred. If he can get to his friends, they'll help him escape before they realize what he's done. We have to box Olson in before he gets too far. To do that, we need more men. Plenty of men. I'm heading to town.

"Berard, I want you and Symington to guard the car Olson stole. He doesn't know Cullie disabled the motor. He might come back for it. Stay out of sight. He's killed and might kill again."

"Got it," said Berard. "Let's go, Frank."

"Chief Sieh, I want you and Hamblin to question John Bluesky's wife. Find out who Ray's friends are and where they live. No rough stuff. Remind her that we have her husband in custody and the sooner she cooperates, the sooner he comes home."

"Where do you want us, Sheriff?" asked Bruckman.

"Burt, you and Will Hanson get the worst job. I need you to stand guard over the bodies until the coroner gets out here. Stay alert. Olson could be a half-mile away by now, or he could be watching us from the brush as we speak. He's a murderer on the run. There's no way of knowing what he's thinking right now."

A shiver went down Wilbur Hanson's spine. "You mean Olson might come back? Might try to finish the rest of us off?"

"I doubt he'd come back. But keep an eye peeled. He's not thinking straight. Unpredictable."

Seehuetter jumped into the patrol car. The starter ground. The engine roared. Siren blaring, the sheriff sped down the gravel road toward town, a cloud of dust billowing behind.

Less than a mile away, Ray hid in the shadows of the West Fork bridge watching for traffic headed east, away from the murder scene. A Buick sedan bearing Illinois plates thundered over the bridge and around the corner, giving way to the quiet of the morning again. Two westbound cars crossed, headed toward Hayward. Three boys on bicycles came next, each carrying a fishing pole. Ray hoped they would not stop to fish from the bridge. They didn't. A Ford with a fishing boat tied on the roof rumbled across before all went quiet again. Minutes later, the high-pitched drone of an approaching outboard motor warned him to keep moving. But the outboard's whine was soon overwhelmed by the loud rumble of a dump truck. Ray saw his chance.

Recalling his many months of jumping railcars, he waited until the truck crossed the bridge. Then, when beyond sight of the driver, he bolted. Running behind, he tossed his shotgun up and over the tailgate and jumped, hoping to follow it in. Grasping the top of the tailgate, he kicked one foot up, then the other. With a mighty heave, he pulled himself up, over, and into the box, dropping onto a load of gravel.

"Let's see you beat that, Jamestown Johnny."

The truck driver rambled down the road, unaware of the stowaway fugitive in the box. A single eagle flew overhead, the only witness to Ray's escape. Mile after twisting mile, Ray lay on his back watching the treetops fly by. When he felt the truck slow, he scrambled across the gravel to the front of the bed. Ray peeked over the front of the box at the road ahead just as the driver made a sharp right turn. Ray fell to the left, smacking the side of the box with the shotgun.

The driver heard the loud thud. He looked in his side-view mirror. Seeing nothing, he continued a quarter mile before pulling into a country diner. Curious about the noise he'd heard, the driver climbed from the cab. He hoisted himself up to inspect the inside of the box just as Ray scrambled out of sight down the other side and bolted into the woods, shotgun in hand, grinning like a truant schoolboy ditching the principal.

Arriving at the courthouse, Sheriff Seehuetter entered his office, going straight to the phone. His first calls went to the sheriffs of neighboring counties and the Wisconsin State Patrol. It was an alert to warn of a desperate fugitive, armed and dangerous, somewhere in the north woods. The public needed to know.

Next, Seehuetter phoned the chairman of the Sawyer County Board who was outraged at the news of the double murder of two deputized citizens.

"I'll get him," said Seehuetter. "I can't say where or when, but I'll get him."

"What can the county board do to help?"

"Authorize funds for bloodhounds."

"How much?"

"A hundred a day plus two hundred to fly them here."

"How long?"

"Until we nab Olson."

"George, I'll see to it you have a thousand for the hounds. More if need be. When can they be here?"

"This afternoon, if they're available."

"All right. See to it. What else do you need?

"Cooperation from neighboring county board chairmen. Tell each one to have their county sheriff round up ten to twenty men. Armed men who know what they're doing. We'll meet at the courthouse for a briefing tomorrow morning. Seven sharp. Tell them that I am in charge. I don't want anybody interfering with my plan. This is my baby. I call the shots."

"You got it. I'll call them right away."

"I appreciate it."

"What about a reward, George? You think it would help?"

"No. It's one thing to ask folks around here to lock their doors and be prepared to defend themselves in case Olson shows up. But it's totally different if there's a reward. I don't want every Tom, Dick, and Harry running around shooting up the woods trying to get prize money. I don't want unorganized, untrained people out in the woods."

"Anything else?"

"I'll need guns, ammunition, teargas."

"Order what you need, George. I'll find the money."

An hour later, five bloodhounds and their trainer were on a plane from La Crosse and a supply of rifles, pistols, and ammunition were on a northbound army truck along with five Thompson sub-machine guns and 100 hand grenades.* Seehuetter's men would be well armed.

The Sheriff's next calls were made in person. He drove downtown, parking in front of Angler's. Staring straight ahead, he wondered how he could break the news to Cullie's wife, Helen, and his brothers, Buck and Oscar—something he'd never done before. Next to seeing his friends die that morning, this would be the hardest part of his job.

*According to the *Chicago Sunday Tribune,* June 18, 1939.

From Angler's, the sheriff drove to the Twin Gables to deliver the same, hard news to Fred Scott's wife. He left the restaurant with a heavy heart and deeper determination to bring in Olson.

At 2 p.m., all northern Wisconsin radio stations broadcast the alert. Word of the murders washed across the Namekagon River Valley and beyond. Groups of angry men, young and old, armed and determined, soon scoured the woods. They checked every resort, entered every cabin, woodshed, and chicken coup within five miles of the crime scene. Gangs of vengeance-seeking amateur man hunters, motored up and down hot, dusty back roads, all eager for a glimpse—or better yet, a shot—at the outlaw. Other well-meaning search parties aimlessly tramped through the woods near the crime scene, destroying any sign left by Olson who now hid a full twenty miles east.

Seehuetter arrived with the county coroner around three. Men from the funeral home prepared the bodies for their final ride to town. The sight of the black Cadillac hearse motoring from the murder scene only fed the furor of Olson's wrathful hunters.

A mile away, at Deerfoot Lodge, Ernie Mercer cried out, "I seen him! I seen Olson! He just ducked into that cabin, there!"

A dozen men quickly surrounded the Deerfoot Lodge cottage, hiding behind trees and outbuildings.

"You sure about this, Ernie?" came a shout.

"Dang right I'm sure. It was him I tell ya. I know it!"

"All right, Olson," shouted one of the searchers. "We know you're in there. We got you surrounded. If you're not out by my count to three, we'll shoot!

"One!

"Two!"

Before the shout "three," a shot rang out. Every man there opened fire, riddling the cottage with bullets. For the second time that day, lead slugs tore through pine walls. Chips of wood and debris flew skyward. Gunsmoke filled the air. The gunfire echoed across the Chippewa flowage as men emptied their weapons, reloaded, emptied, and reloaded again. And kept on shooting.

Searchers nearby heard the gunfire and came running, hoping to get in on the action. More bullets crashed through walls, shattered windows, then zinged high into treetops.

"Hold your fire!" came a shout. "I think we got him."

Slowly five men crept toward the cabin, nerves on edge, weapons at the ready. With great care, they peered through windows. One brave soul looked inside, then entered.

Seconds stretched into minutes. Then, "Ain't nobody here!"

"Nobody? You sure?"

"Yep. Nobody but me. Ernie musta been seein' things."

"Goddammit, Ernie! What you saw wasn't Olson. It was one of us! Jesus! You coulda got somebody killed!"

Disappointed, the search parties resumed their work, checking in and under cabins, up and down the shore.

As darkness fell, some men returned to their homes. Most gathered at their favorite watering holes to compare stories, commiserate, and make plans for Sunday's hunt.

Day one of the manhunt for Ray Olson ended with the wives and families of Cullie Johnson and Fred Scott in mourning, suffering from the shock of the tragic deaths. It ended with hundreds of angry men vowing to capture or kill the fugitive, no matter the cost. It ended with hysterical wives and mothers begging duty-bound husbands and adventurous sons to stay home and stay safe. It ended with maps, guns, grenades, and bloodhounds being readied for tomorrow. Day one ended with Delores Olson caged in a cramped, cold, Hayward jail cell, not knowing her husband was wanted for murder, running for his life.

And day one ended with a remorseful, yet determined fugitive in hiding—hungry and tired—hunkering in a hot, dark spruce swamp, soaked with sweat, picking off bloodthirsty ticks, swatting at swarms of mosquitoes.

And dreading day two.

Chapter 26

At first light, sheltered below the limbs of a balsam tree, Ray woke with his jacket pulled over his face to foil the mosquitoes. But his jacket had slipped during the night. He rubbed his eyes to find the left side of his face covered with mosquito bites and his eyelid swollen shut.

Sleep had helped Ray bury the memory of what had happened. Now awake, thoughts of the preceding day shook him. He jumped to his feet. "East," he said. "Gotta go east."

In the dim twilight, he picked his way through the swamp, then up the side of an oak ridge where he followed deer trails that led him farther from the scene of the crime. The mosquitoes followed. He snapped a bough from a small balsam and waved it as he walked to keep some of the insects at bay. The trail descended to a small brook. Ray lay flat on the bank. Cupping his hands, he drank and drank, then immersed his face in the cool, clear water. His thirst quenched, he sat on a nearby log, swishing and swatting at the swarm of mosquitoes.

"Food," he muttered. "Gotta eat to keep goin'."

He pulled the Colt .38 from his belt and flipped open the cylinder. All six chambers were loaded. He snapped it shut again, returning the revolver to his belt. Next, he felt for his jackknife, finding it in a pocket in his trousers. In another pocket, his lucky rabbit's foot. Ray scoffed, throwing it to the ground, but quickly picked it up again. He brushed it off, dropping it into the same pocket. Patting his jacket, Ray pulled out a pack of Lucky Strike cigarettes, soaked from rain the night before. He squeezed water from the pack, then discarded it in disgust.

"Matches!" he said, fumbling through his jacket pockets. Ray found a dozen stick matches, also wet. These he dropped into a shirt pocket, hoping they might dry.

"Food," he repeated. "What am I gonna do for food? Haven't eaten since yesterday morning. The thought brought memories of the shootout—visions of Cullie and Fred on the ground—bullets tearing through the walls, cutting down his dog.

"What a mess. And why'd they have to go shoot my dog? Kill me, sure. But not my dog. Poor Blackie didn't have a chance. No place to hide. Poor, poor Blackie. Dang them county coppers!"

Ray stood. Trying to ignore his hunger, he crossed the small stream by stepping from stone to stone. He resumed his eastward tramp, shotgun in hand. Ray slipped through the woods step by step, as silent as a fox, the only sound in the forest coming from songbirds now waking. Step by step by silent step he put distance behind. Step by step until … *Woosh!* A ruffed grouse thundered from an overhead branch.

Startled, Ray froze, his heart pounding.

Woosh! Another flushed from its overnight perch.

Ray searched the limbs above. Seeing a third grouse, he drew his pistol, cocked the hammer, aligned the sights, and squeezed the trigger. The sharp crack of the handgun filled the woods. The bird fell to the forest floor, head missing, wings pointlessly pounding and pounding a final, futile flight to nowhere.

Ray picked up the limp bird. He looked at it with a sadness he'd never felt after shooting other grouse. He stroked the bird's feathers, smoothing them, admiring their beauty. Then, as he held it, he felt one final shudder of muscles quivering below feathers and skin. The bird was dead. Nothing more. Nothing less. Alive one moment, dead the next. Gone for good. Gone forever. But not gone for nothing. Its life wouldn't be a waste.

Not like yesterday, that horrible yesterday.

Ray hurried back to the stream. He tore through feathers and skin, exposing the breast. With his jackknife, he separated flesh from bone until all of the bird's meat lay on a flat rock near the water. The rest he set on another rock, a fine meal for some otter, mink, or raccoon.

Piece by piece, Ray washed the meat, chewed, and swallowed, devouring his breakfast. When finished, he rinsed his knife, wiping it and his hands on his trousers as he resumed his eastward trek, wondering, as he walked, how many may have heard the shot.

Miles west, Sheriff George Seehuetter prepared for his early morning meeting in Hayward. The undersheriff, James Berard, took charge of dispensing weapons to those who needed them. Only Berard, Seehuetter, and three sheriffs of neighboring counties would take possession of the teargas, grenades, and the five Thompson sub-machine guns. Each man would oversee his own search team, each team assigned by Seehuetter to a one-square mile section of land at a time. When satisfied that Olson wasn't there, another mile-square parcel would be assigned. Deputy Hamblin and ten men would accompany George Brooks, the handler of the bloodhounds, who had arrived earlier by plane with his hounds. The pilot, eager to assist, agreed to spend his day searching from high above the crime scene. His sole passenger would be armed only with binoculars.

On this warm, still, Sunday morning, Seehuetter and Berard could hear the far away rumbling of approaching cars and trucks. Around half-past six, men arrived at the courthouse, some alone, some in pairs, and others in small groups. Most carried a rifle or shotgun in one hand and a lunch box in the other. Soon, more cars and trucks rolled up Dakota Avenue and more men turned up, milling around, sharing thoughts of the hunt and vows to be the one to avenge the slain deputies. Each man signed the roster and was assigned to one of the five teams.

Hamblin shared copies of a photo of Ray Olson. From the tailgate of his truck, City Police Chief Fred Sieh distributed military compasses and bottles of mosquito dope provided by the quartermaster at Camp McCoy.

Finally, from the courthouse steps, Sheriff Seehuetter blew a sharp whistle to begin the briefing.

"All right, men, pay attention. You've all been assigned to a group. Don't switch groups unless you okay it with me and don't bother asking because the answer is no. Your team leader is in charge of your group. Do what he says and only what he says. He has a map. He will tell you which part of the map you will search and other details. Now, our plan is to carefully and thoroughly beat the brush and comb through every swamp and woodlot until we find Olson or are certain he isn't there. Only then do we move on to the next area.

"Meanwhile, Deputy Hamblin's team will be with the hounds. Should they lead us to Olson, I will pull two teams off their assigned areas to support Hamblin.

"Now, men, it's important that nobody gets hurt out there. Yes, Olson is armed and likely to shoot if cornered. But the bigger risk is from that guy standing right next to you. Now listen and listen good. Under no circumstances do you shoot at anyone or anything unless you are absolutely sure it is Ray Olson and that you won't accidentally hit somebody else.

"And here's something else. We are not the only ones at risk of getting shot. Besides us and Olson, there are people out there. Folks who live around the lakes. Tourists who haven't heard what's going on yet. Or, maybe they have heard and don't have enough horse sense to go back home until this is over. And you know how tourists are. They might be out berry picking or trout fishing or just walking around in the woods for no good reason. For crying out loud, men, don't shoot them! We need those tourists to keep coming back, keep renting our cabins, drinking at our taverns, spending their money. If you should meet up with someone other than Olson, politely let them know it would be wise to stay at their resort for now and not go out wandering around.

"Oh, yes. There's already a pile of newspapermen around, too. And bound to be more soon. Them you can go ahead and shoot."

Quiet laughter rolled through the crowd.

"No, no. Sorry. As much as I hate to say it, you cannot shoot the reporters, no matter how much they get in your way. If they are causing a problem or asking questions or trying to get photographs, get word to me. Let me handle it. Maybe I'll shoot them.

"Okay. One last thing before we get going. When you signed your name to the roster, you became my deputy and a member of my posse. But to make it official, raise your right hand and repeat after me."

Sheriff Seehuetter swore in 205 deputies at once, then ordered the five teams to leave for their assigned areas. By the time the convoy of deputized man hunters neared the scene of the crime, the search plane circled above the Chippewa Flowage.

The hunt for Ray Olson had resumed.

Ray's morning march now took him south to a field planted with Norway pine seedlings. Not wanting to risk being seen, he skirted the plantation, coming to a logging road that snaked through a spruce woods, then out onto fire lane. The plantation and road told him he was between the Loretta Civilian Conservation Corps camp and Winter, a remote, quiet village.

Ray guessed the forty-some corpsmen at the camp would have heard the news. He also knew it was early Sunday and the men would not be working. Would they spend the day looking for him?

His thoughts turned to Delores. "Last time I saw her was three days ago," he mumbled to himself. "No doubt they have her locked up. If I don't turn myself in, they'll probably take it out on her. Aw, the poor kid. She didn't do nothin'. I gotta go back. Bust her out. But how? I can't just walk to town. Everybody must know the score by now. Everybody must be on the lookout—in the woods, on the roads. Lookin' for a fella on foot. Just think. All them suckers after me, Ray Olson. Hey! I bet they're not lookin' in town. I could go there. Sure! With everybody out here, I could hide out in the city till I figure a way to bust Baby out. Then we could hightail it out of that town on the double. But how?"

The faint ring of a distant church bell drifted through the air. Ray stopped.

"A church!" He turned west, toward the sound of the bell. "It's Sunday! There's bound to be cars there. Plenty to pick from. That's it! That's how I'll get to Hayward—to my baby!"

Seeing a huge oak ahead, he ran to it, tore off his jacket, and wrapped it around the shotgun. He stashed the gun in the brush behind the tree. Checking the position of the sun, he took off running straight for the bell's faint ring.

Within seconds, the bell stopped. Ray did not. Keeping the sun over his left shoulder, he bounded through the woods, pushing brush aside, and jumping over fallen logs. He crossed a creek, a logging road, and came to a small pond. Skirting it, he found an abandoned railroad grade that headed his way. Down the grade he ran. In the distance he saw a building, then two, then more. "Winter!" he said. "The Village of Winter!"

As Ray imagined, more than a dozen cars lined the highway near the church. He picked the first Ford, opened the door, and climbed in. No key in the ignition. He tried the glove box, the ashtray, then pulled down the visor. No keys.

"Dang it!"

Ray got out, looking over the cars ahead. He skipped a Chevy, then jumped behind the wheel of the next car. Visor. Ashtray. Glove box. No keys, but a pint of Old Crow in the glove box went into his hip pocket as he left for car three. As he pulled down the visor of the Desoto, a set of keys dropped into his lap. He cranked the engine over. It started. Gently, he pulled out onto the highway and motored off to find his shotgun, again grinning like a kid playing hooky.

"Delores, don't you worry. I'm comin' to get you, Doll!"

At the scene of the homicides, Deputy Jim Hamblin watched as George Brooks let his bloodhounds explore the area before taking them inside the sleep shack. The four dogs sniffed and snorted and smelled the bedding and chair. Brooks gave each a pat of encouragement. "Hunt him up, boys! Hunt him up," he told them. "Find him." The hounds sniffed the bed again before Brooks took them outside where they zigzagged, sniffing, snorting, and searching."

"Brooks," Hamblin said, "try over this way. Olson ran into the brush right here."

Brooks corralled the dogs, walking them toward Hamblin. With a howl, they charged into the brush. "They're on his trail," said Brooks. "Let's go."

Brooks, Hamblin, and ten deputized posse members followed the howling dogs into the brush. An hour later, they came out onto Highway B at the West Fork bridge. The dogs milled around, sniffing, howling, searching for the trail. Brooks had them circle the area, then circle it again. Each time, they returned to the place under the bridge where Olson hid the day before.

"No use," said Brooks. Either he jumped into somebody's boat here, or hitched a ride."

"Is someone helping him?" asked a posse member.

Hamblin petted one of the hounds. "It's true Olson's got friends who might help him. But how would one of them know where he'd be? Or when, for that matter. No, Olson did this by himself. I'll let the Sheriff know we hit a dead end. At least for now."

Chapter 27

In the bright morning sun, a stolen 1934 Desoto sedan cruised down Highway 70, west of the Village of Winter, headed for Hayward. Ray looked at the gas gauge, the needle on E. Ray slammed his fists on the wheel.

"Dammit! I should have picked one with a full tank. Bessie, I hope you can get me out of sight somewhere. Another twenty minutes and church will be out and so will word that you and me is on the run."

Ray pulled onto a side road, headed for the Chippewa Flowage again. "Let's see if we can get some help. It's time to find out who our friends really are."

Turning down a narrow, grassy road, Ray drove the car deep into the woods on the south side of the flowage and shut off the motor. In a few minutes, he had the car hidden with brush and branches from nearby pines. His jacket over one shoulder, shotgun on the other, he tramped downhill to the water's edge, then worked his way along the shore to the Indian Trail Resort.

Ahead, Ray saw a row of wooden guide boats tied to the dock, each with oars and one with an outboard motor. He stood in the shadows wondering if this could be a trap. "Why weren't these boats out on the lake on a nice morning like this? Where are the tourists? The guides?"

The distant drone of an airplane caught his attention. He watched it slowly circle at low altitude far to the north. "A search plane. Looking for me. That's why nobody's fishing. They're afraid they'll run into me! Scared of me. Imagine that."

Ray looked back at the boats, then scanned the grounds. Seeing no one, he strolled to the dock and the boat with the motor. With the shotgun wrapped in his jacket again, he boarded the boat. He put the oars in the locks and rowed away from the resort. Rounding an island several hundred yards away, he primed the motor and gave the starter cord a sharp pull, then another, then another. He unscrewed the gas cap. The tank was half full. He primed it again, pulled the cord, and the outboard came to life.

Ray slowly motored across the flowage, staying between islands as best he could. Nearing the narrows above the dam, he silenced the motor, rowing the final half mile to a camp along the shore. Seeing no one outside, he beached the boat. Leaving the jacket-wrapped shotgun in the boat, he walked up to the shack, and knocked.

"Billy, you here? Billy?"

"Who's there?"

"Billy, I need some gasoline."

"Ray?"

"You gotta help me out, Billy."

"I heard what you done. I don't want no trouble. You get outa here. Go."

"Aw, please, Billy. Can'tcha help me out?"

"Seehuetter's got a posse looking for you. A couple hundred men."

"Jesus! A couple hundred? Out after me?"

"Ray, I don't want no part of this."

"But, it's just a can of gasoline. Who's gonna know?"

I ain't goin' to jail 'cause of you, Ray. Go away."

Ray turned back toward his boat.

"Ray!" Billy shouted from inside his shack. "There's a pickup at the Whitcomb place. They're gone. Won't be back for a week. Arnie keeps his keys in the ashtray."

"You sure they're gone?"

"I drove 'em to the Spooner depot, myself. Pickin' them up one week from today. Don't you tell nobody I said so."

"Won't tell a soul, Billy. Knew I could count on you, pal."

Ray motored up the lake into a quiet cove with a single dock. He tied up the boat, noticing several inches of water in Arnie Whitcomb's fishing boat. Confident in Billy's tip, he climbed the steps to the house and knocked on the door. No one answered.

Ray found the keys to the truck in the ashtray. In the glove compartment, a scrap of paper. Searching deeper, he found a pencil.

He returned to the dock and put a note on the front seat of the boat, setting the anchor on top to hold it in place. He started the motor, then jumped onto the dock and let go of the empty boat. Midway across the bay, he pulled the revolver from his belt and fired into the air, the report echoing down the shore. Ray ran up the steps, two at a time. Seconds later, he was speeding away in Arnie Whitcomb's pickup.

Sheriff Seehuetter got word from the office. A resort owner, hearing a distant shot, had looked out to see a motorboat making tight circles in the bay, no one at the tiller. He'd rowed out to investigate and found the note. Back at his lodge, he called the sheriff's office and read the note into the phone while the sheriff's secretary wrote it down, word for word.

"Who ever finds this Boat Please Return it. am ending my troubles for ever. Ray Olson."*

The search plane circled above by the time Sheriff Seehuetter and two carloads of men converged on the scene. Three rowboats crisscrossed, finding no sign of Olson's body. The plane circled again and again, looking for blood-reddened water as Hamblin and Brooks arrived with the bloodhounds.

"We won't find him here," said Hamblin. I know Olson. He'd sooner go down in a fight than take his own life."

"But, for now, this is our only lead," countered Seehuetter. "He was here. Search both sides of the bay. See if the dogs can pick up a trail. I'm pulling two teams from the northeast quadrant and bringing them here. Olson has to be near."

"Sheriff!" came a shout from the road. "Someone called the state patrol office. Olson's been spotted in Park Falls!"

"Did they say when?"

"An hour ago."

"Impossible."

*Actual wording. Note found in stolen boat, June 18, 1939.

"There's another report that he's in Chicago," said Berard. "And the cities. We can't check them all."

"I'll tell the Price County sheriff to check out the Park Falls report. Chicago PD has men looking for Olson there. Same goes for St. Paul and Minneapolis. But I think as long as his wife is locked up here, Ray Olson will stay here. She's the bacon in our rattrap."

"So, you think he will try to break her out?" asked Berard.

"I'm counting on it. I've increased our watch at the jail. Soon as Olson takes the bait, we'll have him. Meanwhile, we'll scour the woods and patrol every last logging road. Catch him or not, we'll keep him on edge. Keep him on the move. Always awake, hungry, and tired. That, Jim, is how we will bring Ray Olson to justice."

A handful of posse members thought nothing of seeing Arnie Whitcomb's pickup ramble down Highway B. But, then, they didn't notice Olson behind the wheel. Ray was headed west—headed for Hayward—headed for the courthouse, the county jail, and for Delores. Ray pulled the flask of Cabin Still from his pocket, pulled the cork with his teeth, and held it up. "Here's to you, Baby. I'm comin' to get you. I got big plans for us, Doll. Big plans." He took a long drink from the bottle, then looked far ahead. A row of cars had stopped before a barricade stretched across the road.

"Dammit!" he said, making a gentle U-turn."

A glance at the rearview mirror told him he was not being pursued. "Must be some other road," he said as he laid on the gas.

A mile later, he turned north on a side road. It wound around lakes, crossed a bridge, then passed more lakes and ponds before coming to a T. Ray turned left to see a dozen cars and trucks parked along the gravel road. "Posse!" he said, slamming on the brakes.

Ray cranked the wheel, making another U-turn, then headed east down the dusty fire lane. Minutes later, he pulled up to the stop sign at County Trunk S, south of Moose Lake. A car approached from the left. Ray waited. The driver slowed, studying him as he went by.

"Too dangerous driving during daylight," Ray said to himself.

A half-mile later he pulled onto a side road, then down an old logging road. He backed the pickup off the trail between several balsams. In minutes, he had his get-away vehicle covered with brush, waiting for its next run. Back in the cab, he pulled the cork from the flask and finished it off. "From here on out, I'm travelin' only by dark of night."

Five teams of posse members methodically searched the woods near the resort where the suicide note had been discovered. Rows of thirty to forty men, fifteen to twenty feet apart, moved through the forest, under direction of their group leaders. With the descending sun nearing the treetops across the bay, Sheriff Seehuetter decided to call it a day. He joined Jim Berard to compare notes.

"Where do we go from here, George?" asked the undersheriff.

"Tomorrow we'll work our way around the flowage."

"Rough country. Plenty of swampland."

"Makes it a perfect place for a woodsman to hide."

"Some of that land is so brushy, so thick that our men could come within a few feet of him and never know it. Olson could sit tight, lay down in some spruce thicket and we'd walk right past him. Could be we're just spinning our wheels."

"Jim, as long as he knows he's being hunted, he'll stay on the move. Sooner or later, he'll slip up."

"It'll be dark in an hour or so. Olson's bound to try to use the cover of darkness against us."

"I know. The best we can do after dark is patrol the roads, guard the intersections."

"He'll need food, George. We should watch every store, every tavern, every restaurant."

"Good idea. I'll make a list of places. Tell Hamblin I said he should try to round up two or three volunteers to cover each place through the night."

A patrol car rushed toward them, the driver slamming on the brakes. A deputy jumped out.

"Sheriff!" he shouted, "we just got a call. Olson was spotted near Moose Lake."

"Impossible."

"Highway S, Sheriff."

"You sure this fella who saw him is reliable?"

"He said Olson used to work for him. Claimed he was dead sure it was our fugitive."

Seehuetter looked at Berard. "How the hell can he be here one minute and up at Moose Lake the next? I don't buy it."

"I'll take a few men up there to check it out, just in case."

"I doubt you'll see much more than red squirrels and blue jays."

"Say, George, you don't suppose Olson's got his sights set on robbing the Moose Lake Store?"

"Maybe. Go ahead and put some men on it. Overnight watch. But I think it's a waste of time. My money says Olson is here. Somewhere on the Big Chip."

Back in Hayward, a blue Chevy roadster pulled up to the Sheriff's office. A man wearing a plaid sport coat entered with a steno pad in one hand, a pencil in the other.

"Where can I find Sheriff Sea-hunter?"

"You mean Seehuetter?"

"Yeah. That's it. Seehuetter."

"He's out."

"My name's Abernathy. Sherman Abernathy. *Chicago Trib.* I'm here to do a story on ..."

"Yeah, yeah, so are the men in the next room," she said, pointing. "Go have a seat. You'll get the whole story around eight o'clock when the sheriff gets here."

Abernathy stood in the doorway, staring at twelve other reporters, each hoping for a scoop on the Olson manhunt. He pulled a chair up to the table. One reporter hammered away with two fingers at a portable typewriter. Three others played gin rummy. The rest simply sat.

"You fella's all local?" he asked.

"Duluth News-Tribune," answered one.

"Superior Evening Telegram," said another.

"True Detective Magazine."

"I'm local," said the next reporter. *"Sawyer County Record.* Just down the street."

"Me, too, more or less," said the next man. *"Ashland Daily Press."*

"Rhinelander Daily News."

"CBS Radio out of Des Moines."

"Pioneer Press. St. Paul."

"Wausau Daily Herald."

"Cap Times. Madison."

"Milwaukee Journal."

"New York Times."

"The Times?" replied Abernathy. "You mean to say you came all the way here from New York? Seems to me like you'd have plenty of copy to fill your police beat pages without ever having to cross the Hudson, much less coming out to the middle of nowhere."

"East coast crime is nothing like this. A big woodsman on the loose in the wilderness? I'm working the Tarzan angle."

"Huh?"

"Tarzan. You know, the ape man? Johnny Weissmuller? The guy who swings vine to vine like a monkey through the jungle yelling, 'Ah yee-ah yee-ah ye-ahh.'"

"Sure. Sure. Tarzan. I get it. But what I don't get is the angle."

"A new Tarzan movie just came out this week. I'm gonna paint this guy Olson as a backwoods Tarzan from wild and woolly Wisconsin. Big fella who lives off the land, sleeps in the woods way out west. Makes friends with the bear and the wolves and the wildcats so they don't eat him for breakfast. Get it?"

"Won't play in Rhinelander," said the man across the table. "Your description of Olson fits that of most or our readers."

"Way out west," said the Milwaukee reporter. "How typical! I can't get over how you East Coast writers always bundle Wisconsin in with Arizona and Montana. Last time I looked, Wisconsin was

197

still on the *east* side of the Mississippi River, bud."

The detective magazine reporter griped, "Aw, what's the diff? Ask anyone in Montana or Arizona and they'll tell you Wisconsin is back east. Who cares?"

"Say," said Abernathy, "exactly what did this Olson guy do to get into such a fix? I mean, you don't shoot a man in the head with a shotgun for nothing. Not even where I'm from!"

"I've been talking to some of the locals," said the man from Duluth. "Word has it that the first man that Olson killed, a fella named Cullie Johnson, owned a bar downtown with his two brothers. They keep a few slot machines in the basement for the tourists. Olson might have jimmied one of them open when nobody was looking."

"Naw, you got it all wrong," said the Minneapolis reporter. "See, Ray Olson moonlighted as a slot machine mechanic for some Chicago outfit. They have a string of slots in the local resorts. Cullie Johnson didn't want anything to do with this Olson. See, Cullie's machines come out of St. Paul. Cullie told Olson to stay clear of his bar or he'd make Olson's wife a widow. Least that's what I heard."

"That's just barroom talk," said Rhinelander.

"I knew Cullie pretty well," said the Hayward reporter. "If he made that threat, he sure didn't mean anything by it. He might have been a little rough around the edges, but Cullie wouldn't hurt a fly."

"But Olson couldn't know if Cullie was serious or not," said the Ashland man. "Olson ran in some pretty tough circles. He knew men who followed up on their threats."

"Like what?"

"Like three to five in Waupun, that's what."

"What's Waupun?" asked New York.

"State pen. Wisconsin's worst of the worst. Olson went in as an everyday lawbreaker. Came out with a doctor's degree—in crime."

"I don't buy that, either," said the Hayward newsman. "Olson's not big-time. Far from it. Maybe I wouldn't trust him with my wallet, but, compared to most crooks, he's small potatoes."

"Well, he must be one tough character, out there surrounded by a million mosquitoes. Most guys couldn't last a day."

"It's the ticks that I can't stand," said the radio man.

"Imagine this killer, Olson, sleeping out in the woods, rummaging for food. No fire, wet from the rain, insects swarming, biting him every chance. He must be quite the Tarzan, all right."

"And ducking more than two hundred armed possemen and a pack of bloodhounds to boot," said Duluth. "Say, maybe that Tarzan angle fits like a glove."

Abernathy laughed, patting the New Yorker on the back. "I guess that's why this guy works for *The Times* and we don't!"

"Aw, lay off," said the New Yorker. "At least I came up with an angle. Say, what do we do for food around here?"

"Try the Moose Café downtown," said the Hayward reporter.

"Moose Café? Do they really serve moose out here?"

"No, they don't serve moose, but they might serve you as long as you don't tell them you're from New York City."

Chapter 28

Five posse members scoured the southwest end of Moose Lake, looking for signs of the fugitive. They searched in vacant cabins, sheds, and along trails until sundown, when three exhausted men went home. The others remained to stand watch at the Moose Lake Store, hoping Olson would show up after dark. With army blankets wrapped around their shoulders, they sat leaning against trees, their shotguns across their laps.

In town that night, Sheriff Seehuetter walked into the press room at a quarter past nine.

"All right. First off, I've got two rules. Break either one of them and I'll see to it you are escorted to the county line and left there to feed the mosquitoes. First, if any one of you goes out to get interviews or photos, know you are totally on your own. Don't ask for an escort. I need every man I can get to be out looking for Olson. My advice to you is to stay put and let me bring the details to you. If you go poking around, taking pictures, looking for a scoop, you are risking your own lives.

"Next, I'll cooperate with you if you cooperate with me. Now hear this! I don't want any of you to mention slot machines anywhere in your stories. Not one word about gambling, see? It makes our resorts and our community look bad. Any questions?"

He stared into each man's eyes.

"Okay. Here's where we are right now. Two of my deputies were shot and killed by Ray Olson, formerly known as August Frederick Buelo. B-U-E-L-O. He's originally from Waukesha County, down by Milwaukee, and he's not the only crook to come from there, let me tell you. They seem to dish out more than their share. Olson served a stretch in prison for burglary, then ran out on another jail term and hasn't surfaced for years—until now."

"What can you tell us about the victims?" asked Duluth.

"Both of the men Olson killed were well-known and well-liked around here. Fred Scott ran a popular restaurant and bar called Twin Gables. Cullie Johnson owned a bar downtown along with his two brothers, Buck and Oscar. Both Cullie and Fred were cheerful, outgoing fellas who would help you out without batting an eye, no matter what. Hayward lost two fine men. I can't tell you how hard it was to break the news to their wives that both of them died at the hands of this scum, Olson."

"Sheriff," said the *Telegram*, "he has the whole Chequamegon National Forest to hide in. What in blazes makes you think you'll ever find him?"

"Oh, I'll find him. I have a couple hundred men working twelve-hour shifts. It's true that our bloodhounds lost Olson's trail today, but they'll be back on the job at first light along with the rest of us. Look, Olson murdered two of my men in cold blood. Two of my friends. He's out there—armed and dangerous. And, by God, I intend to bring him in, one way or the other."

In the moonlight, Ray hiked along the West Moose Lake Road to County Trunk S, a half-mile from the lake. He stopped every few minutes to listen for sounds of cars on the road, of doors closing, of men talking. His hunger and the silence of the night bolstered his courage, inspiring him to continue toward the Moose Lake Store. When close, he hid in the woods, watching and listening.

Twenty minutes passed. Seeing no one, he crawled on hands and knees to the building. He kicked in a cellar door and entered dark room, bumping his head on the low ceiling.

In the India ink blackness, he reached into his shirt pocket for a match. Kneeling, he struck the match on his zipper. Over and over he struck the matchhead. It would not light. Neither would a second match. Nor a third.

The fourth match came to life on the first strike. Holding the match high, Ray squinted, seeing he was in a crawlspace below the store. Above the damp, musty, shallow cellar, he saw a trapdoor. He shook out the match, pushed open the door, and climbed into the store. Ray stood in silence, letting his eyes adjust to the moonlight coming through the front windows. Then he went to work.

Three packs of Lucky's and a box of farmer matches filled one jacket pocket. Two cans of pork and beans filled another pocket. A bar of soap. A toothbrush. Toilet paper. Lotion for his mosquito bites and mosquito dope to help defend against more. From the cooler, cheese. In the till, he found some change and, nearby, candy bars and gum. Jacket bulging, he opened a loaf of bread, sliced slabs of meat from a sausage, opened a beer, and stood at the counter, eating his midnight snack. Ray popped the paper plug from a quart milk bottle, tipped it up, and chugged half of it down. He walked to the front windows, belched, and watched, stuffing a piece of Wrigley's Spearmint chewing gum into his mouth.

Seeing no one outside, Ray opened the door, then stood in the shadow of the doorway, surveying the road and woods beyond, chewing his gum and listening. Something felt wrong. Was someone aiming at him right now? Waiting for him to step out into the moonlight for a clean shot? He reached into his pocket for his lucky rabbit's foot, then turned.

Ray retreated to the dark interior of the store and left by the back door, staying low and avoiding the moonlight. He crossed the yard from tree to tree. Minutes later, with the Moose Lake Store well behind, he walked up the road to the Teal River. In the moonlight, he descended the bank and once again vanished into the shadowy forest.

The drowsy jailhouse attendant jumped when a man rapped sharply on the glass.

"Miss," said the reporter, "I'd like to see Delores Olson."

"She's in seclusion until they bring in her husband," she replied. "Only the sheriff can ..."

"George said it would be okay."

"At this hour?"

"You don't want to go against your boss's wishes, do you?"

"Well, let me check with him."

"Oh, I wouldn't bother the sheriff right now. It's late. He's had an awful day."

"Well ..."

"Aw, c'mon. Just a few minutes. I'll stay outside her cell. What harm can that do?"

"I suppose. As long as Sheriff Seehuetter said so."

"Yep, he said so, all right."

"You have any weapons on you?"

"Pencil and paper," he said with a smug smile. "The only weapons I've ever needed."

The jailer escorted the reporter down the row of women's cells, all empty save one on the end.

"Say, Delores, there's somebody here who wants to talk to you."

"Ray?"

"Don't we wish!" The jailer walked out. "You got five minutes, mister."

The reporter watched as Delores Olson climbed from her cot, straightened her clothes, and approached the bars of her cell. "Who are you?"

"Bert Williamson, reporter for the *Rhinelander Daily News*. Mind if I ask you a few questions, Mrs. Olson?"

"Look, mister, they haven't let me speak to a soul for four days, other than to let them know the food stinks and I need more toilet paper. Go ahead. Ask me anything you want. I appreciate the company."

"What made your husband snap?"

"What?"

"Why'd he fly off the handle like that?"

"You mean, take off on Deputy Hamblin? Look, mister. Ray didn't steal those plates. He ran off so he could find out who slapped those hot plates on our car, that's all. He'll find the jerk. And, when he does there'll be hell to pay. I sure wouldn't want to be in that chump's shoes."

"Jesus. You don't know."

"What? What don't I know?"

"Delores, Saturday morning, when the sheriff tried to bring him in, your husband shot two deputies."

"What? He wouldn't do that. My Ray cares about people. Goes out of his way to help. You're mixing him up with somebody else."

"He shot two men."

Delores stared at the reporter. "No, you got the wrong guy."

"Oh, it's him, all right. They're out looking for him now."

"Who? Who's looking for him?"

"Seehuetter, Berard, some other sheriffs, the posse."

"Posse? After Ray?"

"Seehuetter had 200 deputized men beating the bush for your husband today. And there's more coming tomorrow."

"Oh, jeez." Delores sat on her cot, holding her head in her hands.

"So, what's your story?"

"What?"

"I need a feature for my paper. Look, this is your big chance to defend your husband in the press. So, what's your story?"

"I don't have a story," she said, sobbing. "Sure, trouble seemed to find Ray from time to time. But deep down inside my husband is a good man. Send that story to your editor."

"What's his angle?"

"Angle? Ray doesn't have an angle. What's *your* angle?"

"That's what I'm trying to find out. Was your husband in with the mob?"

"The mob? No. Well, some slot machine work. Nothing to write home about, though."

"So, he's connected?"

"To the mob? Ray? Not a chance. He does some mechanical work for some guy now and then, that's all."

"The sheriff checked your cabin."

"Our home? What right does he ..."

"Seehuetter says they found tackle boxes, other stuff he figures Ray stole."

"That's all baloney. There's a guy who hired Ray to do some work, then didn't pay him. Ray took some stuff as collateral, that's all. To guarantee he gets his money, see? To make sure the guy pays up. The sheriff had no right to be in our home. We're just regular people trying to get through life like everybody else."

"So, if your husband is just a regular guy, why did he shoot those two deputies?"

"Ray must have thought they were out to kill him. They never should have done that. You corner Ray and he's like a raging wolf. Seehuetter and Berard should have asked me. I could have told them. And I could have talked to Ray—convinced him to face the music, clear his record. Oh, jeez. What's Ray going to do now?"

"Now? Right now he's out in the forest, running for his life. Running like a man wanted for homicide."

"Homicide? You mean ..."

"Neither of them survived."

"They're dead?"

"Stone cold dead."

She lay back on the cot, covering her eyes with her arm. "Oh, Sweetie. What have you done?"

"I'm sorry you had to hear this from me. Seehuetter should have told you."

She stood again, approaching the cell door. "Mister, who were they?"

The reporter checked his notes. "Both of them owned taverns. A Fred Scott and a Carl Johnson."

"Carl Johnson? You mean ... Cullie? Oh, jeez."

"What? What about Cullie, Delores?"

"Cullie's the guy who threatened Ray. Said he was going to make me a widow. Don't you see? Ray must have figured it was either Cullie or him. Oh, Jesus!"

She slunk back to her cot, holding her head in her hands.

"So, give me the story on Ray Olson, Delores."

"You want a story? You want the scoop so you can get your newspaper reporter money? Your bonus? Your promotion? Okay, you greedy bastard. Here it is! I'm his wife. I know him better than anyone. I know him and I can tell you this—he was always good to me. Tell Seehuetter that. Tell Berard that. Tell them not to hurt my husband. Tell them no matter what you people say, no matter what lies you print, Ray is not a bad person. Tell Seehuetter to give the poor guy a chance to turn himself in without fear of being killed. Tell him not to hunt him down like some animal. Tell Seehuetter and Berard if they hunt Ray like a trapped animal, he'll fight like one. Tell them! And tell everybody else. Tell everybody!"

Delores Olson sat on her cot, rocking back and forth, her arms wrapped around her knees. "God, please protect Ray," she sobbed. "He was always good to me."

Chapter 29

Half-past five Monday morning on West Moose Lake Road, Officer Hamblin waited in his patrol car, motor running. He looked at his watch, wondering when the bloodhounds would arrive. The sound of a panel truck rumbling toward him answered his question. Hamblin pulled onto the road, leading the way north to the Moose Lake Store.

"Olson was spotted in a Chevy pickup not far from here," he said to Brooks. "Might as well let your hounds check the store out, then we'll branch out from there."

One by one, the hounds jumped out the back door of the panel truck. They scoured the edge of the parking lot, then worked in the direction of the store when one of the hounds let out a chilling bellow.

"Well, I'll be damned," said Hamblin. "Maybe he *was* here!"

The other hounds soon joined in with howls that echoed across the lake. Seconds later, they stood near the open Moose Lake Store crawlspace. The two sentries who had guarded the store through the night looked on. Four more posse members pulled in to join in the hunt.

"One of you go wake up the storekeeper," said Hamblin. "Get him down here. He'll want to see what went on last night."

"You don't suppose Olson is still inside, do you?" asked Brooks.

"Not a chance. He broke in, raided the place, and snuck out. He's probably miles from here by now."

"We didn't see a thing," said one of the two sentries. "We were right there in the woods, not thirty yards off with a good view of the place. You sure he was here?"

"I'd bet my life on it," said Brooks. "My dogs never lie."

They circled the building, finding where Olson's scent trail crossed the yard a few feet shy of the sentries' hiding place.

"This can't be!" said one of the guards. "If he came that close, we would have spotted him for sure."

"Like I said, my dogs don't lie. You musta dozed off."

"Say! I was wide awake all night!" barked the other sentry. "Olson must be some kind of a magician,"

"Or maybe a ghost?"

"There'll be none of that kind of talk," said Hamblin. "We don't want folks to think this guy is any more than some frightened thug on the run. Meanwhile, there's no point in searching around the Chippewa Flowage any more. I'll get word to the others."

Inside the store, staring at the open bread bag and milk bottle, Hamblin made a call to the sheriff's office. "Get word to Seehuetter," he said. "Tell him the bloodhounds are on Olson's trail up by the Moose Lake Dam. He'll know what to do."

Ray jumped to his feet when he heard the hounds in the distance. He ran west, deeper into the forest, coming to a wide marsh. Not knowing if he could cross it, he turned north, hoping for a stream or a pond he could use to throw the hounds off their course. And on he ran.

Brooks and three posse members scrambled through the woods behind the bloodhounds, trying to keep up. They pushed brush and boughs aside, jumped over fallen logs, and splashed through wetlands. No longer able to see the hounds ahead, they relied on the dogs' loud howling to guide them.

Bounding through the woods now, Ray looked over his shoulder to see shapes, brown shapes, low to the ground, howling, and gaining on him. A stream ahead! He ran faster, sliding down the bank, splashing into the water, running downstream around a bend. He ducked under brush. Jumped over rocks. Rounded another bend, then climbed the bank, circled back and stopped. Below, he heard their howls as they searched downstream. He hid behind a maple as Brooks and the deputies slogged through the creek bottom, following the howls. As soon as they were out of sight, Ray slid down the streambank and headed upstream. Within minutes, the hounds found where Olson stood to watch them pass.

"He doubled back upstream," said Brooks. "He's close! We've got him this time. Let's go!"

Just as the men reached the stream below, raindrops began rippling the water. Within minutes, torrents fell. A lightning flash and a thunderclap followed.

"It's no good," said Brooks. "Bloodhounds can't follow scent in the rain. That's it. We're done. Let's get the hell outa here."

Ray worked his way upstream, hearing no hounds behind and nothing but the pounding of his heart and the rush of raindrops in the treetops. It was the closest he'd come to capture since the Bluesky sleep shack shootout three days before.

Ray slowed his pace. By mid-afternoon, Monday, a tired, completely drenched fugitive stood in the woods where he'd concealed Arnie Whitcomb's pickup truck. Worried that gangs of possemen might close in, he yanked the brush and branches from hood and fenders and started the motor. The logging road took him to a fire lane. The fire lane led to Highway 77. Seeing no one, he crossed the highway, following the road through the woods to the north end of Lost Land Lake.

Again he buried his truck in the brush, covering it with balsam boughs. He climbed into the cab and, windows up, maliciously swatted every mosquito. After killing the last one, he crowded his six-foot-two frame onto the narrow seat. And there, he slept.

Not far south, the posse checked cabins and homes around Moose Lake one by one. Acting on a phone tip, Seehuetter, Berard, and their men surrounded one of several small cottages downstream from the Moose Lake Dam.

"Ray Olson, this is the sheriff," shouted Seehuetter. "We've got you surrounded. Throw out your guns and come out with your hands up." Hearing no reply, he shouted again. "We know you're in there, Olson. Surrender or we'll shoot."

Still nothing.

"Last chance, Olson," yelled the sheriff as he loaded the teargas gun. He leaned out from behind the tree that hid him, aimed, and fired, lobbing the canister through the air, shattering a window.

"Watch it, men" shouted Berard. "He's bound to come out shooting."

Rain began to fall again as Seehuetter loaded a second teargas round, aimed, and fired. It flew high, bouncing off the roof and exploded. A white cloud of teargas drifted across the yard. A dozen possemen retreated to the woods. Seehuetter fired a third round. This canister broke through a bedroom window.

"Nobody could take that, Sheriff," said Berard. "Not even Olson."

"I'm not taking any chances, Jim. All right men," he shouted, "open fire!"

For a third time in three days, they blasted hole after hole through walls, hoping to end the manhunt. Glass breaking and wood splinters flying, they continued the fusillade. One round ricocheted off the chimney and struck a tree hiding a posseman.

"He's shooting back!" he screamed, diving to the ground. "Olson's in there and he's shooting!"

"Give him hell, boys," yelled Seehuetter, loading more teargas. "We've got him trapped!"

In the pouring rain, more ammunition relayed from behind fed the front line as the posse blasted away at the cottage. Occasionally, another round ricocheted toward a posse member or went in one side of the building and out the other, convincing yet another deputy that Olson was shooting back from inside. Finally, after three hours of siege, the sheriff shouted, "Hold your fire!"

"Cover me," said Berard, scrambling up onto the porch. On one knee, revolver in hand, he looked through a broken window. Seeing nothing, he moved to the front door and gave it a shove. It fell to the floor, the door jamb and hinges riddled with bullet holes. Berard looked in, then entered the small cabin. Glass shards, dust, and debris coated everything inside. The cottage and its contents destroyed, Berard walked out into the rain.

"Seems like we got another bum tip, Sheriff," he yelled. "What now?"

"Maybe he's in one of the other cabins," guessed a deputy.

"He's right," said Seehuetter, loading another teargas canister. "Safest thing to do is to smoke each one."

In the falling rain, the posse assaulted one cabin after another with teargas, evicting only a family of flying squirrels. Seehuetter called off the search. Berard and Hamblin assigned volunteers to guard roads, stores, and several of the resorts that had closed due to the manhunt. Their enthusiasm waning, the rest of the posse went home, some for the first time since the search began days before.

Ray remained cooped up in the stolen truck Tuesday as downpour after downpour drenched everything outside. That night, his patience gave out. He turned the key, started the truck, and drove out of the woods, balsam branches scattering along the road. Dark skies and rain veiled his late-night run.

He turned south on 77 and gunned the motor. "I'm coming, Doll," he said over the steering wheel. "I've been on the run too dang long and you've been in jail too dang long. It's time to make things right. Time for me and you to start over. Baby, it's time!"

Time can be your friend. Time can be your enemy. For impatient, spur-of-the-moment Ray Olson, time now tormented him. He'd slept the daylight hours away. Now, wide awake, he headed for town. Ray had no watch. The truck, no clock, no radio. He drove, not knowing the time. Not caring about time.

The pickup truck raced down the wet highway. It flew past the trail leading to cabins shot to pieces by the posse. It sped by the road to the Moose Lake Store and the bridge over the West Fork of the Chippewa River. Ray drove past the Chippewa Flowage and the road to Deerfoot Lodge and the home of John Bluesky, then past the Round Lake Resort and Peterson's Westview Resort.

"I'm coming, Doll," Ray said as the lights of downtown Hayward shimmered in the dark sky.

Rounding the bend, he saw two cars stopped in the road ahead, the glimmer of their brake lights reflecting from the wet blacktop. Just beyond, two more cars stretched across the highway.

"Roadblock!"

Ray slowed, then stopped. Another car came from behind. Nowhere for Ray to go but ahead.

Three men holding two deer rifles and a revolver checked cars. Just ahead of Ray, the driver of a black Oldsmobile sedan laid on the horn, shaking his fist at them. The deputies ignored him. He honked again. He flashed his lights. They waved the first car through. Ray heard the driver ahead rev his motor. Tires squealed as the Olds ran the roadblock, bringing shouts from the deputies.

"Pull over! Pull over!"

"Stop!"

"Stop or I'll shoot!"

The Oldsmobile gained speed. The driver laid on his horn again.

A rifle cracked. A deputy's pistol flashed and banged. One—two—three—four shots. The black sedan raced away. Ray saw his chance.

He pulled up and rolled down his window, shouting, "I'm with Berard's squad. I'll chase him down."

A guard jumped on Ray's running board. "Go! Go! Go!" he screamed."

"Hang on!" Ray grinned. He gunned the motor of the Chevy pickup and popped the clutch. Tires screeched as he turned south onto Highway 63, the deputy clinging onto the door frame. Racing through town, they passed the root beer stand, the Dodge dealer, the feed mill. Far ahead, the Oldsmobile pulled into a tavern, parking under a Fitger's beer sign. Ray followed, turning off the highway in time to see the driver enter the bar. The deputy on the Chevy's running board stepped off, following the driver inside. Ray pulled up to the Olds to see three bullet holes in the back fender. He slowly drove off, the county jail his destination.

"I'm comin', Baby. Nothin' can stop me now. Nothin'."

Miles away, a light glowed from a lakeside home on the south shore of Teal Lake. The kitchen door opened. A woman in her bathrobe placed a wooden box atop the hood of the car in the yard, then returned by flashlight, closing and bolting the door.

"Gracie, is that you?" The man's voice came from upstairs.

"Yes, Carl, it's just me finishing up in the kitchen."

"I thought I saw a light outside."

"You must have been dreaming, dear."

"No. I swear I saw a light. Say, do you suppose it's that maniac, Olson?"

"He's not a maniac. He's a man in trouble. He's probably starving and soaking wet and covered with insect bites, the poor soul."

"Poor soul? You mean you're on his side? For crying out loud, Gracie, he shot and killed two deputies, two good men."

"You don't know the whole story."

"And I suppose you do?"

"Well, I know you can't go by that awful story they put on the front page of the paper. Made him sound like some half-crazed killer out to mow down the whole population. I never met the man, but I doubt he did anything more than try to defend himself."

"He murdered Fred and Cullie. Isn't that enough?"

"You read the *Record*, Carl. You saw what they said. He was cornered in a tiny tarpaper shack, surrounded by nine men with guns. No place to run. Imagine what was going through his mind. Now he's been on the run for days on end without food, without hope, without a friend in the world."

"So, why were you outside?"

"Me? Outside?"

"I saw the flashlight. If it wasn't you, then it was Olson and we should call the sheriff."

"Oh, all right. It was me. I put some food out for the raccoons, that's all."

"When did you start doing that, Gracie? I've never known you to ..."

"Night before last, dear."

Carl came down the stairs. He unlocked the door. Flashlight in hand, he stepped outside. Seconds later, he returned.

"You're a good person, Gracie. I don't approve of you feeding the animals. But if you must, well, I suppose you must. A few leftovers, some bread and butter, an apple. That's fine. But the thermos of coffee?"

"Oh, all right. I'll go get the thermos. Where's the flashlight?"

"Hmm?"

"The flashlight. Where is it, Carl?"

"Um, I left it in the box. You know, for the raccoons. Now come to bed."

Chapter 30

A county jail is no place to be during a rainstorm on a dark, rainy, June night. Not outside. Not in.

Ray parked in an alley a block away. He pulled the Colt from under the seat and flipped open the cylinder to see six rounds ready to fire. Waiting for a lull in the storm, he looked up and down the alley, then left the truck. He stuffed the revolver into a pocket before walking toward the jail, trying to stay the shadows.

Ray made his way to the rear of the jailhouse. He expected the back door to be locked. It was. The thick wire glass window allowed a view of the hallway but not the cells. He crept around the building. A row of high windows, barred and sealed, showed him the location of each cell, but not the occupant. He found a side exit, again locked. A streetlight lit up his last option—the front door. Mustering his courage, he walked into the light. Through the glass, he saw two officers. Beyond them, the night jailer. Ray stepped back into the shadows. A phone booth across the street by the courthouse gave him an idea. He circled back around the building and crossed the street.

Ray flipped through the phone book, then slipped a nickel into the slot—a nickel he'd pinched from the Moose Lake Store cash register. He dialed the jail. It rang only once. Covering his mouth to muffle his voice, he spoke.

"This is Hamblin," Ray said. "I've been shot. I'm at Angler's. Behind the bar. Ray Olson's here. He shot me. Shot Seehuetter. We're trapped. Need help. Hurry!"

Ray bolted from the booth and ran across the street. He circled behind the jail again, reaching the corner near the front door just as the two guards rushed out and jumped into the nearest patrol car. The jailer stood at the open door, watching them speed off. Before the door closed, Ray stuck the barrel of the Colt in the jailer's ribs.

"You got two choices," he said. "Live or die. Pick one."

"Live! Live! Oh, Lord, please don't shoot! Please! I have a wife and kids. Don't shoot me. Please!"

"Who else is on duty?"

"Nobody. The others just left. Are you him?"

"Me? I'm John Dillinger's brother. I'm here for Delores Olson. You're going to help me get her outa here."

"She's gone."

"Gone where?"

"City jail."

"What?"

"Seehuetter moved her there in case Ray Olson tried to bust her out of here."

Olson raised the pistol. "You're lying."

"No! See for yourself. Look, mister, I had nothing to do with it. Oh, please don't shoot."

They walked past the cells on the women's side, all empty.

"Where's the city jail?"

"Two blocks down and one block over."

"Get in the cell."

"What?"

"Get in the dang cell."

"Okay. Just don't shoot."

Ray slammed the cell door. "I'm not out to shoot nobody. Never was. Tell that to your boss."

He knew the two officers would soon return. They'd have a key. Free the jailer. Warn the chief of police. Within minutes, the city would be crawling with lawmen, possemen, and newspapermen.

Ray ran to the truck. Side streets and alleys took him out of town, avoiding the roadblocks. His plan, if it ever was a plan, had failed—this time.

The rain stopped before dawn. But the trees dripped and the undergrowth remained soaking wet from the night before and a morning fog hung throughout the forest. Ray covered the truck as before, then slept, aware that search parties would be hampered by the weather.

After dark, driven by hunger, Ray set out on foot. Vacant cabins along Teal Lake provided little plunder. But the glow of a kitchen light drew him in. On the hood of the car he found a box of food, a thermos of coffee, and a flashlight. His prize in hand, he continued down the shore, wishing he could say thanks. The next cabin offered something more. In the dark, he drank from a half-full pint of gin found far under the sink. A can of peas and another of pork and beans added to his plunder and he was off into the dark woods again.

Undersheriff James Berard and forty men from the Taylor Lake Civilian Conservation Corps camp searched the river bottom south of Teal Lake. Side-by-side, ten to fifteen feet apart, the line of men stretched nearly 500 feet. Reaching the highway, the line turned to the northeast. They regrouped, formed their lines again, and trudged through the next 500-foot strip of underbrush.

Nearing the end of their fifth march, they climbed the shoulder of the county highway, waiting for Berard's order to break for lunch. Far down the roadway, beyond the Teal River Bridge, stood a tall figure holding a shotgun.

"Hey, fellas," said a corpsman, "looks like one of our men got himself turned around. What a stooge!" He waved the lone man to join them. The man didn't move. "Look at him! Just standing there like some kinda dummy!"

"Officer Berard," said another corpsman, "That guy down there—is he one of us? Or is he from Seehuetter's gang?"

Berard pulled his binoculars from his belt. There stood Ray Olson, waving a rabbit's foot.

"By God, that's him!" Berard shouted, raising his rifle. Berard took aim, shouting, "Olson! Drop your gun or I'll shoot!"

Ray grinned, waved, then strolled across the road.

"Olson! Stop or I'll shoot!"

Ray continued on.

Berard fired, the bullet blasting sand into the air behind the fugitive.

Ray jumped from the road, as another shot rang out. Then another, then a dozen more as the deputies fired. He bounded down the bank and along the stream, disappearing into the tag alder underbrush. Bullets whined and snapped through tree limbs above as deputies shot like madmen into the forest surrounding the fugitive. On Ray ran, laughing, again untouched and unharmed.

An hour later, Brooks and Hamblin led the bloodhounds into the same woods, finding Olson's trail and following it upstream. Olson's scent took the dogs and the men down steep banks, through a muddy bog, over windfalls, and through nearly impenetrable brush and briars. Hours later, they found his boot prints in the mud along the edge of a creek, but lost the trail where Olson had waded through the water. Not knowing he had doubled back, the search party stood foiled once more. They turned back, fighting through the same windfalls, brush, and briars. Exhausted, sweaty, and swatting aimlessly at swarms of mosquitoes, the men returned to their cars, abandoning their pursuit for the day.

In town, the jailer unlocked the cell door and swung it open, hinges squealing.

"Delores, there are two FBI agents here. They have some questions."

"Tell them I'm busy. I have a *Saturday Evening Post* here that I've only read nine times."

"C'mon, Delores. They have better things to do than put up with the likes of you."

"What do you mean by that?"

"Oh, pardon me. I meant better things to do than to put up with a jailbird."

"Look, I'm just another waitress at another backwoods resort. I haven't done anything wrong."

"Let's go, Delores. They're waiting in the conference room."

"Conference? Isn't that just like a cop? It's an interrogation room and you know it."

"Dammit, Olson. I don't want any trouble and neither do you.

Either you come with me and talk to these fellas right now or I'll bring them here and you can answer their damn questions through the bars. Take your choice."

"All right. For cripe's sake, simmer down. I'll come."

Two men in dark suits, one with a notepad, eyed her as she entered and sat, then waited for the door to close.

"Are you Delores Olson?"

"You're kidding me, right?"

"Miss, for our records, just answer the question. Are you Delores Olson?"

"Of course. Anything else? Can I go now?"

"Is your husband Ray Olson?"

"Yes."

"Do you know where he is?"

"Not here. And you can bet your bottom dollar he never will be."

"Come again?"

"He's too smart for you. You flatfoots haven't caught him and you won't catch him. Not in a hundred years."

"We're not looking for him, Delores. That's the Sheriff's job. If the FBI wanted him, we'd have him by now."

"Sez you. If you don't care if Ray's on the loose, then what are you doing here? I should think you'd want to be somewhere else. Anywhere else!"

"How long have you and Ray been married?"

"Going on four years, now. Why?"

"So, you were with him in '36?"

"Say, you're pretty good with your arithmetic."

"December twenty-ninth, 1936?"

"Yeah. We were out west."

"Tacoma, right?" The man watched for a reaction.

"Yes. How did you ...? Say, what's the deal? What is it you want?"

The man with the notepad handed her a police sketch of the Mattson kidnapper. "Is that your husband?"

221

Delores laughed. "Hell no, that's not my husband! He doesn't look anything like that."

"You sure? Look again."

Delores studied the poster. "Nope. Not him. Not a chance. You're barking up the wrong tree."

"When did you and Ray leave Tacoma?"

"Jeez, I don't know. Maybe March, April?"

"Delores, you took a train to Milwaukee at nine-thirty on the morning of January tenth, 1937, one day before they found the body of ten-year-old Charlie Mattson out in the woods, beaten, naked, and left to die in the cold. His body was frozen stiff, Delores. And he'd been molested before he died. The poor little guy's head was bashed in so bad we had trouble identifying him. Now you look at that picture again and you tell me that isn't a spittin' image of your husband. Look. Look!"

Delores broke down in tears.

"Look at him. That's your husband in the picture. You know it is!"

"Ray had nothing to do with that little boy being killed. Nothing. Ray's a good guy. He cares about people. He loves kids and puppies and kittens and rainbows and me. You bums are after the wrong guy."

"Yeah, your husband's a real gem, all right. Kittens, puppies, rainbows. Wouldn't hurt a flea—other than the two men he gunned down last week. Delores, he murdered two good men. Now why should we believe he didn't kill before? Kill a poor, defenseless child? Murder little Charlie just like he murdered Fred Scott and Carl Johnson?"

222

"Look. I know what you're up to. And it won't work. If you know what day I left Tacoma, then you know he wasn't with me. Ray left town Christmas Day. Left with some redheaded tramp. Saw the error of his ways and came crawling back a year later. Look. My husband may not be perfect, but he had nothing to do with that boy's death. That's all I'm going to say. Now leave me alone."

"We can offer you a deal, Delores."

"What deal?"

"How old are you?"

"What do you care?"

"Answer me."

"Twenty. Why?"

"Anyone party to the Mattson kidnapping faces a life sentence. For you, that means sixty, seventy years in prison. Think about that, sweetheart. Sixty, seventy birthdays behind bars. Every holiday spent all alone. The Mattson case has been open for two years. We want to close it. You can help us. We know Ray is tangled up in this. Give him up and we will see to it you are never implicated, never connected in any way—and you will never serve time for it. Never."

"So, in order to save my own skin, you want me to rat out my husband for something he didn't do?"

"You learn fast. We can keep you out of prison, Delores. Your husband pulling that trigger last week means he will either end up in prison for the rest of his life or dead. Ray wasted his life. Why should you waste yours, too? You can help us close the case and help yourself at the same time. What do you say?"

"So, that's it, then? I just tell you he did it and I'm free to go?"

"Free as a bird."

"Jailer!" she yelled. "Jailer!"

The jailer opened the door.

"I'm done talking to these pencil-pushing gumshoes. Take me to my cell."

"Think it over, Delores," said the man with the notepad.

"You've got a lot of living to do. Don't waste it in some six-by-six prison cell."

"I don't plan to waste it at all," she said as she left. "I plan to spend it with my husband."

Wednesday night, Ray slogged his way through a dense spruce swamp in the moonlight, then up a slight grade to a brushy, white pine cutover. Swishing at mosquitoes with a short balsam bough, he worked his way around a meadow filled with great stumps left from centuries-old pines. Skirting the clearing, he found the remains of an abandoned logging camp. The roof of the bunkhouse sagged, bent from age and many years of heavy snows. He entered the main cabin, hoping to find any morsel of food left by some transient hunter who'd used the camp for shelter. Finding none, he tried the cook shanty. Discarded tin cans, rusted stovepipes, and cast-off mess tables spoke of winters when able men harvested fortunes for the lumber barons. The musty air mixed with the stench of dead mice and rotting flour sacks. Disappointed again, he checked the other buildings.

Then, hungry, and exhausted, he slept.

Chapter 31

Early Thursday morning, day six of the manhunt, Brooks let his dogs out of the truck south of Lost Land Lake. Hamblin spoke to his small party of deputies as they checked their guns and doused themselves with government-issued insect repellent.

"Men, yesterday Officer Berard got a good look at Olson not far from here. We're going to try to pick up the trail again. Sheriff Seehuetter has fifty men to the northeast and Berard's men are searching south of Highway 77. The other three county sheriffs are not far west of here. We figure Olson is close by. Today might be our day. Okay, fan out. Let's go."

Hamblin, Brooks, and the bloodhounds left the gravel road, heading into the woods. The dozen deputies with them spread out in a line and kept pace. Hours later, they waded through a swamp and then plodded uphill, passing large, decaying white pine stumps in a meadow. Next, they crossed a clearing where the dogs again picked up Olson's trail. Howling now, the hounds ran ahead of the search team.

"Look sharp, men," said Hamblin to the deputies behind. "He could be waiting for us."

The bloodhounds led them along the edge of the clearing to the abandoned lumber camp, then ran straight to the cabin next to the bunkhouse. As the hounds circled, so did the posse, hiding behind tree stumps and dilapidated buildings. Brooks called off his dogs, taking them far back into the woods, beyond range of any gunfire.

"If Olson's in there and makes a break for it, we'll have him cold," said Hamblin. "But we shouldn't try to flush him out without more men to back us up. I need two volunteers to locate Berard and Seehuetter."

An hour later, Berard and his band of CCC men crossed the clearing and joined the others surrounding the camp.

"I think we've got him," said Hamblin. "In the cabin by that old bunkhouse."

"With few trees to hide him, he won't get past us. Not this time."

"Did you bring teargas?"

"Seehuetter has it," replied Berard.

The sheriff and thirty men appeared at the far side of the clearing. Soon, the lumber camp was covered from every possible angle.

"Ray Olson, you are surrounded," cried the sheriff. "Come out with your hands up and you won't be harmed."

Hearing no reply, he aimed and fired, lobbing a teargas canister into the cabin.

"All right men, look alert and keep your heads down. Ready? Set? Fire!"

A rattle of gunfire rose from the deserted camp. Gunsmoke and dust filled the air. On and on they fired into the building, reloading between volleys.

Sensing no return fire, Seehuetter ended the siege, shouting, "Hold your fire!"

"Another false alarm, sheriff?" asked Berard.

"So it appears. Hamblin, keep your sights on that window. Berard, you watch the door. I'll check it out."

Finding no one inside, Seehuetter returned to the firing line. "Someone was in there earlier. Probably Olson. Looks like we need the hounds again. Hamblin, go get Brooks. Let's see if we can pick up his trail."

The bloodhounds circled the cabin, then the cook shanty and bunkhouse, howling outside the doors of each. Men hid nearby, their rifles trained on each building. Seehuetter tossed in teargas canisters. With hammers half-cocked, the men waited, expecting to see Olson rush out, firing blindly. When the teargas finally dispersed, the buildings were checked as before with the same result. No murder fugitive. The dilapidated blacksmith shop, a collapsed horse barn, and a woodshed came next, each shot full of holes. And again, no Ray Olson.

"Brooks, Hamblin," said the sheriff, "have the hounds circle the camp. See if they can pick up Olson's scent."

"I doubt they will," said Brooks. "Between the teargas, the

gunsmoke, and all these men tramping around, there's little chance we'll find his trail."

"Right now, it's our best option," said Seehuetter. "Maybe our only option. He's bound to make a mistake. He's only human."

"I'm beginning to wonder," said Berard.

"We have to keep on him. Sooner or later, he'll slip up," Seehuetter added. "Or kill again."

"Not unless he's cornered," said Hamblin. "In spite of what they printed in the *Record*, Ray's no maniac. He's a fugitive on the run, and a smart one, at that."

"And I'm going to bring him in," said Seehuetter. "One way or another."

After three times around the camp in ever-widening circles, the bloodhounds picked up Olson's trail. The posse waited at the lumber camp while Hamblin, Berard, and Brooks followed the howling dogs. An hour later, they trudged through a dense tag alder lowland and onto a logging road. There, tire tracks told them they were done. Ray Olson escaped again, this time in a vehicle.

"Dammit!" growled the sheriff. "Someone gave him a lift. If I find out who …"

"Maybe not, George," said Berard. "Look where he parked. These tire tracks say the vehicle sat here for a good while. Probably overnight. Maybe two nights. If that's the case, it means Olson stole another car. He could be miles away by now."

"Or close by."

"Or on his way to get his woman," said Hamblin. "But wherever he is, my money says he's tired—tired of being hungry, tired of running, and tired of being alone."

Thursday night, Warden Plante took the call—a tip from a local farmer who found a dead deer not far from Moose Lake. Shot and dressed, the hide had been stripped off from the back of the neck to the rump. Plante loaded a double barrel shotgun with buckshot and drove to the scene. Half an hour later, he called Hamblin.

"Jim, there's no doubt about it," said the warden. "One clean shot. Looks to me like Olson used Cullie's .38 to get some steaks. Both back-straps are gone."

"Any sign of a campfire?"

"Not that I could find. I don't suppose a man in Olson's position would risk giving up his whereabouts by sending out smoke signals. He's too smart for that. I should know. I've been trying to pinch him for fish and game violations. Somehow he always stayed one step ahead of me. No, don't bother looking for signs of a campfire. Not from Olson."

"You suppose he ate that venison raw? Jesus!"

"Well, think about it. Fresh meat. Nothing wrong with it. A desperate man could do worse. I've heard of lost men eating bugs to keep alive. Raw venison sounds a whole lot better."

"How long do you figure the doe's been dead."

"Couple a days. Maybe three."

"Well, if it was Olson, he'd be long gone by now."

"That's what I figure, too."

"All right, Leon. Thanks for the call. I'll let our deputies know to watch for any more dead deer."

Friday morning, Sheriff Seehuetter called Jim Berard into his office. Both men stood at the window, staring at the rain, wondering what to do next.

Seehuetter broke the silence. "Jim, don't let this get out to those newspapermen, but, well, I don't have the slightest inkling where Olson might be. Not a damn clue. We know that he got himself a vehicle. Stole it, I'm sure. By now he could be in any county, any state. Anywhere."

"Could be," said Berard. "But he could still be here, too."

"This morning, I got a call from St. Cloud, Minnesota. Someone spotted him in a barber shop there. Another call came from Duluth. Said Olson was hanging around the railyard, trying to jump a freight. I've had tips from Mellen, Glidden, Park Falls, and Wausau. The sheriff of Eau Claire County said we can call off the search because they caught him and had him in custody. Turned out to be somebody else. Some drifter. By God, if I didn't know better, I'd say Olson was everywhere but here."

"We still have his wife, George. I doubt he will leave without her. My gut feeling is that Olson is out there somewhere, hanging around, waiting for the right time to spring her."

"Jim, the governor called. Said he's concerned about the terrible image this whole deal is giving the state. That was his word for it. Terrible. He asked me why we cater to so many gangsters up here. Can you believe that?"

"Oh for Christ sake! If Governor Julius Heil wants Olson captured, he should send us some state patrol boys, give us some support."

"That's precisely what I said. I told him I'd gladly turn this operation over to him."

"And?"

"That cooled him down. I have a feeling he doesn't want to risk getting involved. If he took over and Olson got away, it would make him look bad, cost him votes come November."

"Meanwhile, we get no support from the state. Wonderful! What about the feds?"

"The FBI has two agents here, but only because of some possible connection between Olson and a kidnapping out west. They're no help to us. More in the way than anything. No, this manhunt is still up to us. But it's gone stale. Jim, I think it's time to change tactics."

"So, where do we go from here?"

"Olson has a thousand square miles where he can hide out. Trying to drive him out of the woods like a buck caught in a deer drive won't work unless we have a good hunch where he's holed up. Not only that, our men are losing interest. Many have jobs they need to tend to. Others are just plain tired out."

"How many are still with us?"

"We've dropped from a couple hundred to around sixty. Just enough to post checkpoints on the main roads."

"I'd better set up a new schedule."

"I'm dismissing Brooks and his bloodhounds. We can't afford to have them sit in their kennels, day after day, hoping for a tip that never seems to come."

"Too bad. Brooks has some good trackers there."

"We can always call them back."

"Okay. What else?" asked Berard.

"Bring Delores Olson back to the county jail. I want her close to us and out of the hands of the city police."

"Got it. Next?"

"We'll continue to spot check empty cabins around the lakes. And we'll follow up on any local tips as best we can."

"Is that it?"

"For now."

"George, I don't have to tell you, after seven days, we're right back where we began. We could be at this all summer. You think the resorts can handle that? Think the local businesses can survive a summer without tourists?"

"I've heard the complaints. I wish I could help them. Right now, our success depends on Olson making a mistake. We have to be prepared to act and act fast when he does."

"*If* he does, Sheriff."

Seehuetter stared at the falling rain. "I'll say it again, Jim. Sooner or later, Olson will slip up. They all do."

Friday evening, hidden deep in the woods near Spider Lake, Ray poured another five gallons of stolen gasoline into the tank, then tossed the can into the brush. Wet and cold, Ray climbed in, swatted the mosquitoes, and started the motor. He let it idle, waiting for the heater to warm him and dry his wet boots. Nowhere to go, he sat back, eyes closed, waiting for his dinner to cook.

An hour later, a pause in the rain gave Ray a needed break. He lifted the hood. With his sleeve pulled over his hand, he removed a previously opened can of pork and beans from the hot exhaust manifold. With his jackknife, he stabbed the sizzling venison steak.

From his pocket, he pulled out a new lucky spoon and a fork, stolen from some cabin.

There, in the wet woods, washing his steak and beans down with a bottle of red wine lifted the night before, he dined, wondering what the suckers at the roadblocks had in their lunchboxes.

Chapter 32

Rain drenched the Chequamegon Forest all day Saturday, the eighth day of the manhunt. It soaked the woods, swelling the streams. The search, though not called off, stood suspended. Most of the possemen stayed home. Only the deputies manning roadblocks remained in the field. Clad in raincoats, they guarded the roadways. Spending most of their time in their cars, they listened to the radio, played cards, smoked cigarettes, and told the same old jokes over and over. They also checked every driver and passenger of every vehicle before allowing them to pass.

Meanwhile, Ray hunkered down in the stolen pickup at a different backwoods hideaway. By nightfall, hunger, impatience, and anxiety drove the stir-crazy Olson into the dark woods. Flashlight in hand, he tramped through the wet forest, searching for cabins to loot. Those nearby he'd already plundered, causing him to venture far, and forcing him to abandon his plan to return before dawn, Sunday.

Light rain falling again, Ray trudged through the woods, out of sight, parallel to Highway 77. He came to a driveway leading to a small house. Hiding in the shadows, he watched the yard. Seeing no sign of anyone, he snaked between trees toward the home. Lone tire tracks in the rain-softened driveway told him someone had left. Thinking whoever occupied that car could be in church, he leaned his shotgun against a tree, straightened his jacket, then pulled a comb from his pocket and combed his hair. Next, Ray boldly walked up to the door and knocked.

No one answered.

He knocked harder, looking through the window.

No one came.

Ray tried the doorknob.

Locked.

He looked under the doormat—no key. He felt above the door frame—no key. He stepped a few feet to the right and ran his fingers below the windowsill—no key. He slid his hand along the frame above the window—there!

Ray inserted the key. The bolt turned. He looked back over his shoulder. Seeing no one, he opened the door a few inches.

"Anybody home?"

No reply.

"Ma? Pa? Hello? Is anybody here?"

Nothing.

"My car broke down," he shouted. "Can somebody give me a lift into town? Hello?"

Hearing no answer, Ray slipped inside, closing the door.

Sheriff Seehuetter took the early Sunday morning call. Arnie Whitcomb returned from a trip to find his truck missing. Its description matched that of one reported seen by a road patrol near Spider Lake. Seehuetter, Berard, and twenty possemen rushed to the scene and combed the woods once more, unaware of the miles of rugged wilderness that now lay between them and their quarry.

"Found something," yelled a deputy. "Over here. Five-gallon gas can. Empty."

"Out here?" questioned Berard. "Must be him. Watch yourselves. He might be close."

"Sheriff," came a call from down the line, "you need to see this."

Balsam boughs lay scattered around a patch of broken brush. Tire tracks led away. The sheriff picked up an empty wine bottle. A deputy handed him a tin can. "We missed him, fellas," he said. "Olson was here within a day, maybe within hours, and we missed him. Dammit!"

"Think he'll come back, Sheriff?"

Seehuetter studied the scene for a moment. "No. He's long gone. All we can do is get word out to our roadblocks to watch for Whitcomb's pickup. That's it, fellas, I've about had it. Let's call it off."

"Sheriff," said Berard, "it's a quarter of ten. You hanging it up already?"

"Yeah. I'm dog-tired. I've been hunting him for ten days and nights. Jim, you take the men and join up with Hamblin. They're working their way around Upper Clam Lake. I'm done for today. I need some sleep."

"I'll have someone drive you home."

"No, I'll make it back to town. You need every man you got."

Miles away, a shotgun leaned against a tree near a small country home. Alone in the house, Ray hastily practiced a familiar line of work.

In the closet near the front door, he found a dark green raincoat and hat. He whipped the belt from the raincoat, then rushed into the kitchen. The salt and pepper shakers on the table went into a jacket pocket. He spread the raincoat out on the table. Ray opened the refrigerator door. Sausage. Butter. A jar of mayonnaise. All went onto the raincoat. A loaf of bread from the breadbox. A spoon, fork, and a can opener from a drawer. Flashlight batteries from another. Cans of peaches, beans, and SPAM from a cupboard. Food and supplies to enable his escape with Delores—get far away—make it to the state line and beyond.

From the bathroom, a bar of soap, a safety razor, and toilet paper added to his plunder. Then, grabbing the corners of the coat, he tied it all together using the belt. He hoisted the makeshift pack onto his shoulder and, stuffing a newspaper into his back pocket, returned to the front door.

Ray opened the door an inch, checked the front yard, then calmly walked across the lawn and into the woods. Grinning like a kid with an all-day sucker, he grabbed his shotgun and resumed his tramp through the forest, headed for his pickup-truck hideaway.

Sunday afternoon, a short, heavy man carrying a black leather bag crushed his cigarette on the porch floor and knocked on the door of George and Eleanor Seehuetter.

"Oh, thank you for coming, Doctor Callahan," said Eleanor. "I hesitated to call you on a Sunday but, well, it's just that I'm so worried about George. All week long he's been out there lugging that heavy gun around the woods, working himself to a frazzle, trying to stay in step with all those young men. When he's not out there, he's at the office. When he finally does come home, George can't seem to sleep."

"Oh, I'm just a little bushed, Doc," said the sheriff from the couch. "All I need is a cat-nap."

"I'll be the judge of that," said Callahan.

Ten minutes later, the Seehuetters listened to their family doctor's assessment.

"You were right, George. You are in need of a cat-nap."

"See, Eleanor? What did I tell you?"

Callahan continued. "A *long* cat-nap. Say, a week."

"What?"

"You're suffering from acute exhaustion. George, I hereby find you guilty of burning the candle at both ends."

"But, a week? Seven days? Nonsense!"

"You, sir, are no spring chicken. I want you to stay put. Get some sleep. Rest up. At least a week. Maybe ten days."

"Doc, you don't understand. I was there when this whole damn Ray Olson mess began. I took charge. I called the shots. Everything went wrong. By God, I have to be there when it all ends. I owe it to Cullie. I owe it to Fred."

"Balderdash! Your health comes first."

"I have a job to do. Men to lead. A murderer to capture before somebody else gets killed, see?"

"George. It's you who doesn't see. You, sir, are suffering from fatigue. You've reached the end of your rope. Unless you want the newspapers to report another tragic result from this ordeal, you will stay here and rest."

"I can't, Doc."

"You will, George. Doctor's orders."

Olson drove north before dawn Monday, soaking wet after a rainy night raiding cabins in search of gasoline and tools—supplies needed to escape with Delores. Nearing Clam Lake, he rounded a bend to find himself confronted by another roadblock. Too late to turn around, he drove on. A man standing in the drizzle waved both arms, signaling him to stop. His partner held a shotgun.

Ray spoke first. "Hamblin sent me. Sheriff Seehuetter's callin' everybody in. They got Olson bottled up down by the Moose Lake Dam and the sheriff wants every man he can get."

"It's damn-well about time! We'll head over there right now."

"Any more men stationed up the road?"

"Two men on the highway east of Clam Lake. Two more on County Trunk D to the west."

"Thanks for the tip."

"Say, it looks like you're soaked to the bone, buddy. How'd you get so wet?"

"Wet? Oh, yeah. I fell in a creek lookin' for that bum, Olson. I figure that's why Hamblin picked me to go spread the word. I think he figures I'm not much good in the woods."

"Hold on, buddy."

Ray's muscles tensed. "What?"

"I got a wool blanket in the car for you."

"Really?" said Ray. "Gee, that's swell of you."

"Here you go," said the guard, handing Ray the blanket. "You can drop it off at the sheriff's office later on."

"Thanks, pal," Ray shouted, driving off. "Good luck nabbing that no-good bum, Olson!"

Ray glanced at his rearview mirror to see the deputies heading south as he drove north. Miles later, he turned onto a remote fire lane, confident it would take him around the roadblock west of Clam Lake. Nearing Garden Lake, he pulled off the road near Castle Creek and backed into a thicket once more. Ray killed the motor and covered the truck with brush before climbing back into the cab. There, he wrapped himself in the blanket and slept the rest of the morning away.

Chapter 33

That Monday afternoon, the tenth day of the manhunt, Ray knelt by Castle Creek. He used the stolen safety razor to shave the ten-day growth from his face. He splashed water onto his hair, soaped up, and then dunked his head. Back inside the truck, he used the blanket to dry himself. A sausage and cheese sandwich provided supper, canned peaches his desert. Far from his previous hideout, he now looked forward to finding new cabins to loot. Content, Ray leaned against the door, waiting for nightfall, reading the paper he'd swiped the day before.

"The officers of Sawyer County are doing everything possible to apprehend this scum of hell," he read.*

"They got a lot of nerve saying that about me," he grumbled. "Scum of hell. All I want to do is bust Delores out, and never come back. It won't be long. First, I'll need a fresh car, a fast one. They're probably lookin' for this pickup by now. I'll find something else. Maybe tonight. Maybe tomorrow night."

Ray read on. *"A skunk in human flesh and a curse to society."*

"Boy! Would I like to get my hands on the good-for-nothing monkey who wrote that! And, get this! *A curse to society.* A curse to society? Okay, I s'pose they think that. Maybe I am, but not because I want it that way. No matter. They can't catch me. Long as I stay one step ahead, they're all just spinnin' their wheels." Ray flipped through the paper. "Swell. The Cubs lost again. What a bunch of bums."

In Hayward, twenty miles west, the chairman called the county board members to the courthouse that same afternoon.

"Gentlemen, I asked you here so we can take up this unpleasant business of that savage fiend, Ray Olson. This is day ten of the manhunt. Sheriff Seehuetter and his posse have failed to bring him in. So far, we've spent over two thousand of the taxpayers' dollars on bloodhounds, guns, and supplies. And yet we're no closer to nabbing him than we were when all this began."

*Direct quotes from the *Sawyer County Record*, June 22, 1939

"Olson's making fools out of us," shouted a board member.

"The longer this takes, the worse we all look," added another.

The chairman continued. "Everybody knows that most of the revenue that supports this county comes from the tourists who visit our resorts, taverns, and stores each summer. In fact, June, July, and August are the bread and butter months for most of our local businesses. Now, most of the tourists—our life blood—have left! And who in blazes can blame them? Every newspaper in the Midwest is running daily updates about the Chequamegon Forest manhunt. They say Olson is a madman, a crazed killer who will strike down anyone and everyone he comes across. Now, we know that's not true, but it sells papers, so they're bound to keep those stories coming. The tourists who read those damn newspaper headlines stay away. Gentlemen, vacationers won't spend a dime here, until we get Olson. This means our county revenue will suffer, too. And I hate like hell to say it, but this could go on all summer long."

"Mister Chairman," came a voice from the floor, "just what do you suggest we do about it? Seehuetter had over 200 deputized men in his posse. He had bloodhounds, a search plane, teargas, machine guns, grenades! For cryin' out loud, what else can we do?"

"That's why I called this meeting—to get your thoughts on how to end this damn carnival show."

"I'll tell you how," said another board member. "We can post a reward. Putting a price on Olson's head will attract bounty hunters—professionals who, for the right amount of dough, will track him down and bring him in, one way or the other."

"I spoke with the sheriff about that last week," said the chairman. "He's concerned about the risk it would pose to his posse and to the public."

"But don't we have a lot more risk from that killer out there? I say we offer a reward, if only to lure in some professional bounty hunters. For Pete's sake, let's get this over with!"

"Too dangerous," said the chairman. "A reward will attract more than bounty hunters. Regular folks will join in, too."

"So, what's wrong with that? Let's give our neighbors a crack at the loot, too. They might remember it come the next election."

"Whoa, now. Before you jump on that horse, just imagine crowds of folks loading their guns and going out in the woods to hunt for Olson. No training, no idea of what or who they might run into. Disorganized. Dangerous. First thing you know they'll be stumbling over each other in the woods, not knowing who's who. And, mind you, carrying loaded guns."

"Well, I say it's the best way to put an end to this Olson manhunt once and for all."

"Mister Chairman, what else can we do? We need to bring an end to this manhunt and get the tourists back up here while there's still some summertime left. I'm all for it. I move that we offer five-hundred dollars to whoever brings Olson in."

"I'll second the motion," said another board member, "but with a friendly amendment."

"And what's that?"

"Make it a thousand dollars. Dead or alive."

That evening, Ray stole along the shore of Garden Lake, moving unseen below windows glowing from lamps inside. A dark cottage became his first target. He crept up to the door and held his flashlight to the glass. The kitchen counter was bare. The door to the icebox was braced wide open. The room was empty. He left for the next cottage, also dark, then hid in the shadows of its garage.

Ray kicked the side door of the garage open. His flashlight beam reflected from a black Buick sedan. No keys in the ignition, ash tray, or glove compartment. None behind the visor. No keys, but Ray had a sneak thief's ace in the hole—time—plenty of time.

His flashlight trained on the dash, he painstakingly removed the ignition switch, pulled out and stripped the ends of the wires, then twisted two of them together. He shifted the car into neutral and hit the starter switch. The engine cranked and cranked. Ray checked his wires, twisting them tighter. He hit the switch again and the engine roared to life.

By the light of a half-moon, Ray opened the garage doors and motored slowly out the driveway and past the cabins with glowing lights. He turned on his headlights when he reached the town road. Minutes later he pulled onto a logging road, looking for a stand of balsams where he could shroud his trophy in pine boughs.

Headlights out now, Ray turned the car around, backing it in between trees. Before covering the car, he checked the gas gauge. Half full. Enough to get to Hayward, free Delores, and make it far out of town and beyond the state line. But they would need more food. Recalling a nearby tavern and store on Lake Namakagon, he again set out on foot in the heat of the late June night.

Sheriff Seehuetter heard news of the reward. That night, ignoring Doc Callahan's orders, he called in those left in his posse.

"Men, we all know that, in spite of all the time and effort you've put in, we are no closer to bringing Olson in than we were at this time last week. Unfortunately, the county board knows it, too. Much to my dismay, the board has thrown a shiny new monkey wrench into the gearbox. Totally ignoring my advice, they have posted a bounty for Olson. This means we're gonna have to watch for people out on their own, stomping through the woods, hunting for him. You might see them poking around vacant cabins. You might see them sneaking down logging roads with loaded guns, hoping to collect that reward."

"Some of them might even look like Olson," added Berard. "This is dangerous. Something we never expected. Never wanted."

Seehuetter continued. "For Pete's sake, fellas, be careful you don't shoot the wrong person. Deputy Hamblin has more copies of Olson's mugshot. Take a good, long look. Memorize that face. We can't afford to make any mistakes."

"We have no idea how many bounty hunters this will attract," said Berard. What we do know is that those who do show up will be armed. And, with a reward dangling over Olson's head, I shudder to say some of those bounty hunters might shoot at any shadow moving through the woods—our shadows, yours and mine.

Because of that risk, we want you to buddy up with someone and always, *always* stay close to that person. If some bounty hunter sees two men together, he's a little less likely to shoot."

"One more thing," said Seehuetter. "Your work was dangerous enough when we only had Olson to worry about. Now it's worse. If any man here wants to quit the posse, I understand. Just let us know so we can try to fill your shoes. Any questions?"

"Just how much is this reward, Sheriff?" came a shout.

"A thousand dollars."

"Holy cow! A thousand bucks?"

"That's what the county board decided."

"Sheriff, can we get in on that reward?"

"The board put no restriction on who brings him in or how it's done. That money is out there for whoever takes him down."

"Even those FBI agents?"

"Yes. Even the feds."

"Well then, I say we get back out there before they do. I could use a new truck!"

Tuesday morning, shortly after three o'clock, Ray hiked along Highway D, now dark and quiet. Nearing Nick Paulsen's Pebble Beach Resort, he waited in the shadows, watching for any movement, any light, any sign of life. Across the lake, an owl in the pines called. A fish splashed in the bay. The incessant whine of determined mosquitoes furnished the only other sound on this, the eleventh day of the manhunt.

Seeing no lights in the cabins along shore, Ray moved toward the building. During prohibition days the sign above read, "Pebble Beach Resort" and "Nick's Store," when two rental cabins and a grocery store served as a front for an illicit saloon. Now, seven years after the repeal of the Volstead Act, the word *Tavern* had replaced *Store*, as spirits still played a greater role in sales than did groceries. Tonight, both food and drink from Nick's would be Ray's prize. A small side window would provide his entrance.

His key? A two-pound rock.

Across the road, Gayle Sleight couldn't sleep. The heat wouldn't let her. She stepped from the cabin into the cool screen porch and sat on the swing in the moonlight. An owl called from the pines across the bay. An otter splashed near shore. Then, the distinct sound of breaking glass. She stood. Saw something. Someone. At Nick's! Under a window! Gayle ran inside her cabin.

"Sidney! Get up! Somebody's breaking in!"

"Here?" Sid Reynolds rolled out of bed, trying to make sense of his sister's words.

"No. At Nick's!"

"What?"

"Pebble Beach Resort! Look! Sid. Maybe it's him!"

"Him? Nick? Why would Nick break into his own store?"

"No, Sidney. Not Nick! Ray Olson!"

"The fugitive?"

"There's a big reward. Look. There he is. See him?"

"Jesus!" whispered Reynolds, grabbing his rifle. He yanked open a drawer. "Dammit, where are my shells?" He rummaged through one drawer after another. "Gayle, did you move my …?"

"No! Hurry Sid! He's climbing in!"

"Found 'em!" Sidney jammed a shell in the Winchester and ran out the back door. "Stay down, Gayle. And keep the lights out."

In his underwear, Sidney Reynolds peered around the corner of their cottage in time to see the intruder's feet follow his legs through the window of the store. Slapping at mosquitoes, he waited for the thief to return—waited for one, clean shot. Seconds passed. Minutes. Then, with his rifle sights trained on the window thirty yards away, something moved. Sidney pulled the hammer back.

"Gayle, can you see him?"

"No. Wait! Look!"

"What was that?"

"Food," said Gayle. "He's throwing cans and bottles out the broken window. Sidney! Get ready to shoot!"

In the dim, four-in-the-morning light, the brother and sister watched as groceries flew out the window, one item after another.

Then a six-pack, then several pints of liquor before all became still.

Tense, Reynolds waited for the thief to climb from the same window. He whisked mosquitoes from his face, arms, and legs, waiting for that one shot that would save the day. Make him a hero. Bring down a murderer. Win the reward.

"Gayle, I can't take these mosquitoes. Bring me my pants and a shirt. And a hat. And mosquito dope. And then call Frostman."

"Who?"

"Frostman. Bayfield County Sheriff!"

Dressing himself, Sidney watched the window. Forty minutes later, Gayle saw the headlights of two patrol cars as they sped toward her, crossing the bridge. They slowed to a stop when she waved a flashlight from the screen porch.

"He's in Nick's Tavern," she told Berard. "My brother and I saw him go through the window about an hour ago and we haven't seen him since. Sidney's behind our cabin with his rifle aimed at the window, waiting to shoot when Olson comes out."

"Are you sure it's Olson? How do you know?"

Gayle didn't answer.

"Go tell your brother he is not to shoot! Tell him! Now!"

The possemen surrounded the store, hiding in the shadows.

"You in the store," shouted Berard. "Come out with hands up!"

Silence.

"This is the police. We have you surrounded," Berard yelled. "Surrender now and you won't be hurt!"

More silence.

"You think we should shoot?" asked someone.

"No," Berard said. "If it was Olson, he's long gone by now."

"How do you figure?"

"He knows better than to stick around."

"And, if it's not Olson?"

"Think about it. Anybody else would have jumped out of that same broken window and Sidney would have plugged him. Would have shot the wrong guy, see?"

"So, what should we do?"

245

"Cover me, men," said Berard. "But mind your nerves. I'd just as soon not be the one getting shot."

With Reynolds and eight possemen aiming at Nick's Tavern from all angles, Berard bolted. He bounded up the steps. He kicked in the front door. No shot rang out. No fugitive attacked.

Nine men scoured Nick Paulsen's store inside and out, trying to determine the thief's escape route.

"Found something!" Reynolds shouted from outside. "Looks like Olson went northwest along the lake."

Other deputies joined Sidney, holding his rifle in one hand, a pound of butter in the other. "He must've dropped this on his way."

After analyzing the clues, Berard concluded the culprit pitched bottles, cans, and boxes of food out the broken window, then left by a side door. He then circled the store, probably on hands and knees, scooped up his bounty, and headed northwest, unseen and unheard.

"I want four men to take my car two miles up the road," said Berard. "Post there while the rest of us fan out and work our way toward you. He's bound to be hiding somewhere near Mumms Bay or Eagle Point. With luck, we'll flush him out like a scared rabbit."

Berard's men searched north along the east shore of Lake Namakagon, hoping to trap Olson. But, although Ray had thrown a pound of butter that way, he had not escaped up the shore. Instead, he'd retraced his steps, heading back to his new hideaway.

Now, with Tuesday's rising sun peeking through the trees, he tossed his pack of goods into the Buick's back seat and climbed in for a breakfast of cold bologna and root beer. A thunderstorm ushered in another all-day rain. Ray didn't mind, comfortable in the plush rear seat of his new car. After a long snooze, he turned on the radio, tuned in a ball game, and spent the afternoon growling and grousing at the Cubs and Cardinals. Later, he opened a can of beans and a box of crackers, washing it down with warm beer before setting out on foot—a final quest to stock up on food and supplies before rescuing his sweetheart.

Chapter 34

The telephone at the Seehuetter home rang and rang before the sheriff picked it up, James Berard on the other end.

"George, I'm up at the Pebble Beach Resort on Lake Namakagon. Olson broke into Nick's Tavern around four this morning. Got away with food, some supplies, some change Nick left in the till."

"Are you sure it was him?"

"No question about it. He left on foot. We figure he's still nearby. I have three patrols scouring the area, looking for signs."

"Jim, I'll try to get ahold of George Brooks down in La Crosse and see if I can talk him into flying his dogs up again. Now that you have a hot trail, his bloodhounds might put an end to this nightmare. Meanwhile, you might want to call in the Taylor Lake CCC boys again. They know that Namakagon and Grandview country better than we do."

"Sheriff, are you coming up?"

"'Fraid not. Much as I'd like to be there, Doc Callahan put me in shackles for a while. I guess that means you're in charge now."

"All right. I'll call Taylor Lake. You get some rest. And tell Eleanor I said not to take any guff from you."

"Look, Jim, I don't care how you do it, just get Olson, see?"

"I'll do all I can, George."

"Get him!"

Wednesday night, knowing the road would be watched, Ray pirated a rowboat from a vacant cottage on Garden Lake. With an empty packsack along, he rowed for the cabins and cottages lining Anderson Island's east shore. Stroke by stroke, he slipped through the water, watching the headlights of cars motoring along County Trunk D. He passed Pebble Beach, Burgundy Point, and Forest Lodge. With lights from Lakewoods Resort to his left, he rowed north, passing Paine's Island. A south wind helped him skirt Eagle Point. With the lights of the Pla-Mor Tavern on his right, he rowed for the channel between the mainland and Anderson Island.

Approaching the bridge, he spotted two men checking cars. Ray smiled and waved, then changed course. The west side of Anderson Island would have to do.

Rowing north, midway between Junek's Point and the island, he watched ahead for dark cabins. But along Chicago Avenue, yard lights and headlights warned him to stay away. On he rowed, crossing the lake to Missionary Point, where he tied the boat to a tree, double-knotting the rope. Leaving his shotgun in the bottom of the boat, he explored the shore.

As his first plunder, Ray chose a large farmhouse with no lights burning, no car in the driveway. He climbed the back steps and knocked on the door of the home of the Victor Anderson family. Hearing no reply, he knocked harder. Sliding the blade of his knife between the lock and the doorjamb, he felt the latch release.

"Anybody home?" he yelled. "Ma? Pa? Anybody?"

Confident he was alone, Ray lit a Lucky Strike and went to work filling his packsack with canned goods. Next, he made a sandwich of bread from the breadbox and ham and cheese from the icebox. He washed it down with cold milk before fading into the night once more.

Down the shore, Victor, his wife, and their twin boys visited friends who had rented one of the Anderson's summer cabins. They chatted while listening to a boxing match on the radio. Heavyweight champ, Joe Louis, after being knocked down in the third round, came back in the fourth to knock out Tony Galento.

The fight over, fifteen-year-old Dean and Del, bored with the adults' conversation, asked to walk home. A quarter-mile later, they crossed the yard and climbed the back steps to find the kitchen door unlocked.

"Looks like Pa forgot to lock up," said Dean.

"Gee-whiz," said Del. "You'd think he'd be more careful with that madman on the loose."

"Wait! You smell that?"

"Cigarette smoke?"

"Del, look at the table. Milk. Ham. Ma's bread! Somebody's in the house! Cripes! Let's get outa here!"

On the way out, Del eased the door shut, locking it. "Run for it, Dean!" he whispered as they jumped off the back porch. The twins sprinted across the yard. Glancing over their shoulders again and again, they raced back up the road.

"Ma! Pa!" Dean flung the front door wide open. "Somebody's in our house!"

"There's dirty dishes on the table!" added Del, catching his breath.

"Well!" said their mother. "I certainly would not leave any dishes unwashed."

"Ma, you don't get it!" shouted Dean. "We smelled cigarette smoke!"

"It's that outlaw!" said Del. "Pa, he was in our house! I know it! Might still be!"

"Del's right, Pa! You gotta call the sheriff!"

"Hold on, boys," said their father. "Sounds to me like your imaginations are playing games on you."

"No, Pa! Look! The door was unlocked. There were dirty dishes and stuff left on the table. We smelled cigarettes. I'm tellin' you, somebody broke in. Somebody was inside our house! Who else could it be but that outlaw who robbed Nick Paulsen's place?"

"Victor," said their mother, "Delbert is right. We should call the sheriff."

"All right. It won't hurt to call. I'll go have a look-see."

"Can we come, Pa?"

"You know the answer to that, boys. You help keep an eye on things here. I'll be right back."

Along the water's edge, Ray unloaded the goods from his pack into the boat, then walked up the shore to find another cabin to raid. Ducking below sight of the windows, he avoided the glow of the lamplight coming from the first cabin. The next two cottages stood dark. No cars. No tourists. Ray walked up the steps onto the porch of the second. He pulled his cigarettes from his pocket. He struck a match on the door jamb, lit the Lucky Strike and waited, listening, looking, smoking his cigarette to the butt before he knocked. No one answered. He turned the knob. The door opened. Ray crushed out his Lucky and walked in like he owned the place.

"Anybody home?"

No answer.

"Ma? Pa? Anybody?"

No answer.

His flashlight lit the pantry. As Ray filled his pack with crackers, candy bars, biscuits, and bananas, he heard the crunch of footsteps on the gravel pathway. Packsack in hand, he ducked into the bedroom seconds before a young couple entered. Flashlight off, Ray hid behind the half-open door, listening and watching through the crack between the hinges.

The woman flipped on a light switch and snuffed her cigarette out in an ashtray.

The man opened the pantry door. "I'm having another drink," he said. "Join me?"

"Sure. Pour us a nightcap, honeybunch." She flopped onto the couch with a magazine.

"Now, where'd that bottle of gin go? I could swear it was right here when we left."

"Oh, keep looking, Harry. You'll find it."

"Sometimes I think little elves sneak in and hide things when we're gone."

"Maybe it's the shoe fairies come to help clean up by drinking your gin!"

"You're a funny gal, Violet. Almost as funny as a bottle of gin vanishing into thin air."

"It's there, silly. Keep looking. Okay?"

Harry rummaged through the pantry. "There ought to be a law against elves and fairies stealing my gin!"

"Look under the sink."

"Nope. It's gone, I tell you."

"Really?"

"I'm calling the cops!"

"Hang on, I'll come help find it." She rose from the couch.

"Say! Here it is!" he said. "The elves hid it in the icebox."

"Oh, my stars. Honey, I completely forgot I put it there."

"So, you've joined the ranks of the elves and fairies?"

"Sorry."

"All is forgiven, seeing as how I found the gin. Now, where do you suppose the elves hid the highball glasses?"

"In the cupboard, Harry."

"Where?"

"In the cupboard."

"Where?"

"In the cupboard, dear. C-U-P-B-O-A-R-D."

"Here they are, Vi. They were in the cupboard."

"Say, you ever wonder why it is that, when you're searching for something, it always shows up in the very last place you look?"

"How's that?"

"Oh, never mind. Fix us a drink."

From behind the bedroom door, Ray watched the couple slump back into the sofa, kick off their shoes, and finish off the bottle of gin. Violet then tottered toward the bedroom.

Silently, Ray pushed far back into the corner. With soft light shining in from the next room, he watched Violet struggle to strip off her sweater and slacks. Laughing, she fell back onto the bed.

"Time for bed, Harry," she said with a slur.

Harry turned off the light and followed Violet into the bedroom. In the dark, he pulled off his shirt and wriggled out of his trousers, leaving them on the floor near the bed. He flopped onto the mattress, pulling the blanket over both of them, unaware that a fugitive wanted for a double homicide stood only feet away, afraid to make a sound or move a muscle.

Undersheriff Berard got the call around ten-thirty that night. Someone had broken into Victor Anderson's farmhouse, four miles north of Nick's Tavern. Though he questioned validity of the report, it was his only lead. He hand-picked a small team of men.* Together, they would surround the Victor Anderson farm in the dark. If the report held true, the prowler, perhaps Ray Olson, would be flushed out at first light.

In a lakeside cabin not far from the Anderson farm, Violet and Harry quietly cuddled under the covers while Ray watched from a dark corner a few feet away. Then, as silent as a cat stalking a bird, he crept closer and closer to the couple. Inches away now, he slowly reached down, listening to the heavy breathing coming from beneath the blankets. Harry's wallet the target, Ray picked up the trousers. Harry's car keys slipped from a pocket, striking the floor.

"Harry!" said Violet from under the covers.

"Hmm?"

"I heard something."

"Must've been those shoe fairies, Vi."

Ray's heart pounded. Step by step, he silently backed out of the room. Reaching the kitchen, he pulled the wallet from Harry's trousers, stuffed it into his packsack and headed for the door.

Ray passed the dark cabin and the one with the lights glowing, then heard voices ahead. Two men. Coming his way. Nowhere to go, Ray walked up to the lighted cabin door and knocked. A man holding a handful of playing cards answered the door. Inside, other players sat around a table.

"Yes? What is it?"

"Oh, uh, I'm lost, mister. I've been rowin' and rowin', tryin' to find my way back to Lakewoods. Can you point me in the right direction?"

*Constable Ernie Moore, Tom Farley, Frank Flowers, Otto Huddleston, Bill Bernohoft, and Frank Junek, all from Cable. From Hayward, Police Chief Fred Sieh, Bob Couture, Rod Ogren, Ted Bloom, and Clyde Johnson. Led by Sawyer County Undersheriff James Berard. [According to *Official Detective* magazine.]

"Why, sure." The man with the cards walked onto the porch with Ray. "See them lights shining through the trees on the island?"

"Yeah."

"Just head straight for them lights, pal."

The two men passed by.

"Then, when you get beyond the island and out a few hundred yards more, you'll see a smaller island. Champagne Island, they call it. Lakewoods is a bit to the right. Watch for a Hamm's Beer sign, pal."

"Gee, thanks, mister," said Ray, turning toward the lake. "Y'know somethin'? You're a real lifesaver."

Far down the shore, Berard spoke with his men, laying out his plan. Someone approached. Twelve guns suddenly whipped around, hammers clicking back, all muzzles trained on Victor Anderson as he appeared in the beam of Berard's flashlight.

"Guns down," ordered Berard. "Jesus, Victor! You damn near got yourself killed! What the hell are you doing out here?"

"I'm out protecting my family, that's all."

"Looks to me like you're trying to horn in on the reward," said Moore. "Go back home, Vic."

"I got a right to be here as much as you, Ernie."

"That's enough," said Berard. "Okay, Victor, there's a way you can help. Take your rowboat out into the bay. If the prowler tries to make his escape by water, give us a good holler."

"What if he shoots?"

"It's probably not Olson so there's not much chance of that. But, just in case, stay out of range of his shotgun. You have a rifle, and the advantage. If it is Olson and he shoots, well, use your best judgement. But don't put yourself at risk. That goes for everyone. Now, spread out. Surround the farm and wait till first light. At precisely four-thirty, we move in. Watch that you don't shoot at any tourists or each other. And one more thing. Stay alert. Remember what happened at the Bluesky shack. Don't let it happen to you. Any questions?"

"So, is Victor part of this posse, or not?" asked Frank Flowers.

"Yes. You got a problem with that, Frank?"

"Nope. Not a bit. It's just that, well, Victor makes thirteen."

"Come again?"

"Thirteen men on the thirteenth day. Kinda funny, don't you think?"

"Not funny at all, Frank. Okay, men, move out."

Three lawmen and nine volunteer possemen silently slipped through the dark woods. Working in pairs, they surrounded the farm. Down the shore, Victor Anderson shoved off in his boat. He rowed out through the fog, his loaded deer rifle beside him.

Meanwhile, up the shore, the man holding his playing cards watched the late night visitor disappear in the darkness. When near the water's edge, Ray turned, following the shoreline toward his boat. His quest for supplies satisfied, he would now head back to the Buick to finalize his plan to rescue Delores. Crickets chirped from the forest floor. An owl hooted from the woods across the lake. And a man coughed. Ray froze.

Seconds, then minutes lapsed before he realized not one, but two men hid between him and the stolen rowboat. He backed up slowly, wondering if there could be more. Ray turned, retracing his steps. Above the bank, he saw a tractor shed—part of Victor Anderson's farm. There, he could hide until the faintest pre-dawn light would show him the best way to his boat, his chance to steal away unseen and unheard.

The fog grew thicker. Frank Flowers saw someone behind a woodshed and raised his rifle. The ghostly vision faded into the fog. Frank watched, rifle ready.

Nearby, Tom Farley whispered to Frank, "Look! Over there. Next to Victor's car. Something's moving."

Frank saw a dim figure thirty feet away and moved in closer.

"Tom, did you see him?"

"Don't know. Maybe it's just my nerves."

"I hear ya, brother."

Minutes crawled by. Farley squinted at his pocket watch.

"It's four-fifteen, Frank," Farley whispered. "Still a quarter-hour to go."

Beneath the faint glow of the eastern sky, Flowers saw a face appear in the doorway of the shed. "Who's there?" he said. "You in the woodshed! Come out or I'll shoot!"

Creeping low, Berard and Moore joined Frank Flowers and Tom Farley.

"I got a look at him," said Frank. "I'm pretty sure it's Olson."

"Pretty sure?" asked Berard. "Not good enough.There's no room for error. We'll wait for more light."

"Wait?" whispered Moore. "And lose him? I say we rush the bastard right now."

"No. Too dangerous. We wait," said Berard. "Besides, there's no way for him to get off this point unless it's through one of us."

"I'm not so sure," said Farley. "Look what happened at the Bluesky ..."

"There!" said Flowers. "In the woodshed."

The men peered through wisps of fog to see a face staring back at them from the shadows. As quickly as it appeared, it vanished.

Berard checked his watch. "The others are counting on us to follow the plan. Eight minutes more."

Seconds crept slowly along. Moore moved to the right for a better view and a clearer shot. Flowers and Farley moved up. Berard checked his watch. Other deputies moved closer.

"It's time." Berard pocketed his watch and shouted, "Ray Olson. We have you completely surrounded. It's over. You don't stand a chance. Surrender now and I'll see to it that no harm comes to you."

Again Olson's face appeared in the doorway—then vanished.

"Come out with your hands up, Ray," shouted Flowers.

The air dead-still and a veil of fog masking the dimly lit landscape, they waited, crouched behind cover. Knees ached. Hearts pounded. Eyes strained to see through the fog.

The shed door flew open. A man darted across the yard.

"Did you see something?" shouted Farley. "Was that him?"

255

"Where?"

"Headed for the woods!"

"No! He's in the shed!"

"I think he ran toward those trees out on the point!"

"Move in, men!" Berard shouted.

A dozen deputies closed in on the scene, unsure where Olson had gone. Berard kicked the shed door open, finding only a khaki-colored packsack, two banana peels, and a half-eaten Baby Ruth.

"Look sharp," shouted Berard. "He knows we've got him boxed in. Farley, move left. Otto, Clyde, keep an eye on the road. Ernie, Frank, watch the slope to the lake. He might try to run along the shore. Everybody stay low."

Guns raised, six of the twelve men took new positions overlooking the thicket of trees. Moore moved closer to the lake, stopping a few yards above a rowboat tied to a tree along shore. Like a soft, gray glove, fingers of fog drifted in. Everyone remained still. Watching. Listening. Nerves on edge.

Crickets chirped. A dog at a far-away farm barked. A rooster crowed.

"There!" yelled Berard. "Running for the shore! Olson! Halt!"

Ray ran with all his might and all his heart, bounding like a deer over brush and between trees in the dim light. He raced across an opening through thick and thin fog. Forty yards. Fifty. Sixty. Closing in on his boat now. As he crested the bank above the lake, a gunshot shattered the quiet morning. Then two shots—three—four. Then a clattering of rifle fire, shotgun blasts, and the rapid, rhythmic rattle of a Tommy gun. The sound of chaotic gunfire echoed from across the lake.

Unscathed, Ray raced for the water's edge, vaulting through the air toward the boat when a single buckshot pellet struck his neck. He lurched, sliding down the bank. Blood from the wound soaking into his collar, Ray jerked at the rope, trying to untie the boat.

Standing only a few yards above, Ernie Moore took aim and fired, then levered another round into the chamber, firing again. And again. And again. And again until his rifle emptied. One of his seven rifle bullets tore through Olson's gut and pelvis. Ray reeled, the Colt .38 revolver flying from his belt into the lake. He stumbled, reaching for the boat, but fell short. Ray landed face down on the sandy shore, half-in, half-out of the water as a load of buckshot tore into his ribs.

"I got him!" shouted Flowers. "I got Olson!"

"Me too," Moore yelled.

"I hit him two or three times!" said the next guy.

"You'll find my lead in him, boys," another man boasted.

Within seconds, the posse stood over Olson, their hearts pounding, their muzzles pointed at him, hammers back, safeties off, each man eager to fire, hoping for any prompt or provocation.

"Guns down, men," said Berard. "Olson's done running."

Helpless, stretched out belly-down near the boat, Ray coughed up blood. "Oh, please … pull me onto … shore."

"Ogren, Farley, pull him up," said Berard. "Go easy."

They pulled the gut-shot fugitive from the blood-stained water, dropping him face down.

"Roll me over," Ray begged. "Let me see … the sunrise."

Berard handed his Tommy gun to Flowers before stooping to roll Olson onto his back.

Ray looked up, into the eyes of the undersheriff. "I seen you … before. By the bridge. You took a crack … at me."

"I did."

Ray grinned. "Missed … pal."

Victor Anderson joined the deputies, followed by a handful of tourists from nearby cabins.

"All right," said Berard. "No point in crowding him. Everyone step back. Victor, I want you to call Cable. Get ahold of Doc Neer. Tell him we need him here right away."

"What the hell for?" someone yelled. "Let him die."

"Victor, go call Doc," Berard repeated. "And call Sheriff Seehuetter. He needs to know."

Then, turning to Ray, "Who helped you escape?"

"No … nobody."

"I don't believe you. Someone *must* have helped you."

"Just ... me."

"What about Tacoma?" asked Chief Sieh. "Did you murder little Charlie Mattson?"

Ray replied with a rasping moan.

The crowd of spectators grew, gawking, staring, some laughing.

A newspaperman appeared out of nowhere. "Officer Berard, I need to document this for the *Evening Telegram.*"

"Go ahead. Take your pictures." He turned to Ray again. "Olson, the Mattson boy. Did you have a part in it?"

"I'm ... thirsty. So thirsty."

"Otto, find a bucket," said Berard. "Get this man some water."

A boy looked up at his father. "Pa, is the bad guy gonna die?"

"We hope so, Freddy," someone shouted from behind.

"Oh, that poor man," cried a woman. "Show some mercy."

"Like the mercy he showed Fred and Cullie?"

"That's enough!" said Berard.

More people gathered, crowding in for the photos.

"All right, folks," said the newsman, "I want those deputies who captured Olson to gather behind him. Now, squeeze together and smile at the camera. That's it. Hold still." The camera flashed. "Got it! Okay, let's try another. This time, wave at the camera."

Berard questioned Olson again. "Ray, did your wife know about the cabin break-ins?"

"Aw, let her ... go. She's ..."

"What, Ray? She's what?"

"Just ... a kid."

"Did Delores help you steal the Plymouth?"

"She never done ... nothin'," he replied in a guttural tone. "Let her ... go."

"Can you tell me about Charlie Mattson?"

"God, I'm ..."

"What, Ray? What?"

"Thirsty. So ... thirsty."

Berard turned. "Where the hell's that bucket of water?"

"I'm coming," yelled Otto, carrying a bucket.

"Wait! Hand it to me," said a man in the crowd, as he snatched the bucket from Otto. "Here's your damn water, Olson," he yelled, throwing the water in Ray's face. "I hope to high heaven that's the last drink you ever taste."

Ray looked up at Berard. "Tell Delores ... goodbye," he said, his voice faltering. "Tell her ... I love ..."

"I will, Ray. I will tell her."

"I'm so ... cold" he whispered. "Dear ... God ... I'm ..."

Ray Olson exhaled, then lay motionless.

Berard checked for a pulse. "He's gone."

"Good riddance," somebody shouted. A woman cheered. A man behind laughed. Onlookers shook deputies hands and patted their backs.

"All right, folks," yelled the photographer. "Anybody here who wants to be in tonight's newspaper, just gather in tight behind the body and I'll take some more pictures. Okay. Ready? Ready?"

Officer Berard turned away.

"Everybody smile!"

THE CAPITAL TIMES

Ministerial Body to Eye **Sharpshooting Posse Kills**
Barring of Rev. Eddy **Ray Olson, Fugitive Slayer**
In Senate After Prayer **$1,808,300,000 Relief**
Bill Passes Senate, 55-0

The Sawyer County Record
AND HAYWARD REPUBLICAN
DEVOTED TO THE INTERESTS OF SAWYER COUNTY IN PARTICULAR AND NORTHERN WISCONSIN IN GENERAL

HAYWARD, WISCONSIN, THURSDAY, JUNE 29, 1939

Slayer Is Dead After Twelve-day Hunt

No Moaning At The Bar As He Puts Out To Sea

American Legion Convention
Was A Credit To Hayward

Hayward Region Famous From **Grasshoppers** **Road Hearing**
One Coast To The Other **To Be Ended** **Is To Be Held**

TARZAN SLAIN BY POSSE
Dramatic Photo on Page 28

Woods Outlaw
(Story on page 1.)

[Associated Press telephoto]
First picture of Ray Olson, slayer of two deputy sheriffs, who is quarry of one of the biggest man hunts ever held in northern Wisconsin.

POSSE CHEERS AFTER SLAYING KILLER

TRAPPED
IN WOODS
LAKE

Chapter 35

By the time Doc Neer arrived, over fifty people had gathered to see the dead fugitive and hear the story of his final foiled break for freedom. Doc pronounced Ray Olson dead as of 5:30 a.m., Thursday, June 29, 1939, on Missionary Point, located in the north end of Lake Namakagon in Bayfield County, Wisconsin. The death certificate noted that Olson's death was a homicide and the victim was *"shot by posse on farm."** The cause of death was listed as *"gunshot wound of pelvis, colon, and jejunum,"** part of the small intestine. There was no mention of wounds from the shotgun pellets. The death certificate was filed with the Bayfield County Register of Deeds where it would remain unseen for seven decades.

Undersheriff James Berard stood before Delores Olson's cell.

"It's about time!" she said.

"What?"

"You're here to let me out, right?"

"I'm here for something else, Delores. It's about Ray."

"What about him?"

"We caught up with him early this morning."

She sighed. "Is he here? Can I see him?"

"He was shot while trying to escape from my deputies."

"Shot? Is he all right? Is he in the hospital? I have to go to him. Take me to him. Please!"

"You don't understand. Ray's not in the hospital."

"Where, then? Where is he?"

"Delores, Ray wanted me to tell you … Well, that's why I'm here—to grant his last wish—to offer you his goodbye. He died early this morning."

"Oh, jeez, no." She slumped back onto her cot. "Oh, Ray."

"He wanted you to know he loved you."

*Actual wording, hand-written on Ray Olson's death certificate, June 29, 1939

261

"He was always good to me."

"I'm sorry," Berard said, handing her his wallet, pocket knife, and a rabbit's foot.

She stared at them before dropping them on the cot.

"Don't make me laugh, Berard. You're not sorry. You and Seehuetter's army of bloodthirsty killers will be celebrating for weeks. I'll bet most of them are down at Angler's Bar right now, getting drunk, bragging about how brave they were when two-hundred armed predators shot down one, lonely, frightened man."

"Delores, I am sorry it turned out this way."

"But, don't you see? It didn't have to turn out this way. Ray wasn't evil. He wasn't a madman, some crazed maniac like the press was led to believe. My husband was a good man, good at heart. Sure, he made some bad choices. But it wasn't until you cornered him that everything went wrong."

"He could have surrendered to Hamblin when all this started. Or at the Bluesky shack. Or this morning. Or a half-dozen other times. Now, it's over. He's gone."

"Did you shoot him?"

"No. But it makes no difference who. It was bound to happen."

"So, he was murdered by your men?"

"Not murdered. Shot while trying to escape."

"If he was trying to get away, then he was no threat to you."

"We found a pistol and a shotgun."

"Let me guess. He didn't fire either one."

"No. He didn't."

"You and your gang of armed executioners against one man, running away, fearing for his life."

"A cold-hearted criminal."

"Running away. No doubt shot in the back."

"Your husband was a coldblooded killer."

"Thanks to you and your boss."

"What?"

"You turned him into a killer, Berard. You and Seehuetter. Just like you've now turned your men into killers."

262

"C'mon, Delores. Your husband was as crooked as they come."

"Crooks belong in jails, not coffins."

"He got what he deserved."

"Wait your turn."

"What?"

"Berard, we all get what we deserve … sooner or later."

The officer stared at her through the bars. "Look, Ray was a two-bit hoodlum. A criminal. A fugitive from justice."

"You never knew him. I did," she sobbed. "He was good at heart and *always* good to me."

"So, tell me, if Ray was so good, why did he take off when Deputy Hamblin pulled him over for stolen plates?"

"He was afraid."

"Of his past?"

"No. He was afraid of your boss. And of your pal, Cullie."

"Why?"

"Like you don't know."

"I don't, Delores. Tell me."

"Ray had been tampering with their slots. Jamming them."

"The sheriff doesn't have anything to do with slot machines."

"Who do you think you're kidding? Everybody knows the law looks the other way when it comes to gambling in the taverns and resorts up north. My husband had friends who wanted part of the gambling action. Ray messed with Cullie's slots. Cullie called him on it. Ray had a notion someone would be after him."

"That's why he ran?"

"What'd you expect? He was scared. Scared of what would happen next. So scared he couldn't think right. He went to pieces. He just took off. Can you blame him?"

"He wouldn't have been hurt."

"Oh, really? I heard that two days later, you and eight other armed men swarmed in on him like a cloud of wasps. How would you react if you were in Ray's shoes?"

"Had he not panicked, not shot Cullie, your husband would be alive today."

"I know Ray. I know he would not have pulled the trigger unless he feared for his life."

"I suppose that doesn't matter anymore, does it? He turned into a killer. Now he is dead. And here you are, Delores. Left alone without a dime to your name and about to stand before the judge. What are you going to say? What are you going to tell him about you and Ray?"

"Something you and Seehuetter and the rest of your kind overlook."

"And what's that?"

"The truth."

Downtown, in Grey's Barber Shop, details of the Olson manhunt dominated the morning gossip.

"Say, get this," said a man reading the *Evening Telegram*, "*The body of 30-year-old Ray Olson, also known as August Buelo, arrived in Hayward last night from Lake Namakagon where he was killed. Hundreds of persons filed past the body of Olson as it lay in a Hayward mortuary last night, some coming from out of state to view the shrewd woodsman who killed two deputy sheriffs and, in turn, was shot down by posse's rifles yesterday.*"*

"Boy," said the next man on the bench, "would I like to shake the hand of the guy who cut him down."

"That would be Ernie Moore," said the barber. "They say he's a regular sharpshooter."

"No," said the man in the chair. "Frank Flowers made the killing shot. Twelve gauge shotgun with double-ought buckshot. Ask him yourself. He's been over at Angler's all day telling the tale of Olson's final attempt to escape."

"I hear Jim Berard had a Tommy gun," said the next guy in line. "You can't miss with a Tommy gun."

"Say, I wonder who they'll give the reward to."

"I say they should split it among the thirteen men who brought him down. That's only fair."

"Even the men who never saw Olson until after he was shot?"

**Superior Evening Telegram*, June 30, 1939

"Yep."

"Baloney! Only the men who pulled their triggers should get in on it."

"He also serves who stands and waits. Remember that one?"

"Sure. General Pershing."

"Nope. Shakespeare."

"Both wrong," said the next guy in line. "Milton."

"Milton-shmilton. It was Pershing."

"Nope. Milton. Look it up."

"So, you say even the fellow hiding behind a tree while the others are ducking Olson's bullets should get part of the reward?"

"Yep."

"Ducking Olson's bullets?" said the man in the barber's chair. "Ray Olson never fired. You can't duck bullets what ain't been shot. So, split the dang money thirteen ways and be done with it!"

"Fiddlesticks!" said the barber. "You're all wrong. Best bet is to give the loot to those two fifteen-year-olds who tipped off the sheriff. If not for them, we'd still be out there tramping through the swamps. Maybe tramping till freeze-up. Give it to the boys."

"By golly, George, I think you've got something there. I'm going to suggest that to the county board chairman this very day."

"You'll find him over at Angler's, too. Along with about half the men in town."

The man with the paper read on. *"Olson's burial is expected to be in Hayward as his mother, Mrs. Emil Buelo of Mukwonago, Waukesha County, said she was unable to bear the expense of having her son's body transported home."** He lowered the paper.

"Can you beat that? They're going to plant Ray Olson's corpse right here in Hayward. Lord! Haven't we suffered enough? Must we face life knowing his body shares the same soil with that of Cullie and Fred? Fellas, I say we take up a collection to ship his sorry carcass back to Waukesha where it belongs."

"I'll chip in two bucks toward that," said the barber.

"And I'll match it," said the man in the chair.

Superior Evening Telegram, June 30, 1939

By noon, the men at Grey's Barber shop had raised enough money to cover the freight charges. The Anderson Funeral Home delivered the body to the depot. The Buelos would bury their son without a ceremony in the family plot near Vernon, Wisconsin. Still jailed, Delores Olson would not attend.

Two days later, Deputy Hamblin turned the key, opening her cell door. "Delores, Officer Berard put in a good word for you. The D. A. decided you've endured enough. As long as you stay in the county until this case is closed, he says you are free to go.

"Jeez, how kind of him. Did Berard mention that I shouldn't have been jailed in the first place? You know it. He knows it. Everybody knows it. Seventeen days! You cops had no right."

"Well, you can go now."

"Go where? And with what? Ray left me with six dollars to my name." Delores gathered her belongings and followed the deputy down the hall. "Some friend you turned out to be, Hamblin. Thanks to you and your boss, my husband is dead and I'm damn near dead broke."

"Here. Take this," he said, handing her a ten-dollar bill.

She took the ten. "I suppose this is from your share of the reward? The blood money you and your pals got for killing my Ray?"

"No, Delores. It's a gift from me to a young woman who could use a break right now. Good luck, kid."

Delores crossed the street to the payphone. Twenty minutes later, George and Nora Peterson, owners of Westview Resort, pulled up. In tears, Delores climbed into the back seat.

"You're welcome to stay with us, hon," said Nora. "We know you're a good person. Stay on as long as you want."

"Oh, thanks, Nora. But I don't think you'll want me hanging around. There'll be gawkers coming to stare at the child-bride of the mad maniac, Ray Olson. And you'll have paying guests who will go elsewhere so their kids don't bump into me and get led astray, tainted by some gangster's gun moll. No, Nora, as soon as I can scrape up a few bucks, I'll be making myself scarce."

"We understand, Delores," said George. "It must be awful tough to be in your shoes right now. But if anyone can take it, we know you can. Meanwhile, stay with us. Please."

Bookings at most of the Hayward area resorts fell to an ominous low in July 1939, thanks to a flurry of exaggerated newspaper and magazine stories about trigger-happy lawmen, illicit gambling, and gangsters hiding out in the Chequamegon Forest. Uneasy tourists, unwilling to risk visiting a region gone wild with gun-toting woodsmen took their vacation dollars elsewhere. But at the Westview Resort, business flourished.

As Delores predicted, curiosity seekers came to see the twenty-year-old wife of the criminal who survived thirteen days on the run in the Chequamegon Forest. Meeting Delores Olson meant visiting the resort's dining room. Tips left by diners soon eclipsed her earlier earnings, as she told hair-raising tales about Al Capone, John Dillinger, Baby Face Nelson, and other gangsters who vacationed in Hayward years before. But she remained silent when questioned about her husband and what he'd done to achieve notoriety.

One night she served a young couple who didn't mention Ray's past—or hers.

"Travel far?" asked Delores, making dinner table small talk.

" I'll say," said the young woman. "Buddy and I have been on the road twenty-one days."

"And still eleven hundred miles to go," said Buddy. "We thought we'd spend a few days in Wisconsin before heading back."

"Where's home?"

"Boulder, Colorado. Ever heard of it?"

"Colorado? Sure, but not Boulder."

"It's a nice little town north of Denver," Buddy replied. "You'd like it. Beautiful mountains. Lots of birds, wildlife ..."

"And not too many people," added his wife. "At least, not yet."

"I think I'd like a place like that. A place where nobody bothers you, right? Not like here. Not these days."

"I can't imagine how you feel." She turned to her husband. "How about we ask Delores to come along with us? We have room, don't we, dear?"

"Room in the car? Sure. Fine with me."

"Aw," said Delores, "that's awful nice of you, but …"

"Oh, c'mon. The owners told us your story. You need to get away from this place. Come stay with Buddy and me in Boulder for a while. Heck, if you don't like it, take the train someplace else."

"Jeez, thanks, but I don't know. Jobs are awful hard to find these days."

"Nonsense," said the young man. "Why, even when times are hard, folks have to eat. I'll bet you can find yourself a good waitressing job almost anywhere."

Four days later, Delores left Wisconsin in the rear seat of a car bearing Colorado plates. As they crossed into Minnesota, she breathed a sigh of relief, a sigh different than those she'd breathed crossing state lines while on the run with Ray. Next to Delores, a single suitcase carried all she had—all save her most prized possession—a stolen Zenith Stratosphere console radio, her reminder of the man she'd loved and lost in northwest Wisconsin's Chequamegon National Forest.

The End

Epilogue

I didn't bother knocking. I knew at nine-thirty in the morning my editor would be behind his desk, reading the newspaper. He expected me. I walked right in. He didn't lower the paper.

"James," he said into the *Times*, "I finished reading your manuscript yesterday."

"So, what do you think?"

"It's good. I enjoyed it. But there's a problem."

"A problem? What do you mean? I've researched this case from stem to stern. Covered every angle. Sheriff's reports. FBI files. Court records. I haven't missed a stitch. Weather Reports. News stories. Death certificates. The works! And I interviewed anyone and everyone still alive who knows anything about the Ray Olson story."

"Not everyone."

"All right, spit it out!"

He finally lowered his newspaper. "You missed someone, James. One of the deputies. Ninety-two years old last month. Said he was at the Bluesky sleep shack when the gunfire broke out. He got word you were working on a book about the Ray Olson manhunt. When he couldn't locate you, he spoke with me."

"And?"

"He said the newspapers, the radio, even the court documents had it all backwards."

"What do you mean?"

"Backwards. You know, the order reversed."

"Reversed?"

"According to him, it wasn't like they said. Something went wrong. But it all happened so fast, the men there didn't know what to do—didn't know how to keep things on track. So everyone there agreed to tell the same story. Well, all but one of them agreed."

"I don't get it. What was backwards? What was out of order?"

"He said they knew Ray Olson was in Bluesky's sleep shack."

"Right. They'd been told Ray was in there. It's in my manuscript. So what?"

"According to him, although they'd been told Olson had no gun, they didn't trust the source. They had to assume he was armed. That's why they shot the cabin full of holes. To get Olson before he could get one of them."

"What?"

"This old man insisted that they shot the cabin full of holes *first*. Only after they were dead sure Olson could not have survived, did Cullie Johnson kick the door in."

"But, that means ..."

"Yes. I know what it means. And that, James, is the problem with your manuscript. You'll need to make some changes—say something about this—let people know."

I stood in silence, waiting for it to sink in before I said, "So ... this old timer told you that Ray Olson shot Cullie Johnson *after* the siege on the cabin, *after* they all shot the place up?"

"That's what he said."

"And you believed him?"

"He's ninety-two. Why would he lie? Look. He said they shot into the cabin until they figured Olson was dead. That's when Cullie kicked in the door just as Olson climbed down from the rafters. Olson shot Cullie point blank, then took off, his shotgun in one hand and Cullie's Colt in the other. This changes everything."

"I don't buy it. How does that explain the death of Fred Scott?"

"Scott? Well, you see, he was the one man who didn't go along with their story."

"But that means ..."

"I'm afraid so."

"Oh, Jesus!"

"That's precisely what I said, James. Now you see what I meant by 'there's a problem.'"

I collapsed into a chair, contemplating this new angle, wondering what to do.

"How do we break this to the families? What ... what do we say?"

"We, James? Thank God I'm only the editor."

###

Addendum

September, 1939, *Official Detective* carried a long, stylized feature article about the Olson manhunt. Parts of the article were accurate.

Undersheriff Berard (left) & Sheriff George Seehuetter.

The west end of Nick Paulsen's tavern was built over the water. Nick was the author's great-uncle.

A few of the Taylor Lake CCC men who participated in the manhunt. The author's great-uncle, George Loken, sits lower right.

The facts behind the fiction within
James Brakken's *Alias Ray Olson*

Alias Ray Olson is based on true-life events and experiences of August Frederick Buelo (1908 – 1939), aka Ray Olson. Research for the novel included 1939 newspaper accounts, court documents, interviews, and anecdotes. Details of his life and death include:

Buelo was born in 1908 in Vernon, Wisconsin, near Milwaukee. Unemployed during the Great Depression, Augie turned to petty theft. Arrested for burglary, he served 2 years in Waupun State Prison.

During Augie's prison term, Warden Oscar Lee had prison inmates bused to Bayfield County to build a cabin for him on Cable Lake. (Still known as "the Lee cabin" by some.)

Augie married Delores Olson, a cousin 10 years younger. At age 16, she left with him for Tacoma when he fled from a 6-month jail term for stealing, then illegally selling muskrat pelts.

Heading west, they passed through Spokane around the time of the murder of Marshal George Conniff, probably by Spokane Police Detective Clyde Ralston. Ralston was accompanied by an unidentified man. Augie Buelo may have been involved.

It is likely Buelo (now going by the name Ray Olson) was part of the December 26, 1939, kidnapping of 10-year-old Charlie Mattson, a Tacoma doctor's son. A police sketch of the kidnapper is remarkably close to Olson's mugshot. (See cover.) Olson left Tacoma immediately after the abduction, disappeared for over six months, then hid out in northwest Wisconsin, where he trapped, guided, and worked at resorts. The Olsons lived in the back room of a combination grocery store and tavern now known as Musky Tale Resort on Sawyer County Highway B, near the bridge over the Chippewa River's west fork.

Though illegal, taverns and resorts had gambling machines in the 1930s. Ray was known to have tampered with slot machines, jamming them with slugs. The author agrees with those who say he was mixed up with racketeers who dealt with slot machines.

Angler's Bar in downtown Hayward, owned by Oscar, Buck, and Carl (Cullie) Johnson, had slot machines. Many felt Cullie and Ray butted heads over damaged slots.

On Thursday, June 15, 1939, Sawyer County Sheriff Deputy James Hamblin pulled Ray and Delores over for suspicion of stolen license plates. Olson escaped after a high-speed chase through downtown Hayward, ditching his car near the Namekagon River. Hamblin took Delores to the sheriff's office where she was jailed

273

without charge. She remained in the county jail for the next 17 days.

That night, Olson stole a car east of Hayward. After returning home for his shotgun, he broke into the store next to where he lived, stealing supplies. Late Friday night, Game Warden Leon Plante, informed Sheriff Seehuetter that he saw Olson driving near the John Bluesky cabin on the Chippewa Flowage. Saturday morning, Seehuetter and three other lawmen, plus five armed Hayward citizens, surrounded a small, tarpaper "sleep" shack near the Bluesky cabin.

Seehuetter, Hamblin, and Cullie Johnson broke down the door of the guide shack. Johnson was killed instantly by a shotgun blast to the head. The remaining lawmen emptied their weapons into the shack, hoping to subdue Olson. Minutes later, Fred Scott, owner of Twin Gables, a restaurant and tavern, was killed by a shotgun, though it remains unclear who fired. With the lawmen out of ammunition, Ray escaped into the woods.

Sheriff Seehuetter put out a call for volunteers. Over 100 showed up, creating a disorganized posse of vigilantes intent on revenge. Seehuetter also ordered bloodhounds to be flown in from La Crosse, hundreds of hand grenades and tear gas bombs, plus five .45 caliber Thompson sub-machine guns.

Saturday afternoon, the posse shot up a cabin at nearby Deerfoot Lodge where they thought Olson hid. Not finding Olson in the bullet-riddled cabin, the posse shot into the other empty cabins before realizing Olson had again escaped.

Ray stole (or was given) a boat from the Bow and Arrow Resort. He rowed across to Arrowhead Island where he spent the night. Sunday morning, he rowed up Hay Creek and, after writing a mock suicide note, fired his shotgun, then set the boat adrift. A neighbor saw the empty boat and called the sheriff. Finding no body, the lawmen knew Olson escaped a fourth time.

Ray fled northward, probably given a ride by a friend. Sunday evening, a Moose Lake resort owner he'd once worked for spotted him. The bloodhounds were soon on his trail until a thunderstorm stopped the chase, Ray Olson's fifth escape.

Supposing Olson to be hungry, Sheriff Seehuetter sent men to guard taverns, resorts, and stores. While two exhausted sentries slept nearby, Ray broke into the Moose Lake Store and Tavern on Highway S, now Charlie's Fine Foods. He entered via a crawlspace and came up through a trap door. Ray ate, grabbed some supplies, and left by the back door.

Monday, when the bloodhounds led lawmen to the store, the guards were embarrassed to learn the fugitive had walked within yards of their posts, the sixth time he avoided capture in five days.

Seehuetter organized the possemen into four teams of fifty led by Undersheriff Jim Berard and sheriffs from neighboring counties. They searched Moose Lake cabins and homes, occupied or not, without search warrants. More cabins and an abandoned logging camp were shot up. Roadblocks were set. Armed possemen stopped all cars. When one motorist misunderstood a wave to stop as a wave to go, he drove off in a hail of bullets, some striking his car.

About a mile north of the Moose Lake Store near the Teal River Bridge, Officer Jim Berard and his posse spotted Ray Olson crossing the road. They fired at him. He didn't return fire, but ran into the woods. The bloodhounds later picked up the trail but lost it where Ray had waded into the river, his seventh escape.

Wednesday night, Warden Leon Plante received a call. A farmer had found a dead doe with some meat removed and covered by brush. Men were stationed in the surrounding woods to watch for Olson to return for more meat. Ray did not take the bait. Instead, he broke into several more cabins near Teal Lake and Spider Lake over the next three nights, before stealing another car and fleeing north through the fire lanes to Bayfield County's Garden Lake, near Lake Namakagon.

Newsmen flocked to Hayward, hoping for a headline. Many sensationalized their stories, making Ray Olson sound like a crazed madman bent on killing anyone in his path. Anxiety among area residents and visitors grew day by day as the manhunt dragged on. While he hid in the forest, false reports of sighting him came from towns and cities near and far.

Controversy grew regarding whether Olson was unfairly accused. Some believed at the Bluesky guide shack, Ray fired on Cullie Johnson after being told to surrender. Still others believed the lawmen emptied their guns on the cabin *before* Johnson kicked in the door. Many believed Olson did not shoot Fred Scott. Some wondered if he actually killed anyone at all. Although most people feared Olson and hoped he'd pay dearly for his crimes, some felt sympathy, even putting out food for him at night.

Rainy weather and insect bites plagued both the fugitive and the possemen. One paper reported that Sheriff Seehuetter suffered from exhaustion and remained in Hayward during the second week of the manhunt. In his office, he found the Tacoma police sketch of the kidnapping suspect that resembled Olson. He alerted the FBI. Two agents came to Hayward, but didn't participate in the manhunt.

Resorts suffered. Worried the manhunt might last all summer, businesses pressured the Sawyer County Board into offering a one-thousand-dollar, dead-or-alive reward on Monday, June 26. Many residents began their own search for Olson, endangering the possemen, other members of the community, and themselves.

Around 3:30 Tuesday morning, Olson broke into Nick Paulsen's Pebble Beach Resort. Nearby, Gayle Sleight heard a window break. She alerted her brother, Sidney Reynolds, in the next room. While she called the sheriff, Sid took aim, waiting for Olson. Instead, cans, bottles and boxes of food flew out the window. Olson exited by another door, crawling around the building to retrieve the plunder. He escaped along the lakeshore, foiling lawmen the eighth time.

Wednesday evening, fifteen-year-old twins, Del and Dean Anderson, returned to their parents' Missionary Point home to find the door open, food left out on the table, and the smell of cigarette smoke. Knowing something was wrong, they ran from the house. The sheriff was called. Undersheriff Jim Berard hand-picked 12 deputies. In the pre-dawn light, they saw Olson. Berard called for him to surrender. Olson bolted. The men opened fire, missing shot after shot.

Unscathed, he untied the boat he'd left along shore. A shotgun pellet grazed his neck. From only a few yards away, Cable Constable Ernie Moore emptied his rifle at Olson. Only two of Moore's bullets struck, but they tore through Olson's pelvis and abdomen, ending Olson's flight.

Doctor Wilmer Neer was called from his home in Cable, 15 miles away. Onlookers soon began arriving, including a neighbor and his 9-year-old son, Freddy Meyer. (This author interviewed Fred Meyer, now 87, the only known surviving witness to the Olson case. Fred provided key details to Olson's demise.)

Undersheriff Jim Berard asked Olson if anyone aided in his flight. Olson insisted nobody helped him. When asked if Delores had a part in his crimes, he simply said, "Aw, let her go." When someone in the crowd cursed Olson for shooting Fred Scott and Cullie Johnson, he denied shooting Scott, thus adding to the controversy.

A *Superior Evening Telegram* newspaperman took photos of the dying Olson and the cheerful possemen and onlookers. When Olson complained of thirst, someone threw water in his face. About a half-hour after being shot, Olson asked Berard to say goodbye to Delores for him, then muttered, "I'm cold" and "Oh, dear God," before dying.

The photographer continued shooting various poses that included guns placed across Olson's body with possemen waving. The photos appeared in newspapers nationwide, causing northwest Wisconsin to be regarded a crime-laden gangster hangout and a dangerous place to vacation. The local economy would not recover for two years.

When Doc Neer arrived, he pronounced Ray Olson dead as of 5:30 a.m. Thursday, June 29, 1939. The death certificate notes Olson's death was a homicide and the victim was *"shot by posse on farm."* The cause of death was listed as *"gunshot wound of pelvis, colon, and jejunum,"* part of the small intestine. Newspaper accounts reported 20 to 30 bullet wounds. Most may have been from shotgun pellet wounds.

The controversy regarding Olson's case remains to this day. In an article about Olson, historian and posse member, Eldon Marple, wrote that some people believed Cullie only kicked the door open _after_ the nine men riddled the Bluesky guide shack with bullets. This author has interviewed descendants of those involved who say Olson was misguided, but not a bad person and definitely did not kill Fred Scott and perhaps did not kill Cullie Johnson.

Twenty-year-old Delores Olson remained in jail 17 days though never charged. When released, she left the state, spending the balance of her life in Colorado, working as a domestic. Never remarried, she died in 2003 at the age of 84.

Mrs. Victor Anderson suffered anxiety attacks for years due to intrusions by a constant flow of curiosity seekers looking for souvenirs. The Pebble Beach Resort and Nick Paulsen (the author's great uncle) have been gone for decades.

The Moose Lake Store is now Charlie's Fine Foods (and rightfully named). Angler's Bar is now Angler's Bar and Grill and still a popular downtown Hayward stop. (Check out the 1930s photos on the back wall.) Musky Tale Resort and Deerfoot Lodge welcome tourists, as do the woodlands and waters of the Chequamegon National Forest, a place August F. Buelo, *Alias Ray Olson*, once loved and lost.

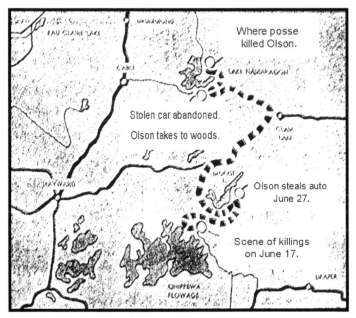

This *slightly* accurate map appeared in many papers nationwide.

Below, L to R: Frank Flowers, Ernie Moore, Mrs. & Mr. Victor Anderson.

Photo by *Superior Evening Telegram.*

Labels on map:
Where posse killed Olson.
Stolen car abandoned.
Olson takes to woods.
Olson steals auto June 27.
Scene of killings on June 17.

Play Part in Olson Manhunt

CABLE.—These people had a hand in the final tracking down of killer Ray Olson. At left are Mr. and Mrs. Victor Anderson, at whose farm home on Lake Namekagon east of here Olson was trapped. At right: Edward Flowers, state guide, and Ernest Moore, Cable marshal, both of Cable, who joined Sawyer county possemen in the grim hunt.

Spoiler Alert! Reading this first will ruin surprises and twists in the story!

Deputy James Hamblin (R) with a pump 12 gauge shotgun. The rifleman is Jake Bloom.

Below, John Bluesky, was one of Ray's friends jailed without being charged during the manhunt.

L to R: Buck, Oscar & Cullie Johnson in the lower bar at Angler's. Four weeks after Cullie's death, Buck died suddenly from a rare stomach illness while fishing with Jake Bloom on Teal Lake. Oscar ran the tavern for decades.

OLSON MANHUNT

Fugitive Shot Near Cable

Killer Cornered After Taking Refuge at House on Shores of Lake Namekagon; 30 Bullets Rip Into Body

(By Telegram Staff Correspondent)

CABLE—In his own blood at daybreak Thursday Ray Olson paid the price exacted by the smoking guns of a relentless posse—a price for the death of Carl (Cully) Johnson and Fred Scott.

So ended a grim and dogged pursuit of 13 days, a pursuit through woods and swamp, across river and lake, that began June 17 in a little tarpaper Indian shack 20 miles east of Hayward.

There Olson gave no mercy to deputies who sought to arrest him.

Thursday, at 5:30 a. m. on the shores of Lake Namekagon, possemen showed that same mercy to the fugitive killer. When his body lay riddled with

Telegram Scoop!

Associated Press equipment for transmitting photographs over telephone wires arrived in Superior from Minneapolis by plane Thursday morning, to rush Superior Evening Telegram photos on the Olson case to the nation.

This was recognition by the national news service that the Evening Telegram had scored a clean "scoop" on photos and news from the scene of the killing.

It was the second time in recent years that the Evening Telegram had scored such a beat. The other occasion was the Inez kidnaping case at Spooner, when the hideout of John headland revealed the bodies of two men and G-men swooped into that area to solve the case.

0 bullets, an outstretched arm grasping for freedom that never could be, then possemen laid down their guns and wept in sheer relief.

As though signifying that the hunt was over, possemen laid a pistol on the riddled body of Olson. It was the same pistol Olson had snatched from the bleeding body of Cully Johnson on that fatal Saturday morning 13 days ago.

Greatest Manhunt in State.

It wrote the end to as merciless a manhunt as the state of Wisconsin has ever seen. Time and time again 300 possemen drove Olson into swamplands, cornered him in small patches of wilderness, and forced him to break for freedom. Five times the fugitive gave his pursuers the slip, but on the sixth time Olson met a death that had been sworn for him by the grief-stricken city of Hayward.

Death came swiftly to Olson, and came soon after the last fresh clue in the hunt.

Top: The *Superior Evening Telegram* provided the best coverage of the manhunt. George Seehuetter and Joe Cox celebrate the end of the ordeal.

Across from Angler's Bar, Grey's Barber Shop, remains Hayward, Wisconsin's best place to get a quality haircut and all the latest news.

More great reading from James Brakken's
Badger Valley Publishing

James Brakken's *Chief Namakagon Series*
A Timber, Treasure, & Treachery Trilogy
Set in northern Wisconsin's 19th century wilderness.

Historical fiction at its best. Thrilling, fact-based northern Wisconsin novels by James Brakken. Set in the 1800s in Wisconsin, Minnesota and Michigan. Stand-alone novels, written & illustrated for adults but suitable for ages 12 and up. Available in large print.

THE TREASURE OF NAMAKAGON

Book 1: Live the old "lumberjack" days in far northern Wisconsin. Button up your mackinaw, grab a pike pole, and plunge into 1883 "pinery" life. Meet legendary Chief Namakagon. Explore his secret silver mine. Join the lumberjacks as they save the camp from disaster in this thrilling, fact-based north woods wilderness adventure. **2nd PLACE WINNER in Amazon's 2013 BREAKTHROUGH NOVEL AWARDS (ABNA) out of 10,000 novels entered worldwide!**

TOR LOKEN & THE DEATH OF CHIEF NAMAKAGON

BOOK 2: A shipwreck, a lost map, river pirates, lumberjacks, miners, charlatans, ne'er-do-wells, and the 1886 murder of Chief Namakagon for his silver treasure! And all based on fact! Follow the true trail of clues in this thrilling mystery novel. Solve the twisting, turning, 13-decade-old murder case as penned by the Bayfield County author whose research finally unlocks the truth. Includes maps to the Marengo silver fields, the likely location of Chief Namakagon's legendary lost silver mine.

THE SECRET LIFE OF CHIEF NAMAKAGON

BOOK 3: Who was he before he came to NW Wisconsin? Was he a fugitive in hiding? Was he wanted for murder? The answers will amaze you! Follow his fascinating life among the Chippewas and fur traders of the north. An adventurer caught between two worlds, his life story propelled him into fame before jealousy and greed changed everything. Share his courageous story— the true tale of a feared warrior—an Anishinabe leader, woodsman, and war hero destined for our history books.

All three are fact-based, illustrated, historical fiction novels.
Find special Trilogy pricing & free US shipping at BadgerValley.com

DARK - A CAMPFIRE COMPANION

56 very scary short stories & delightfully frightening poems. Spine-tingling tales of ghosts, dragons, ne'er-do-wells, and monsters—each waiting to raise goosebumps. Every story is morbidly illustrated by long-dead master artists of the macabre. Chilling, yet wonderful fireside reading. A "must-have" for every cabin bookshelf and home library. Ages 12 and up.

THE MOOSE & WILBUR P. DILBY
Plus 36 Fairly True Tales from 'Up North.

Thirty-seven short stories straight from the heart & the heart of the north. All fairly true, more or less. Some are sad, some shocking, most are hilarious. Small town tales of baseball, fishing, and hunting, tavern tales, jokesters, murderers, gangsters, and flimflam men. Lost treasure, lumberjacks, and legends of the north. Includes a 1-act play and several short stories based on the Chief Namakagon trilogy. Written for adults but fine for age 12. **Features *two* 1ˢᵗ place award-winning stories.**

SAVING OUR LAKES & STREAMS:
101 Practical Things You Can Do Today

A handbook for all who care for our lakes and streams. Simple tips, ideas, and articles from award-winning conservationist and author, James Brakken. Foreword by Dan Small, host of Wisconsin Public TV's "OUTDOOR WISCONSIN." 200-pages, 101 tips, 75 articles, 75 photos. Discounted at BadgerValley.com. All ages. Great fundraiser! Ships free. (Up to 33% off & factory-direct shipping to conservation groups, lake associations, & lake districts.) Profits help support efforts to protect and preserve Wisconsin's waters.

Secure online ordering at BadgerValley.com where the WI sales tax is pre-paid and US shipping is still free!

BADGER VALLEY PUBLISHING
45255 East Cable Lake Road
Cable, Wisconsin 54821
715-798-3163
TreasureofNamakagon@gmail.com

Badger Valley can publish YOUR book, too!
Now accepting new book proposals.

The Treasure of Namakagon
Our "flagship" lumberjack novel and best seller by far.
Book 1 in the award-winning Chief Namakagon trilogy:

2nd PLACE WINNER out of *10,000* worldwide entries in the 2013 *Amazon Breakthrough Novel Award* competition!

A young lumberjack, his Indian mentor, and a lost silver mine—a fact-based tale of timber, treasure, and treachery in America's 19th century wilderness. Following a daring rescue from a dangerous child-labor scheme in 1883 Chicago, an orphan is plunged into the peak of lumberjack life in far northwestern Wisconsin. There, an Ojibwe chief teaches him respect for nature and shows him to hidden treasure—an actual mine, lost when the chief died in 1886 and yet to be rediscovered.

You'll meet young Tor Loken whose family owns a wilderness lumber camp. You'll join the fight when a sinister timber tycoon takes control of the river, threatening the Lokens' future and the lumberjacks' dollar-a-day pay. You'll be in the cook shanty before dawn for breakfast, then out into the cuttings where, knee deep in snow, you'll help harvest giant pine logs. Hitch the Clydesdales to the tanker. Ice the trails for the giant timber sleighs. Take the train to town but keep one eye peeled for hooligans seeking an easy swindle.

Back in the bunkhouse, spin a yarn with colorful lumberjack friends. Next, it's a Saturday night of merriment in town. Dress warmly, though. It's a three hour sleigh ride back to camp at twenty below zero.

Come spring, you'll drive the timber down a thundering, icy river, jumping log to log as they rush downstream, danger around each bend. Finally, payday! Time to celebrate. Keep your pocketbook buttoned up, though. Scoundrels are eager to separate you from your winter wages.

Put on your red wool mackinaw. Grab your pike pole. You are about to plunge into 19th century lumberjack life *The Treasure of Namakagon*, a thrilling adventure, thick with twists and turns, researched and illustrated by an author who lives there.

And, yes, the girl wins the boy's heart!

Tor Loken and the Death of Chief Namakagon

Lace your calked boots and button your mackinaw once again. You are about to plunge into a twisting, turning, thrilling north woods mystery: *Tor Loken and the Death of Chief Namakagon.*

Based on the suspicious death of Chief Namakagon in 1886, this tale depicts a time when rugged lumberjacks and miners brought civilization and wealth to Wisconsin's wilderness, while corrupt, ruthless opportunists devoured all they could.

Following a devastating blizzard, Namakagon's body is discovered near a secluded silver mine. Only nineteen-year-old Tor Loken can prove murder. Suspicious accidents soon plague his father's lumber camp. Tor and his sweetheart, Rosie, risk their lives to capture the killer and protect the tribal treasure. With you, they will solve the dark mystery surrounding Namakagon's murder in this fast-paced, fact-based thriller by the award-winning Wisconsin author whose research now unlocks the truth.

History tells us Chief Namakagon traded silver for supplies in Ashland in the 1880s. Several miners tried to get him to disclose the source of his silver. One man came close but, when a large bear blocked their trail, Namakagon took this for a bad omen and refused to continue. Following a fierce 1886 blizzard, Namakagon's remains were found along a trail that may have been very near his silver cache. Many suspect he met with foul play. Suspicions remain regarding the cause of his death. The location of the lost silver is still unknown.

In this mystery-adventure, Tor loses his mentor during this snowstorm. Tor is determined to solve the mystery of Namakagon's death. Suspicious accidents plague the Loken camp as Tor and Rosie risk all to stop the murderer.

Learn more about the rich history of the lumberjack days, help solve the mystery, and gather your own clues about the likely location of the legendary silver mine of Chief Namakagon.

243 pages. Illustrated. Written for adults though suitable for age twelve and up. **Maps to the 19th century Marengo silver fields, the likely location of Chief Namakagon's lost silver mine, are included in this novel.** This is a thrilling read and a book you will treasure in more ways than one! Available at select outlets and BadgerValley.com where the sales tax is pre-paid and nationwide shipping is still free.

Grab a paddle and step into your birch bark canoe. You're off to the early 1800s and a fascinating, factual dramatization of the early life of Old Ice Feathers. It is a novel you won't want to put down.

Book 3 in the trilogy:

The Secret Life of Chief Namakagon

When, in 1886, his friend and mentor dies, young Tor Loken learns of Namakagon's previous life. But why, four decades earlier, did he isolate himself in this uninhabited northern Wisconsin wilderness? Was Namakagon running from a troubled past?

Now James Brakken's research reveals Namakagon's life *before** he came to his northern Wisconsin home. His is an amazing true-life adventure—a tale of a child abduction by renegades, then 30 years living as an Ojibwe. Caught in the middle of a bloody civil war between the Hudson's Bay Company and the North West Fur Company, his people reject him. He tries living among the Whites but is unable to adjust. Loved by few and despised by many, he can't find his niche in life—a life torn in two by others. All odds are against him until he meets a doctor who helps him write a book about his life with the Indians. But even his world renowned book cannot stop his downfall.

*When, in 2014, James Brakken's research verified the original identity of Chief Namakagon, he solved a 168-year-old cold case that historians have pondered for over a century. Since northern Wisconsin was settled in the 1880s, nobody knew that Chief Namakagon was actually a man who disappeared after being accused of a Michigan murder in 1846.

Then, accused of murder in 1846, he flees and begins a new life, that of an Indian hermit in northwest Wisconsin where he becomes Ice Feathers and discovers a secret silver mine. (A map in this book gives the best clue yet to the lost mine's likely whereabouts.)

These adventure-filled pages unveil Chief Namakagon's secret and offer a captivating, stand-alone novel written for all readers who enjoy a fusion of thrilling fiction and fascinating history. This illustrated novel is suitable for readers age 12 and up.

Find your *TREASURE* and 7 other James Brakken books, written for young and old and *made in the USA* at BadgerValley.com, select Indy bookstores, and other preferred outlets. Sample excerpts, discounts and secure online credit card ordering are available at James Brakken's official website, BadgerValley.com.

James Brakken's
Annotated Early Life Among the Indians
The 1892 Memoir of Benjamin Armstrong

A firsthand portrayal of northwestern Wisconsin life in the mid-1800s as European settlers changed Native American life forever.

James Brakken has "rescued" this rare book and reprinted it with clarifications designed to aid the reader in understanding the archaic writing style and outdated terms.

Not only is this a fascinating look at northern Wisconsin in the mid-1800s, the Armstrong memoir also corroborates the existence of Chief Namakagon's silver mine. Ben Armstrong knew Namakagon, had a 1-pound silver nugget given him by the chief, and may have been inspired by Chief Namakagon to write this memoir.

Included among many of Armstrong's adventures, you'll find …

- The Wisconsin Trail of Tears.
- Indian councils with President Fillmore and Abe Lincoln.
- Indian laws, customs, and religion.
- The treaties of 1837, 1848, and 1854.
- The Black Hawk War.
- Sioux and Ojibwe wars.
- The Battle of the Brule.
- Revenge of the Sioux.
- Origins of the Ghost Dance.
- Fur trader tales.
- Tales of Great Buffalo and other chiefs.
- Lost silver mines in northwest Wisconsin.
- Ojibwe stories from times long past.

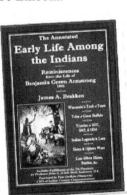

Commentary by Wisconsin author and historian, James Brakken, who connects this 19th century account with contemporary times and issues. **Includes illustrations and original photogravures. 222 pages.**

Foreword by Paul DeMain. *A must-have for your "up north" library.*

Saving Our Lakes & Streams:
101 Practical Things You Can Do Today
Written for *all* who care for our waters.

- Great self-help gift for newcomers to lakes and streams.
- Foreword by Dan Small of "OUTDOOR WISCONSIN."
- 200-pages, 101 tips, 75 articles, and 75 photos.
- Up to 33% off to conservation groups for quantity purchases.
- Perfect gift for recognizing volunteers & directors.
- A "must-read" for all your local & county officials.
- Share news of this with your local & school librarians.
- Great for resorts, short-term renters, and campers, too!
- Special pricing and free shipping at BadgerValley.com

James Brakken's Awards & Honors:

- 2013, 2014, & 2016 Lake Superior Writers Award
- 2014 Wisconsin Writers Assn Jade Ring Award
- 2nd place, 2013 Amazon Breakthrough Novel Awards
- 2001 Wisconsin Lakes Stewardship Award
- Director Emeritus & past president of Wisconsin Lakes, Inc.
- Northwest Waters Consortium president
- Bayfield County Lakes Forum past president
- Cable Lakes Association past president
- Namekagon River Partnership director
- Wisconsin Conservation Congress delegate
- Author of 8 books to date.

Deep Discounts for Schools, Conservation Groups, & Lake Associations!

The Early Life and True Identity of Chief Namakagon
James Brakken
If it waddles like a duck and quacks like a duck ...

When, in 2008, I began *The Treasure of Namakagon,* I did not intend to write a sequel, much less a trilogy. But research for book one led me to these two conclusions: 1, the chief really did refuse to disclose where he was getting silver. And, 2, his death involved foul play. Compelled to share what I discovered about his silver mine and the suspicious facts surrounding his death. I wrote *Tor Loken and the Death of Chief Namakagon,* a fact-filled murder mystery.

My research soon had me wondering why, in the mid-1840s, this man came to a remote, uninhabited lake in northern Wisconsin to live a hermit's life. Why did he isolate himself in this distant place? And how was it he could speak English, extraordinarily uncommon of Natives then?

I imagine the November, 1880 arrival of the railway turned his life on end, especially when newspaperman, George Thomas, stepped off the train and sought out the only English-speaking, long-time resident of the area. The reporter's interview helped answer some of my questions: According to Thomas, Namakagon came from Sault Ste. Marie decades earlier. Why? Because a dream revealed a fire and a death. Thomas wrote that this dream made Namakagon fear he'd be executed for a murder he did not commit.

By itself, this statement shed no light on my search for his previous life—until, that is, I traveled to the Sault where a deeper investigation revealed a murder *had* occurred there—in 1846. Fearing execution, the accused man fled—*a statement nearly identical to that given by Namakagon to George Thomas!*

I exposed many more clues and convincing details, but positive proof came while scouring the old land records, looking for the location of his silver mine. *The official records, buried for decades, disclosed the "early" identity of Chief Namakagon.* Eureka! I'd solved a *168-year-old cold case*—the solution to the 1846 disappearance of an innocent man wanted for a cold-blooded murder. The official government land records, along with the sheer number of clues, statements, and facts provided by professional historians, were clear evidence that the hermit of Lake Namakagon was, indeed, a fugitive who hid for forty years in the Wisconsin wilderness. I'd unveiled compelling, reliable verification of Namakagon's early life.

So, research for my fact-based murder mystery, *The Death of Chief Namakagon,* led me to write *The Secret Life of Chief Namakagon,* a book about the first half of his life. It's a fascinating, wilderness adventure based on his own words and those of historians—historians who, by the way, knew only part of his colorful life. My first two Chief Namakagon books shed light on the final half of his intriguing life and still-suspicious death.

Secret is a window into the world of a woodsman with an amazing history, an adventurer, a war hero who evaded death many times, a celebrated author forced to turn fugitive and become Mikwam-mi-Miguan, or Ice Feathers, the legendary hermit we now call Chief Namakagon.

Take pleasure in sharing his journey and learning his story in book three of the trilogy, *The Secret Life of Chief Namakagon.*

~~~

Did you enjoy a James Brakken book? A few ways you can help:

Unlike writers tied to brick and mortar publishing houses, *Indy* authors like James Brakken must rely on readers to stimulate interest in their books. *If you enjoyed this book, please ... 1. Tell friends, neighbors, & others; 2. Ask a library to order copies; 3. "Like" us on Facebook at Jim.Brakken; 4 Give it 5 stars at Amazon; (Search: James Brakken books.). Or, better yet, purchase another James Brakken book from BadgerValley.com! Thanks for your interest and your support!*

Critical reviews of James Brakken's 8 books and more than 100 short stories and poems:

"Wonderfully written .... Compelling" "A good piece of writing with suspense and action ..." **Jerry Apps, award-winning Wis. author.**

"Weaving mystery into history, James Brakken's writing vivifies the tumultuous nature of 19th-century life in the legendary north woods." **Michael Perry, NYT bestselling Wisconsin author**

"Open with caution. You won't want to put this one down." **LaMoine MacLaughlin, President, Wisconsin Writers Association**

"A fascinating tale ... "Rip-roaring action ..." "So well-written." "Difficult to put down; a great read." **Publisher's Weekly Magazine**

"The writing style of this piece is its greatest strength." "The flow of the words is like an old fashioned song." **Amazon Books**

"It's the dialog and characters that drive The Treasure of Namakagon, a book that, if the audience for (adventure novels) was more like it was in the 1950s, would likely be sitting at or near the top of the best seller's lists. It appears as if author James A. Brakken is determined to make a go of this series, and ... he's made at least one fan of this reader." **Judge at 22nd Writer's Digest Book Awards**

"James Brakken has captured all of the current science, technology, and leadership necessary to preserve our lakes and streams." **Mary Platner, Founder and Past-president of Wisconsin Lakes.**

"Brakken has provided a timely handbook for citizens ready to play their role in realizing the state's Public Trust Doctrine." **Eric Olson, Director, UW Extension Lakes**

"A twisting, thrilling mix of mystery, adventure, and legendary treasure. Wisconsin history buffs will find this book a treasure in itself. An exciting adventure for all ages." **Waldo Asp, AARP Chairman**

"In scene after scene, the reader is surrounded by the beauty of pristine woods and lakes, rooting for the good guys to beat out the greedy." **A. Y. Stratton, author of Buried Heart**

"I thoroughly enjoyed it!" **Larry Meiller, WI Public Radio host.**

About the Author

The writing career of Bayfield County author, James Brakken, began in college when his story of a fishing trip with his father, "Muskie Madness," was published by *Boy's Life Magazine* in 1974. More articles followed in *Sports Afield, Outdoor Life, Field & Stream,* and other publications.

His first novel, *The Treasure of Namakagon (2012),* features a boy in an 1883 northern Wisconsin lumber camp and a legendary lost silver mine. The suspicious 1886 death of Chief Namakagon and the 1846 disappearance of a murder fugitive led to two more in the trilogy, *Tor Loken & the Death of Chief Namakagon* and *The Secret Life of Chief Namakagon.* Brakken's *Annotated Early Life Among the Indians* is an 1892 memoir by Benjamin Armstrong, adopted son of Chief Buffalo. It corroborates the existence of the mystery silver mine. Both Armstrong and Namakagon lived in northwest Wisconsin during the mid-1800s.

Treasure won 2nd place out of 10,000 worldwide entries in the 2013 Amazon Breakthrough Novel Awards. Brakken also received the 2013, 2014, and 2016 Lake Superior Writers Award and the coveted Wisconsin Writers Association Jade Ring Award for a short story in his collection, *The Moose and Wilbur P. Dilby plus 36 Fairly True Tales from Up North.* The author earned statewide recognition for conservation as reflected in his self-help book, *Saving Our Lakes & Streams: 101 Practical Things You Can Do Today.* (To protect our waters, lake associations, conservation clubs, and realtors often purchase large quantities of *Saving Our Lakes & Streams* at big discounts to give to those who own waterfront property.)

Of Brakken's writing, *Publisher's Weekly Magazine* and *Amazon Books* said, "Difficult to put down. ... A great read," and "the flow of words is like an old fashioned song." Brakken publishes his own books, and those of other authors. See them at BadgerValley.com where the sales tax is pre-paid and nationwide shipping is free.